My Long Journey To Sincerity

..

Elana Mayne

by

Jason Ellis

My Long Journey To Sincerity

..

Elana Mayne

Published by JTT Publishing

ISBN 13: 978-1-906529-57-4

Dedication

For my family. I write, you all make me smile and laugh. I talk for hours about plots, characters and oh-my-goodness-that-is-so-amazing twists. "Sounds great," you say. ;)
For my friends.
For all the readers.
I have to mention Happy Days because of the daily laughs, boulders ... and Queen Bee arenas!
Cenx and Redigit - Mr. and Mrs Terraria. When is the author NPC being added? :)
And Jessica Heeren. A unicorn, sewing, and a bald cat. Even with my imagination, that wasn't a dream! It really happened :)

A message from the author.

Some time ago, I began working with Louise Sargent. We planned to publish a book together, based around a main character with Myalgic Encephalopathy (ME), and Chronic Fatigue Syndrome (CFS).
Unfortunately, I never managed to complete the story. I couldn't seem to do it justice (I'm extremely harsh with self-criticism) and writer's block soon kicked in as well.

Louise has suffered with Myalgic Encephalopathy for many years and launched M.E. Support to raise awareness.

Louise kept in touch - she remembered to post Christmas cards, I forgot most years … I'm terrible, sorry, Louise ;)
Recently, we started talking about the book again. As I was completing this title, I had the idea to aid Louise's work a slightly different way. I shall now be donating a percentage of royalties from the sales of this book to help Louise, the volunteer base, and her support websites:
www.mesupport.co.uk
www.facebook.com/MESupportUK

••

M.E. Support was founded in 2001, and is one of the leading websites on Myalgic Encephalomyelitis, providing information, advice and support.

Chapter one

"Stop! Put your hands out to the side!"

What's happening?!

The unexpected voice startles me as it booms through the hallways of the college building, echoing off the blank walls.

My fear spikes as I see a couple of Community Guards standing in the middle of the corridor, pointing their weapons directly at my head. I move my arms up as instructed, then freeze. The barrels of the handguns are two feet away at the most, staring me down like silver eyes in the moonlight.

The familiar black uniforms confront me as if stone statues have punched out from the ground: boots, khaki trousers and a thick jacket. I know that others are behind me as well, forming an impenetrable barrier. I can hear thick rubber soles thudding on the plastic floor tiles as they manoeuvre to set positions. I dare not move to check if my assumptions are correct.

"Keep your hands up! Stay exactly where you are!" orders one of the guards.

I tense every muscle, willing myself to comply, although my body is shaking and I'm finding it difficult to stand still. It is an impossible situation.

One of the guards steps forward, never letting his aim falter. I can't see his face - all guards wear a helmet with tinted visors, regardless of their division. It has the letters *CG* embossed on it in a dark red colour, surrounded by a circle.

A gloved hand reaches towards one of the many equipment pockets attached to the belt around his waist. Without lowering his weapon, or moving it by even a single centimetre, he pulls out a small metallic device. It beeps once before he runs it along my limbs and body, seemingly paying particular attention to my hands. Then, he holds it close to one of my blue eyes, recording and checking the retina.

As I stand here, waiting for the scan to finish its cycle, all I can do is wonder what he could possibly be looking for - no crimes, abstract or physical, have been committed.

I've done nothing wrong!

"She is clean! Stand down!"

The guns lower, yet are not holstered.

"Elana Mayne, yes?"

It is so difficult to speak clearly, yet the words make their way out of my dry throat, somehow. "Ye … yes … I am Elana Mayne."

"Slowly, and without any sudden movements, reach for your identification card," says the guard. He speaks with determination and clarity.

I lower my right hand down to the waist of my trousers and unclip the laminated card, holding it out at arms length. My hand is visibly trembling and I am having trouble fighting it off.

The Community Guard takes it and uses the same metallic device to scan the information. "Have you seen anyone else in the college library today?" he asks while waiting for my identification to upload and record.

"No, I was just here to …"

An arrogant and authoritative hand shoots up, stopping me from continuing the sentence. Everything after the word 'no' is irrelevant information as far as he is concerned. "Did you speak to anybody?"

"No, I've only just arrived," I answer, keeping my words short and to the point.

Another of the guards walks forward, carrying a thick book. She holds it up so close to my face that I have to blink in order to refocus my eyesight.

"You were reading this book during the past week, yes?" she asks. "We have you on surveillance, so don't even try to deny it."

I gently nod in agreement. *If she already knows, why bother to ask me? And why are they so interested in the books I've been reading?*

"Have you seen anybody else reading this book recently?"

"No."

"Did you notice anything different about it? Did you alter this book in any manner?"

"Erm … no … I didn't do that! I don't understand!"

I'm pleading my replies now, hoping for the situation to be over. I'm angry with myself as well because I shouldn't hesitate when answering their questions. I know such actions are considered as a weakness of character, possibly brought on by guilt. That's how the guards surrounding me could see it. They are trained to see it that way.

Silence follows for half a minute, although it feels a lot longer for me. I can hear the thumping heart in my chest as the seconds tick by and sense the visored eyes all pointing at my face. The world is now a paradox for me: a speeding heartbeat yet time has slowed down.

"You may leave, Elana Mayne," says the guard as he returns the ID card back to me.

With no further words, or hint of an explanation, the

group of Community Guards march off through the corridors of the college library.

I may be physically and mentally shaken by all of this, yet I'm accepting of the situation, too. After all, this is normality. This is life for me ... for everyone. The decisions and actions of Central Government, and its various departments, are not to be questioned. *'Know that we are always working for you. We make the decisions, so you don't have to. We make the laws to ensure that you are always safe. Trust our judgement.'*

The hallways return to complete silence once more.

Calm down ... pull yourself together! You have to! The interrogation is soon ...

••

I sit at a desk in one of the side rooms that are built off of the main library auditorium, studying the thick textbook in front of me: *Scientific Principles in post virus society, by E. Volf; CGSc. Central Government approved author, #131.* I have already passed the examination, so this is more of a recap session, *and* a welcome distraction.

The imminent presentation to designated university representatives needs to be perfect. It is the chance - the *only* chance - to promote my abilities, intellect, and character. The selection process is a daunting experience, yet also an important and crucial rite of passage, compulsory for all sixteen year old students, signalling the transition on their path to adulthood. It is officially titled as the *day of progression.* The title that all teenagers whisper, yet never dare to voice out loud - *The interrogation.* Some have spoken of how they were questioned for hours, yet some for a much shorter time. The anticipation has become more frightening than the actual event for a lot of people.

My entire future - the future of all the sixteen year old

students in *all* the communities - depends on the grades we have received so far in academic testing. They determine which Central Government department may choose us for their training initiatives. Our entire lives will be planned, waiting for us to obediently follow, based on this one meeting.

After a few more minutes of reading, I check the digital clock on the wall, seeing it is 10:31. I need to leave the college library straight away and travel to my interview in the centre of the Community Zone. Fortunately, as the poster on the wall next to me states - *The wise and caring Central Government always keep the public transport systems running smoothly and efficiently.*

It isn't a difficult task in all honesty - only two methods and routes exist: trams either continuously hum around the square perimeter, or cut through it, delivering people to their homes, places of work and education, or trains venture further afield, to another community. The railway network connects the entire globe, with only some long distances - those across the oceans - carried out by an automotive or water-craft service. All air travel is restricted to military personnel or selected members of the government.

"If you don't feel ready now, you never will," I mutter to myself. "Come on, get up. Let's go!" I add, just for a push of confidence.

I stand up, take the textbook back to its shelf, then head for the exit. On the way, I visit the toilets so I can check my reflection in one of the wall mirrors. I want to make sure my appearance isn't at fault. The interrogation will be tainted if I turn up looking unkempt.

Hair is neat. Fingernails clean and filed ... and my clothes are fine, I think as I look down at my permitted outfit, all Central Government issue: a white tunic, black trousers, and a pair of laced plimsolls in grey. I have three more of all these items back at my living quarters. They are delivered

5

weekly to all the residents, and the worn clothes are taken away at the same time for cleaning. Yet another example of the efficient world I live in.

The college library looks like every other building in the Essex Community Safe Zone, every other building in all the Safe Zones if the truth be told. They are grey and bland ... sterile and fortified. Smooth concrete walls are always set at perfect right angles, creating an inner network of corridors that mark out the different library areas. The inside of the main college building is exactly the same, as are the schools, and the majority of housing. A design must have been agreed upon and then repeated and resized as many times as the architects decided was necessary. Build ... stack ... repeat.

A few minutes later I walk through the steel doors of the South wing, stepping outside to the college train station. I see two Community Guards nearby and, for a few nervous seconds, expect them to turn and aim their guns at me, as they did earlier. *They're just on a normal patrol ... nothing else ... just a normal patrol ...*

Growing up in a safe zone is a double-edged sword most of the time. I've seen violence and ... *justice*, carried out swiftly and with cruel precision. It still sickens and terrifies me ... *everyone.* The price of security is worth paying, though, if it keeps danger, trouble - or possibly worse - out of the communities. These are the only habitable areas created by Central Government, varying in size and number of residents. Some are entire countries from the old world, others mere pockets of society, such as the one I live in. The rest of the planet is either designated as a Wild Zone - they house many of the dangerous animals of the world, those which did not succumb to extinction when the virus hit - or an Inhabitable Zone. These are dangerous, contaminated areas. People who have tested positive for the virus are exiled there. Even those with a possibility of infection, or showing symptoms such as erratic thoughts or behaviour; *fifty-fifties* as they are colloquially known, are sent to such horrific places. As far as I know, these unfortunate individuals either die soon from the infection, or manage a few years of prolonged existence, scavenging through the old world, surviving by any means possible.

Today is a warm Friday in the middle of May and the late spring sun is shining brightly, despite a few clouds floating across the sky. They are like random dabs of white paint, smudged to near transparency. My straight black hair, cut a couple of inches above my shoulders, occasionally blows across my face because of the mild and cooling breeze.

I take a look at the digital information screen on the wall, seeing that the next line of train carriages will arrive in seven minutes time. A few other people stand around on the platform, waiting with me. Some read newspapers while others speak with colleagues or friends. There are only a handful like me, alone and quiet with their own thoughts. More guards patrol the area - the ever present force of security - and CCTV cameras are placed everywhere, watching all of us.

A speaker on the wall of the library sounds a dull siren in monotone bursts, each lasting for a couple of seconds. It is a signal from Central Government, a mandatory calling: an important message is about to be broadcast. Along with all the other people, I turn to face the large television screen on the wall of the station platform behind us, as we have been taught to do. We behave like domesticated pets, acting with loyalty, facing our master.

The screen fades in from black and a man appears, sitting behind a desk, holding a printed report in his hands. I recognise him from previous security broadcasts that have played in the past. He looks very smart in a grey suit, and his hair is styled neatly with a central parting. He emits the appearance of a serious professional, a person I can trust completely. I'm smart enough to know this is a fabricated image, purposely created to reassure me and everyone else who is watching.

'Residents, I speak to you today about an important security matter. We have a male Rogue on the loose. He has been categorised as level three, which, as you all know, means there has been no previous history of violence, although he could easily develop an unstable attitude, or cause harm, if agitated by a situation.
Do not approach him.
If seen or encountered, contact your local Community Guard office.
Be safe, and know that your Government is here for you. This threat will be eliminated.'

All the people on the platform sound and act shocked on hearing this news. They begin talking to each other in fast and broken sentences, gasping at the unexpected announcement.

I am also worried to hear about a criminal walking the streets where I live and a few thoughts darts across my mind. *Was he in there ... with me?! Did I see him without even realising? Has he been tampering with books?*

An understanding of my ordeal inside the library earlier this morning begins to unfold with the help - unneeded help - of my fear fuelled thoughts.

The criminal class of 'Rogue' is given to those questioning any laws, or spreading propaganda in an attempt to corrupt the behaviour of others. It could be as simple as whispering an idea to another resident, planting the first spark of distrust. I've even been told stories about deranged individuals, screaming lies as they run through the streets.

Rogues were initially categorized and considered dangerous by researchers from the Science Department of

Central Government. They discovered evidence which proved the unusual actions - often non-conformist in their nature - also indicated early symptoms of infection from the virus.

Stay calm. The Community Guards will deal with it! I think to myself, slightly easing my own fears.

An image appears on the television screen of a man in his mid-thirties. His brown eyes are menacing and bloodshot which makes me relieved that I don't recognise him from the photograph. His appearance scares me, sending a shiver up my spine as I imagine him walking through the library.

Familiar words flash across the screen: *'Central Government is always here for you.'*, followed by their instantly recognisable insignia, all in grey tones. Using various shapes and lines sat inside a square, it illustrates society, Central Government departments, security services, and the safety of the Community Zones. The outer square is always deemed as the most significant, especially by parents, teachers or Government officials, because it represents the perimeter, the border that keeps every resident safe inside. The methods used differ, depending on the community and geographical layout: an electrified fence, a thick wall built ten feet high, a deep trench or moat ... my own community has a mine field. Many pressure activated explosives are buried under the soil, reaching for a quarter of a mile. The fifty-fifties or wild animals will never be able to enter here. *I've never seen any, though, or heard older people speak of them trying to.*

If they were to ever make it through, Community Guards are stationed close by with more automatic weapons and fire-power than I care to imagine.

The screen fades and a different message begins to play - smiling children and their equally content parents. After ten seconds it will change again to another similar one, or show a montage of Government officials with messages of inspiration typed underneath: *I am Minister Howle. I am in charge of the Department for Housing, always working to keep your home sterile, safe, and comfortable.*

With gentle vibrations in my feet and legs, plus a low hum, the train arrives and I step on, finding the nearest empty seat as quickly as possible. I still want, and need, to sit down after the Community Guards stopped me earlier. The journey will hopefully provide the perfect opportunity to compose myself before the progression interviews. *I'm already nervous, I don't need it to get worse ...*

A memory surfaces, caused by the train jolting forwards, replaying in my head as I stare out of the window at the buildings.

At the age of eleven, shortly after beginning my first year of senior education and career decision, all the children in my geography class were taken to one of the communities near the old city of London. History lessons have taught me that it was previously a bustling and highly populated city, prominent too - the capital of England up until the year the virus grabbed the world in its fatal grip. London is now the same as every other community, though, and holds no standing in the country. The power in the world doesn't have a residence. It moves around ... an unseen entity, following all those privileged enough to wield it.

Our class passed through a Wild Zone on that day. We were all fascinated to see the lush trees, acres of green grass and various flowers, yet filled with fear on seeing a pride of lions prowling through an open field. It was the first time any of us had seen such creatures first hand. They looked savage, dangerous, and majestic. In bewildering contrast, part of the old London could be seen from the safety of our train. The Science Department quarantined the area many years ago, finding it to be contaminated with pathogens and uninhabitable to those fortunate enough to live in the Community Zones.

I remember the dust and grey earth blowing in the

wind. It swept across empty roads and moss covered buildings. Some of them had become victims of time and weather erosion, crumbled to near ruin. I imagined a giant walking through the city, destroying buildings with every footstep.

Photographs and video recordings do exist and are still used for educational purposes, although they show nothing but the deserted streets - post virus devastation at its most basic level. Tall buildings, vast road networks, monuments built to praise people of historical significance ... yet, because there are no people in those images, there is no life. The whole story can't be told or imagined with any detail ... with any heartbeat.

The innocent recollections fade away to the back of my mind as the reality of my location takes over - the Essex Community Jurisdiction Bureau looms only minutes ahead. The size of the building always intimidates those who see it or visit here, and Central Government are known to renovate regularly, adding more extensions in thick concrete. Build ... stack ... repeat.

The exact dimensions or number of staff are unknown to me, yet I do remember from leaflets sent out to schools that it is approximately a mile wide. A whole mile of concrete domain, sitting high above everything else. It is placed centrally in the community, with a barracks containing Community Guard housing, plus armed forces as well, surrounding the complex. Air defence hangars contain fighter jets and helicopters, ensuring that every location in the zone can be reached within forty-five minutes. All situations, trivial or major, are dealt with swiftly and safely. As I am often told by those in power: *The normality of life has to be maintained.*

The Bureau building always reminds me of the housing estates that I know so well, although it is an amplified, exaggerated version of them. From birth to the age

11

of eleven, I lived in one myself. I was the proud and content occupant of living unit 903, 9th floor, South Quarter. Once my father achieved a promotion, he also earned relocation privileges, meaning we were then permitted one-level living quarters. It resembles the design of the estate unit, yet is much larger inside, with more hours of rationed water included.

The train slows down as the large station appears. It looks completely different to all the others I have used in my life. They are mundane and purposeful, nothing else, yet this demonstrates why career progression, status, and reward for serving Central Government are values in life to aim for. In full view, for all to see, coloured kiosks are built on the platform, allowing fruit flavoured juices to staff members of particular grades, plus, these extras won't be deducted from their weekly food rations either. There are also delicacies that I've only heard of: peanut butter sandwiches, plain sponge cake, decaffeinated coffee.

I always remember an important Central Government ideal when I see or think of this place:

'Aspire to serve your Government. Be a person of virtue, of understanding, of loyalty. Work hard and you could be rewarded.'

The train stops and the doors open. I politely let a woman step out first - I am in no rush whatsoever to begin these interviews because anxiety is controlling me now. I take in a large gulp of calming air, then step off the carriage.

••

The main lobby of the Jurisdiction Bureau surrounds me like a huge concrete hand. I'm barely allowed a second in time to take in the vast space before an assistant in a light-grey tunic approaches. He taps at the screen of the digital pad which he is holding, then looks at me with what seems to be impatience.

"Follow me, Elana, I'll escort you to the interview," says the young man as he turns his attention back to the display. He is in his mid-twenties with short blond hair and green eyes. The abrupt nature of his words and body language put me on edge.

"Thank you," I reply. I am instructed immediately afterwards - with nothing more than a few waves of his hand - to hand over my ID card.

"This way," he says as the digital pad scans my card.

I don't even know his name. He could have at least introduced himself. He knows how intimidating this place is ... especially today!

After being escorted through the building for ten silent minutes, along many corridors - all that seem to have no end - I finally reach a small room.

Without a hint of manners or politeness, I am directed to wait inside until a representative of the Education Department calls for me.

On the wall opposite my chair, a television screen replays the warning message that I watched earlier at the college library train station, with an update added to the end - the Rogue male still hasn't been apprehended. Apart from that, there isn't anything else to look at. No photographs have been placed on the walls showing content families, smiling at each other.

"Elana Mayne."

The female voice comes from a speaker somewhere in the room, although it is completely hidden from view.

"You may now proceed to your interview. Leave this room, turn left, enter the first door on your right. Introduce yourself, then wait for further instruction."

I stand up and shake my arms and hands with vigour and too much strength. They feel hot and overly sensitive, as if pins and needles are trying to set in. *Here we go!* I think, encouraging myself to be successful.

I follow the directions and soon find myself in a large and windowless hall. Thick panels of transparent plastic separate it in equal sections, and a couple of chairs have been set out, facing each other. They seem too close. Intimidating. *Do I sit? I haven't been told to ...*

I immediately notice others there too, all looking as nervous as I do, all standing by the chairs, wondering who might soon sit in them. *This is it. I wonder if it really is as bad as I've heard?*

Loud clicking noises from the heels on a pair of shoes sound behind me as a woman walks in through the same door I used: late-forties in age, her hair is tied up in a neat style, and she has serious hazel eyes. She wears a beautiful red dress and matching shoes, making me wish that I owned such clothes.

As the woman stops, I speak straight away. "My name is Elana Mayne. I reside in the South Quarter of the Essex Community." My words are rushed yet coherent.

The woman doesn't respond because she is too focused on reading through a file in her hands. I have a terrible feeling she is scouring my personal information for a reason to complain ... something, *anything,* to pick up on.

The wait makes me even more nervous, yet I manage to hold myself together. I am the prey ... and she is a coiled snake. At any moment she will lunge forward, striking with venomous fangs.

Breathe ... breathe ...

"Let us begin," she says. Her face is very sharp - every chance it has to point, it does: her chin, her eyebrows, even the corners of her mouth. She is created from angled stone. "I see you've presented yourself well today. Always a good start."

"Thank you ...," I fumble at my words and panic, realising I am unsure how to address this woman correctly. Is it Professor? Minister? How have I overlooked such a fundamental part of this day? "… ma'am," I say after an awkward length of time.

"You may call me *Miss* Collins."

"Thank you, Miss Collins," I add with an apologetic smile. I doubt it will help.

"I have no concerns about your academic record, Elana, so some of the departments won't need to see you today. Perhaps a little bit more of an effort could have been shown in some of your weaker subjects, though …," says Miss Collins with a few taps of her pen. "… but I won't hold that against you. Others might."

Weaker subjects? I'm slightly confused and thrown off my guard by those two words. I honestly wasn't aware I had any because all of my current grades are eighty-five percent or above. I flick a nervous glance around the hall, seeing all the others in here are now being greeted in a similar fashion. A tall and muscular man, late forties as well, stands in the section to my right, talking to a boy I recognise from college … *Good luck, Andrew.*

"Yes … adequate … I see no real problems here … apart from distraction. Are you easily distracted, Elana?"

"No, Miss Collins. I'm only taking in my surroundings … and the situation." I cough the last part of my sentence. My voice has turned a little croaky because my mouth feels dry. "Interviews, especially one as important as this, will no doubt make everyone nervous."

"No, Elana, they won't. I am not nervous, not in the slightest bit." Miss Collins raises an eyebrow. Her eyes widen and her lips scrunch together with disapproving tightness.

The hunter isn't scared of the prey …

"Kindly keep your eyes on me and ignore your surroundings. Now, tell me, Elana, which department interests you? Where do you see your career path heading?"

Her eyes look up and grab me in a stare that will not

let go.

"Any of the sciences, Miss Collins. They interest me a great deal and are my strongest subjects, as my grades show. I enjoy studying them at college … I always have. I believe I will be able to serve Central Government in that field, if they choose to further my training, of course."

"The sciences?" asks Miss Collins. She looks and sounds a little disappointed with the answer and her hazel-eyed stare grows in strength, drilling beyond my eyes. Her body doesn't move, as if she isn't even breathing.

"Yes …" I desperately want to add something else, yet I also don't want to repeat my first statement. I'm trapped in silence by hesitation.

"So, not able to provide me with a specific answer? A little bit of indecision as well. What a shame. I shall have to make a note of that." Miss Collins scribbles in the file as she speaks to herself. "… indecisive attitude … distracted …"

Again, I feel the urge to add more, yet now it will seem as if I'm doing it for all the wrong reasons: trying to impress Miss Collins, or changing my answers because I have been prompted to. I admit to myself with a sigh and the threat of tears that this interview … the *interrogation* … has not begun well for me.

"And … this surprises me a great deal, Elana, a great deal …" Miss Collins pauses as she flips over pages in her file, scanning the print with excruciating precision. "… I can't find any incidents in your records where you have felt the need to speak to the Community Guards. We've all seen crimes or indiscretions in our lives, all of us. Why haven't you ever reported any?"

My mind empties. It is completely blank and no answer appears.

"… inability to form suitable replies … possible willingness to ignore fundamental law …," says Miss Collins as she scribbles once more, then locks me in her unnerving glare. "Trust me, though, Elana, that soon fades with the onset of adulthood … and the responsibility that accompanies it."

I simply nod, wanting her eyes away from me.

••

The next hour continues in a similar fashion. Various representatives move about and through the sections, each with their own brand of questions and demeanour. The man I'd seen to my right when I first entered is here on behalf of the military - Commander Ward. His uniform has three black CG insignia placed on both the shoulders of his thick green jacket, indicating rank and which department he works for. Just to ensure I felt clouded by rudeness for the whole day, he never even took the time to introduce himself.

Within ten seconds of our encounter, Commander Ward looked at my average body size with frustration, measured my five-and-a-half feet height with a digital scanner, then, with a bored look on his face and a loud sigh, asked me to tense '*whatever biceps I might have*'.

After doing so, he rudely walked off without another word, immediately deciding I wasn't worth interviewing at all.

When Miss Collins returns she is still impossible to read, still angled and made of sharp stone. Her unashamed mannerisms tell me that she is rarely impressed, or ever genuinely pleased with results.

Does she have to act like this? Is this her natural personality, or is it part of her career description to be so searching, so unpleasant?

"I shall forward your details to all the relevant departments, Elana. You will be notified of the outcome on the fourteenth of July. You may leave now."

Finally, I think with a hidden breath of relief, *it's*

over!

"Thank you, Miss Collins," I say and head towards the door. I notice the scared faces of all the others still being interviewed as I politely walk out of the hall, eager to escape this concrete fortress and see the outside world again.

••

With the Jurisdiction Bureau looming behind me, I somehow manage to relax myself, yet I can't gauge if I have failed miserably or managed to impress any of the representatives at all.

"I'm sure it will be fine … won't it? Miss Collins said that my grades were adequate … she saw no problems … I should have chosen a specific area of study, though … but … but that can't be too bad, can it?"

I mumble more retrospective conversations to myself while waiting for the train to arrive. I had been expecting a lot more involvement in the proceedings … a chance to prove myself with some intellectual or practical tasks. Not an hour standing in a room being questioned. *Why bring in chairs if we weren't even allowed to sit on them?*

Complete and utter embarrassment hits me as I remember more details, making my face glow hot and red. Commander Ward so easily dismissed me as a viable investment choice for further training because of my size and apparent weakness. Yes, I agree completely with his decision - I'm definitely not cut out for the military. I often make the same face as he did: usually when my mother cooks a thick, and not particularly appetising, fish stew.

The train arrives so I get up and walk towards an open door on one of the carriages. Then, something happens - something so quick and unexpected, my mind doesn't even have a chance to comprehend or explain it. One second my eyes are looking at the train, the next I'm laying face down on the floor. The entire front of my body aches because of the fall, especially my left hand. It feels warm as sharp pains shoot through my fingers.

"You must ask yourself … How could I know any of this? Unless …?" says a woman's voice, although it isn't familiar to me. It's very soft and delicate, as if spoken in a breeze.

I try to turn my face so that I can look behind me but the pain, confusion, and shock are all still too fresh.

"What … what happened? Did I trip over? Was I pushed?"

Other voices grow louder as they arrive near to me, also wondering why I'm face down on the platform.

"I didn't see anything!" says a male voice. "Did anyone?"

"I think she's hurt herself!" says another - a young man.

"Come on, child. Up you get … it will be fine. Sit for me so that I can check you over," says a different woman with a broader, mature tone. "Are you hurt?"

I have to force myself to think about the answer as I hear the sound of the train moving away. Most of the pain has lessened, except for my hand. "I … I think so. My hand really hurts … and my fingers … they're stinging …," I say

"I'll take you to a medical booth, child. Come on. Your fingers look swollen and need to be examined. Just hold them still for me, as best as you can. Don't move them …"

I try to piece together the last minute. I want to remember what happened to me, what caused me to fall, but the only thing pushing to the forefront of my mind are the words of the unknown and unseen woman. *Who spoke to me? What did they mean?*

As I look about, I completely forget the mature woman's advice - because my thoughts are elsewhere - and push down on the floor as I try to stand up. A chilling howl of pain leaves my throat as I grab the woman's hand in agony, then roll back to the ground in tears.

Chapter two

I sit in my bedroom - four square metres of privacy - inspecting the white bandages and surgical splint now wrapped around, and along, my left fore and middle fingers. After medical inspection at the Jurisdiction Bureau, the in-house doctor confirmed they were both broken during my unexpected - and inexplicable - fall on the train platform.

Despite the pain still pulsing through my hand after every slight movement, I still find myself more concerned with the performance at the progression interview, and the mysterious words I heard: *You must ask yourself ... How could I know any of this? Unless ...?*

"What do they mean? And who spoke them to me? ... *And* why?" I whisper to myself.

My parents are in the lounge, unaware of the full story. I have not told them about the woman's voice and I'm not sure if I will at any time soon. I can hear Miss Collins, the angled snake made of stone, whispering in my ear ... *We've all seen crimes, Elana ... ALL OF US!*

I shake my head to make her hissing words disappear and refocus on my parents. They are reading through the official medical report of the accident, and also the statement I had to complete - a mandatory requirement, caused by the

21

situation with the Community Guards in the college library. I may have been scared, intimidated, and had guns pointed at my head, yet I am still required by law to document all the facts.

As soon as I returned home, I discovered that a statement request had been delivered, addressed to my parents. They are content with my innocence in the matter, but only after hearing the story in full, twice, and once their own questions had been answered satisfactorily. If I break the law, they are breaking the law - unsatisfactory upbringing of a minor. Central Government manages to control parenting as well, to a certain degree.

Luckily for me, I am right-handed, so the injury didn't hinder my ability to write out a personal version of events straight away. My parents did not want there to be any delay in replying to the Community Guards, and have made this very clear to me as well.

Nicholas Mayne, my father, knocks, pauses, then enters the bedroom. He wears the same style of clothes as I do, only in dark blue. This indicates to all that he is an adult male resident, working for the Information Department. He has the same blue eyes as myself, stands six-feet in height, and has neat black hair, brushed backwards.

"This all seems adequate, Elana," he says. His eyes mix between concern for me and the need to obey the law.

There's that word again ... adequate.

"Your mother and I will sign it immediately and return our copies tomorrow morning," says my father as he folds the paperwork and taps it on his palm.

"Thank you, Father. I'm ... I'm sorry. I must have been in the wrong place at the wrong time. I didn't mean to worry you, or Mother." I am speak truthfully.

"Don't apologise, Elana. Like you said earlier, you are innocent. No crimes have been committed here. It is just standard procedure, as you know. I'm more worried about those broken fingers."

I nod my head in agreement because I'm worried about them as well. Terrible pains have been corkscrewing through my hand regularly over the past six hours. The doctor assured me they would set and heal without any further complications, though.

Anne Mayne, my mother, walks through to my bedroom as well, joining the conversation with a sympathetic face. She is wearing a lilac outfit: adult female resident, working in the Housing Department. We look very much alike, except she is a taller and more mature in appearance.

"We'll be leaving for the community social in about fifteen minutes. I've prepared your clothes for you," she says as her eyes move towards my dresser in the corner of the room. "Do you need any help getting dressed, Elana? It might be difficult with your broken fingers."

I decline the offer with a forced smile. "No, Mother, thank you anyway. I think I'll be fine."

My mother carefully lifts my injured hand to inspect the bandages. This is easily the tenth time it's happened since I arrived home. She winces with maternal worry at the dark bruising that is creeping out from underneath, spreading down the skin on my hand, like a purple and blue web. "Call me if you need help," she repeats, then kisses me gently on the forehead.

"Come on, Anne. We'll leave her to get ready," says my father as they both leave the bedroom.

I look at the white dress folded on the top of my dresser and the very ordinary shoes resting on the floor: black with flat soles. I remember the brief encounter with the sharp-faced Miss Collins earlier this morning, specifically her amazing red dress and high heels. One day in the future, possibly, I might be allowed to wear such clothes, yet it would mean many years of career progression first. For now, I'm stuck with the tunic. For now, I blend in with all the others.

With a lot of care and attention, I stand up and unzip my tunic. I slowly take it off with my right hand, being careful not to move my broken fingers too much.

What's that? A soft noise sounds as I feel something brush against the top of my bare feet.

I look down to see a folded piece of paper has fallen to the floor. "Where did that come from?" I whisper to myself. It definitely does not belong to me.

I pick it up, unfold it with shaking hands, then begin to read the handwritten words.

Whoever you are, and however I managed to get this to you is irrelevant. Read my words. Memorize them if you can. Tonight, at approximately nine, you will see, and hear as well, an explosion. Look in a NW direction. The news will report it almost immediately as an accident in one of the steel processing plants. But, as you probably heard me say, how could I know any of this? How does one know of accidents before they occur?

The woman's voice! The woman on the train platform!

I want to drop the note but can't let go. "She hid this in my tunic?" I say, lowering my voice mid-sentence. I stare at my bedroom door, hoping I haven't grabbed the attention of my parents. "It must have been when I fell over? ... Or ... did she push me? Is that when she put it there?"

Keep your eye on the newspapers and media broadcasts. There will be an announcement soon that will make every resident feel that Central Government is rewarding them. I am unsure yet what this will be.

A change in law is imminent. Recent activity, some of my own doing, has caused a reaction. It will involve security, that is all I can estimate at the present time.

A train disaster will be narrowly avoided this week. A driver recently contacted the Community Guards with crucial information about abstract crimes in his department. He is to be rewarded for this. The cover story from the media to the residents will portray him as a heroic individual.

A fifty-fifty could be discovered in the community, very soon. He, or she, will have been caught entering the perimeter. I do not want to imagine what this might lead to. I'm afraid to say this is yet another staged incident. Central Government needs to show strength, always, and this is how it will happen.

If I am not caught and eliminated within two days, there will be a public warning issued.
If I am apprehended, expect a resident to be harmed in the process. Of course, I will be blamed, yet, and I know you have no reason to believe me, I will not be guilty of this. I expect the Elimination Squad, or Plain Sight Guards will be ordered to carry this out.
I'll find another way to contact you again in a few days, if it is possible.

I've lost count of the times today where my body has physically shaken with fear. I have no idea what to do but my fingers still won't loosen their grip on this note.

False stories, fifty-fifties in the zone ... secretive guard departments ... I don't want to think about any of this!

The fact that someone has contacted me is enough to cause panic, yet the consequences could be far worse. Central Government and its associated Security Department will question me until they are fully satisfied that there isn't any involvement. Saying that I know nothing - and have no idea how the piece of paper ended up in my possession - will not be enough. Why would they even believe that someone else had planted it inside my tunic?

Don't forget, they could just as easily claim it is your note ... you wrote it ... you are committing abstract crimes and have unstable thoughts.

I feel physically sick. My stomach churns over and over with fear. I look out of the window in my bedroom, then, with a swift push of my legs, move myself across the room quickly to pull the curtains shut. I'm suddenly paranoid about being seen and tell myself there are people from Central Government watching me. The low street lights become eyes, every noise is a guard watching me, every voice outside is talking about me.

HIDE IT! HIDE IT!

I refold the note, slide it underneath my mattress and sit on top of it on the bed, breathing deeply, trying to decide what to do next. Speak to my parents? Contact the Community Guards? None of the options calm me down.

"Elana!" my father calls. It is followed by loud knocks on my bedroom door.

My heart has had enough of today, yet it still manages to jump around inside my chest again. "Ye ... yes?"

"Are you nearly ready? We're leaving very soon," he says.

"I'll ... I'll be out in five minutes. I'm just putting my clothes on," I call back in reply, hoping I don't sound too guilty. *But ... what am I actually guilty of?*

I stand up on hearing my father walk away from the bedroom door, push the note further underneath the mattress, then finished getting dressed. The adrenaline pumping through my body helps me a great deal with ignoring the pain in my fingers.

••

After a ten minute tram journey, I arrive at the community social with my parents. My mother is wearing the same dress and shoes as I am, and my father looks smart in a grey suit.

This is a weekly event held inside one of the spacious rooms of the Town Hall building. We meet and talk with each other while enjoying a small selection of fruit and refreshments, provided by Central Government. Personally, I enjoy visiting because it is decorated with such contrast to all the other buildings. Here there are mahogany panelled walls, cream curtains draped around the windows and soft carpets under my feet.

The social isn't compulsory by any means, yet it is enjoyed by all who choose to attend. Even the mayor, Charles Hartner, and his family, show up at least twice a month. *Probably why the décor is so different.*

"Elana!" calls an excited voice as I enter the lobby, lit by hanging brass chandeliers.

"Jackson!" I shout back with a welcoming smile.

Seeing my lifelong friend, standing with his parents at the side of the room, clears my head momentarily. My mind is in a chaotic state and I need it to slow down.

Jackson Miller always cheers me up, no matter the severity of my thoughts, because we share such a strong friendship. Just one of his awkward smiles, a look at his brown eyes, or the way he plays with his short blonde hair. It's enough for me. It pulls me back from the sadness.
A lot of girls in the community like him, and with good reason as well: he is handsome, tall with a muscular physique, and he carries a dry wit. There is also an unusual birthmark coiled around his wrist. It granted him the nickname 'Snake'

27

from a very young age.

"Mother, Father, may I leave and talk with my friend?" I ask as we walk through the tall doors to the hall.

"Of course. We will be up at the front, sitting at the tables," replies my father as he waves at a work colleague.

"Be careful with those broken fingers," says my mother.

"Thank you. I will." I rush off and join Jackson at a table by the wall. His parents have also left him so they can mingle with others and socialise.

I play out a scenario in my clouded mind, completely hypothetical, where I tell him everything about the note and the woman on the train platform.

The hall is filled with nearly three-hundred people - about a tenth of the population for the Essex Community - yet, as I walk over to my friend, I notice a lot of students, especially those in my year, are absent. *Probably because of the interrogation. To be honest, I'm not exactly in the mood to be out tonight.*

"What happened to you?" asks Jackson. His eyes, distracted and concerned, stare towards my hand. He didn't even get out a proper hello.

"What?"

"Your fingers? The bandages? What did you do?" He reaches to grab my hand and inspect it but stops himself, worried that any kind of contact will hurt me.

I explain to Jackson about the fall at the train station, yet, as with my parents, I deliberately omit the details about the woman's voice. I also recall the rather short and embarrassing interrogation interview as well. He doesn't see it as negatively as I do, though.

"Or you impressed them so much that they didn't need to keep you there for very long." He points to the centre of my forehead. "That brain of yours had to get noticed … eventually."

The sarcasm in Jackson's voice flies straight over my head as I continue to worry. "But … it was over within an hour! It worries me, that's all. As if I did something wrong but haven't realised."

"Mine lasted for about the same amount of time," says Jackson as he hugs me, smiles, then whispers in my ear. "Can I talk to you about something? Come and sit with me, Elana, please? Away from everyone else."

I notice that Jackson's eyes look familiar. I'd had the same expression earlier this evening, after receiving the note. It is an unspoken, secretive fear. Something you want to let out, yet can't.

"You know I trust you, right?" asks Jackson as he sits on a bench at the end of the room, near the entrance. There are less people mingling about which gives us both some privacy. A few girls stare and smile at Jackson, hoping he will notice them, however, they don't approach us.

I nod as I sit next to him. "Of course. What's the matter with you?"

We have known each other since the age of four - starting nursery school at the same time - and we were residents of the same housing estate too, before my relocation. Jackson and his family still live there.

He looks around the room a couple of times before staring at me. "The progression interview … they said I'd do very well in a military career."

I'm not sure exactly what I was expecting to hear. This doesn't seem bad to me, though. "Well, that's great! Isn't it? You should have seen the military representative at mine … he couldn't get away from me fast enough! I don't think I have a future there. I'm just too … small and short!" I say, managing to add a laugh through my words.

Jackson laughs a little with me, yet he soon looks disappointed again. "Is it great? There will be so much change … *too* much change. Then there's relocation, Elana.

I'll be training for six months before a division is chosen. I'll be sent to a community in the North, where they house the recruits."

"I know, but … this is great, Jackson! It's an amazing career choice," I say. Yes, I'll miss him. I'll miss him with every inch of my heart, yet if the military is to be his path, I have no place in it.

Jackson doesn't share my enthusiasm. "Choice? There wasn't any bloody choice in it! I … don't want to go … but, if that is what they've decided, then … then that is what I have to do." He punches gently on his thighs a couple of times and puffs out lungfuls of air. "Do you know how much I hate that? I should get a say in my own life, Elana, not have it set for me!"

I'm sitting so close to Jackson that I clearly hear him curse under his breath. I look about quickly, double-checking to see if any eyes are pointed in our direction, worried that someone might have overheard his rant.

"Calm down, Jackson! Take it easy! You're going to get yourself in a lot of trouble if you speak like that!"

He takes my advice and sits quietly for a few minutes. I don't speak either, content to be the great friend he obviously needs at this very moment, even without words passing between us. We watch the people around the room, talking with each other and smiling.

"Do you want to come outside for some fresh air?" asks Jackson, eventually. Thankfully, he doesn't have an angry expression any longer, so sharing his fears with me must have helped.

"Yeah, sure. I'll just go and tell my parents."

Outside, with a cooling breeze swirling through the streets, I soon realise that Jackson's mood has only been put on hold. If anything, he has grown more negative. He repeats, over and over, that he should be able to choose for himself, not be told by someone else where his life is heading. It isn't the first time I've heard such words from people my age. I've had a few similar thoughts myself over the past year. Yet again, though, it is something that must be buried inside, kept a secret, made silent. It can never be spoken to others.

"Jackson, you have to calm yourself down. Please. You're worrying me." I lower my voice. "It isn't fair, I get that, okay? But, there isn't anything you can do, is there? I mean, how many people do you know of who have changed their career? I can't think of a single name, can you?"

"There's a first time for everything." Jackson shakes his head after speaking, knowing I'm right. "And … I'll miss … everyone."

I nudge him in the arm as we sit on the high steps that lead up to the Town Hall building. "Yeah, but that's just part of it, you know, life I mean. Look at Anna … she left for a position on the other side of the world. We will probably *never* see her again, but she still writes whenever it is possible," I say, mentioning a mutual friend. "You could see the world too, you know that, right? The military are one of the few departments that travel to other countries on a regular basis. I'd like to see Japan, I think … and Europe too. I'm worried they won't look as beautiful as they do in the photographs I've seen in college, though. I doubt any of the old world looks beautiful any longer … not now."

You're talking too much. He doesn't want to hear any of this.

"True," agrees Jackson as he shifts about awkwardly on the step, edging a few inches closer to my side. "And … you, Elana. How am I going to get along without you there with me? We've known each other for so long now. It … it annoys me, you know?"

I have much to say in reply. Instead, I completely change the subject. "What time is it?"

Jackson turns his head just enough so that he can see

31

the nearest train platform. The street lighting raised to night level about twenty minutes ago, mixing with the sunset, bathing everything in a yellowy-white glow. "As long as my eyesight isn't failing me, it's eight-forty three. We've got about an hour left. What are your plans for the weekend?"

"I expect I'll be reading, studying … or helping my parents with chores at home. You?"

"Maybe I'll go to the library … cram up on my sciences or political studies. I could avoid the military grabbing me then!" says Jackson with a sarcastic laugh. "I might practice saying no. It'd be interesting to see what happens."

"You might want to practice accepting it," I say and think about the note I received again. I feel another urge to tell Jackson everything, to share my fears, just as he has done about having decisions made for him. Instead, I laugh at the thought of him inside a library, without it being related to college studies. He just isn't the type and has always been more athletic than academic.

Nothing yet … she lied to me! I've been warned so many times about people like her - Rogues! They spread rumours … I should report her straight away … and …

I don't get to finish my line of thought. A plume of orange flames rise in the distance, followed a few seconds later by a dull sound, rumbling like thunder crashing high above.

"What was that?" Jackson jumps to his feet, spinning in a complete circle. "Look! Elana, look! Can you see that? Over there!" he exclaims as his eyes focus in on the origin of the noise and light.

No! It can't be! I think, not entirely sure which fact has surprised me more. I am watching an explosion, booming with power and energy. More crucially, the note predicted it correctly.

Jackson stares, both shocked and enthralled by the

distant flame. His mouth drops open just after he curses once again.

"How could I know any of this? Unless?"

I close my eyes tightly because I can hear the words from earlier this morning. They are so clear in my mind, it sounds as if the woman is right beside me again. A shot of pain darts through my fingers to remind me of the moment when it happened.

"Jackson! Watch your language!" I have to warn him after hearing more words that he should keep inside his head.

He continues to stare, now mindful of himself. He definitely doesn't want to get in any trouble with the Community Guards for using unnecessary or obscene language in a public area. He is still classed as a minor in the eyes of the law, until he reaches eighteen years of age, so all crimes will be partly shared with his parents.

Another boom spreads slowly and I reach for Jackson's hand at the exact same moment that he reaches for mine. We both hold tightly. The initial shock and uncontrollable excitement has transformed, morphed now to brutal reality, bringing fear and concern with it.

"I wonder what happened?" asks Jackson. "This is … this is really bad. What do we do?"

"Elana!" cries my mother from the top of the steps. She is followed closely by my father. They stop worrying once outside, satisfied that their daughter is safe.

More residents appear on the steps, their eyes instantly sparkling with the reflection of the far away orange flames. Everyone is drawn to it, like a magnet. It's terrifying, yet pulling all of us in. The flames continue rolling upward, reaching for the night sky in giant rings.

Every person from the social stands still, transfixed with utter disbelief as Community Guards begin to appear in large numbers. They run down the street or jump off trams to line up at the bottom of the stairs, staring like everybody else.

"Stay calm! We are awaiting information. You will all remain here until I receive notification that it is safe for you to travel through the zone!" shouts one of them.

Amongst the crowd, many voices gasp and whisper, some cry out in shock. I never let go of Jackson's hand as I start to try and answer the questions on the note. I don't want my mind to follow that path, though. I squeeze tighter, using his touch as an anchor to the world I know.

There are no questions to be answered! my thoughts shout at me. *I shouldn't have put any belief in that note ... I shouldn't be thinking this way. Does it mean that I ... I am getting sick? Am I possibly infected?*

A Community Guard walks to the top of the steps and all the residents shuffle back slightly, giving him some space to move.

Don't tell me this happened at the processing plant! Don't say those words. The note is wrong!

"I have just been informed that a news bulletin is imminent. Direct your attention to the nearest screen." He speaks loudly and with authority, pointing behind him.

I sway from side to side, pushing on my tip-toes, trying to see the large screen on the right side of the doors to the Town Hall building. The crowd is now blocking my view, all bustling together, all needing immediate answers.

"I've got an idea," says Jackson. He walks down the steps, quickly leading me across the street. The Community Guards don't try to stop us, although they watch our movements every step of the way.

Jackson continues to walk with his hand firmly around mine. I entertain an unusual thought in which we keep going, then, we start to run. I don't know where we will go, but it doesn't seem to matter. *Why am I having such strange thoughts?*

We could both run away from this day - no note, no disappointing interrogations for either of us. We wouldn't be troubled … it would be as if nothing happened at all.

"Come on!" says Jackson with a squeeze of his hand. It brings me out of the daydream. "We can watch it on the screen at the medical booth. Hurry, I want to know what's going on."

Me too! I quicken my pace to keep up with his longer legs. I am just as intrigued and need to hear how the news will explain this terrible event, albeit not for the same reasons. My questions are a lot different to those of everyone else in the community.

Residents, this is an emergency announcement.
Stay calm.

I look over my shoulder. *Every single person from the social is outside!*

The crowd on the Town Hall steps are approximately three hundred feet away, all quiet, eagerly staring at the screen, listening to the broadcast.

There has been an explosion at the steel processing plant in sector 1.
The Emergency Services Department has been deployed to the scene.

No … I feel my heart sink and head spin. Sweat appears on my palms and forehead.

Details have not yet come forth concerning injuries or fatalities, although there has been contact by a representative of Central Government. We have been assured that the buildings destroyed were storage facilities. It is highly unlikely that any staff were inside at the time of the explosion.

I hear a collective sigh from everyone gathered

outside the Town Hall. I know that some of them will have relatives working near to the explosion. *They must be so worried!*

As always, do not panic. We will update you with any new information as soon as we receive it.
Remember, Central Government is in control of the situation and will always ensure the safety of its residents.

The screen fades out and I look at Jackson. "We should get back to the Town Hall and our parents. The Community Guards will tell us what to do next," I say, hiding the real worries inside me. *She was telling the truth! The woman on the train platform was telling the truth. But ... who is she?*

Chapter three

I can't get to sleep tonight, despite many attempts. I have already kicked off my duvet twice, then replaced it again in case the warmth in my room is causing me to stay awake. It isn't making any difference to my restless behaviour, though. Every noise outside still makes me jump as well, despite no solid reason for such actions. After the explosion, I can't shift the idea that the note has somehow put me in serious danger.

Everything that has happened to me creates unwanted thoughts as well: the college library, my progression interview, breaking my fingers on the train platform, the note and the explosion. They are all fighting their way for supremacy.

I have two possible answers for the questions which the enigmatic woman - the Rogue - asked me. *"... How could I know any of this? Unless ...?"* The first - the woman knew about the explosion because she was, in some way, responsible. The second - *someone* knew about it, and the woman discovered this information. I am equally scared of both solutions.

I hear a hum in the pipes, then running water as it drums on the metal sink in the kitchen for a few seconds. *Is someone else awake?*

I get out of bed and walk quietly to the bedroom door, opening it a fraction so I can check. I see my father out there, sipping at a glass of water as he stands by the sink. He is dressed the same as me in a loose, airy t-shirt and thin trousers.

I can't see his face properly, yet I know that he is very tired as well. The slumped shoulders and the way his head hangs forward are all the evidence I need.

I should talk to him. Has he already heard something from his department? I wonder if he is allowed to talk about it, or if he has to wait until it's reported on the news?

"Father? Is something the matter?" I ask as I leave my room and join him. "You aren't usually up at this time of the night."

"Elana, you should be asleep. It's very late," he says with exhausted and forlorn eyes. They look at the clock on the wall. "It's not long after midnight. You must be so tired?"

"I think the explosion is playing on my mind. It's keeping me awake, I know that much," I explain.

My father sips some more water, then takes a seat in the lounge on our sofa. I pour myself a glass as well and sit opposite him on an armchair, bringing my feet up next to me. Only the strip-light in the kitchen was switched on when my father came in here, so the rectangle area containing the lounge and kitchen - twenty square feet - looks cramped, gloomy and eerie.

"Have there been any other news bulletins? Do we know if anybody got hurt at the processing plant?" I ask, only wanting to hear a positive answer. I have a feeling I'm going to regret asking any questions.

"I'm afraid so, yes." My father wipes his tired eyes, apologising to me with words and his facial expression. "Do you remember John Wright? He lived in the estate for a few years while we were housed there?"

I nod, then a terrible sadness fills me. It's like a cold

band grabbing my bare feet, working its way up my body. John Wright has a son - Blake. I'm not particularly close to him, yet we always talk when seeing each other in the community, or at college.

"Is he …?" My face drops, scared that John has been killed. My eyes flick towards the bedroom door. I subconsciously let my vision extend to the edge of my bed, almost as if I am walking there. My searching daydream stops at the side of my bed, close to where the note is hidden.

"No, nothing like that," reassures my father, "but he was very close to the building where the explosion took place. The news bulletin says that he is recovering well in the hospital, yet there has been serious damage to his leg. It's a terrible thing, truly terrible. I hope I am allowed time to visit. It should be granted, because of our friendship."

"Oh, no! That is horrible!" I cry. "I think I'll drop by to see Blake tomorrow. He will need friends around him, especially now," I add, then remember to check my manners, having briefly forgotten them because of the unexpected news. "I mean, if that is allowed, Father? I can still find time to help with the house chores and complete any college assignments when I get back."

My father hadn't noticed my mistake. He smiles and moves next to me, perching on the armrest of the chair. "Take as long as you need, Elana," he says as he puts his arm around me in agreement. There seems to be more to his behaviour, yet, if there is, he's controlling it - acting normally because he has to do so.

"Try to sleep now, Elana. Don't let this bother you too much. I know that is a very difficult thing to do, but you must try, you must." My father hugs me again.

"I will, Father. Goodnight."

I did try, and I managed to sleep for a few hours. Mostly, though, I fidgeted and stared at the ceiling, inches away from the note that is still slipped underneath the mattress. I can almost sense it there, pushing on my skin. I desperately want to take it out and read it again, but resist. *I can't risk it being discovered ... and ... and I'm scared for myself too. How much of it will I believe? Will anything else on there actually happen?*

••

Blake Wright and his family live twenty minutes from my home, in a two storey unit close to the school and college complexes. Apart from Blake and John, there are also eleven year old twin girls, Katrina and Ellysa, and his mother, Louise. Because of these family space requirements, the Wright household are permitted three bedrooms. John's career position too - a managerial post at the steel processing plant - stipulates that he be rewarded with a larger residence.

I could cut my journey time by three-quarters if I jump on a tram, yet choose to walk instead. After yesterday and lack of sleep during the night, I feel the need for some quiet time to myself, just with my own thoughts. Unfortunately, the fears are threatening to multiply beyond control.

Today has brought sunshine again, teasing me with the onset of summer, drawing me outside.

After leaving my residential line, I turn left, walk for a few minutes along the street and reach the Plaza. It is an area designated for rest or gentle recreation activities, such as reading, light studies, or social conversation. There are benches, a few trees, and some potted plants full of marigolds, asters and peonies.

Only one family are present here today. The parents sit with their two children, both boys. An image from a positive government message has jumped off the screen in front of me. Four content, smiling faces, showing everyone else their happiness, reminding me why I should obey the rules.

After ten minutes, I stand at the edge of one of the grass covered areas in the South Quarter. These are always popular - especially with the younger children - as a place to run free, roll about and have fun. At the moment it looks green, lush and inviting, however, within a month or two, the grass will yellow. Before the end of summer, it will become dry and worn, flattened by thousands of footsteps. Central Government has always stated that clean, unpolluted, water is not freely available to maintain it throughout the entire year. Such matters are deemed trivial needs.

I see a few families from this neighbourhood on the grass today, enjoying time in the sun. The children play games together, mostly chasing each other around in large circles. One little girl with curly auburn hair has recently learnt to walk. The clumsy movements and jittery actions of putting one foot in front of the other make me giggle to myself. She is so proud of her new skill - smiling and clapping triumphantly on steadying herself after two steps. Her actions display such an innocence, a care free nature. Not a single worry has made its way inside her young thoughts.

"So cute," I say, lost in the glorious smile of youth.

The final minutes of the journey take me by an estate block. I remember my time living in one of these with very fond memories. It is almost a small town within another. People would visit each other regularly - we all lived so close - or talk on the balconies. Birthday celebrations were always memorable too, simply because of the amount of people who would drop by to offer their congratulations. The joyous occasion countered for the uncomfortable and cramped space inside.

I turn right at the end of the estate building and walk for another five-hundred yards. The living units grow larger and larger, yet they are different to the others. Instead of the concrete design replicated so many times throughout the community, these are large metal containers, stacked on top of each other. They have been modified by government engineers, with windows and doors cut and set in, bringing them in line with housing regulations. I've been inside a few of them and they are always made welcoming and a place to call home, not just a steel shell with some furniture added.

This one is Blake's. Maybe I should just keep walking? Am I right to come here? He might want to be alone?

I take a deep breath and ignore myself and the spreading doubts. I know that in a time of need such as this, I would be comforted with my friends close by.

While the inner argument about whether or not I should be here continues, my legs ignore every thought and take me to the front door.

No turning back now, I'm here. I bang my fist on the metal, wondering what my first word or reaction will be.

A tall boy answers the door: broad shoulders, dark skin and cropped hair. He looks so tired, yet strong enough, both physically and mentally, to deal with what has happened.

I hope you are that strong, Blake ... I really hope you are ...

His brown eyes are slightly red, indicating a mixture of broken sleep and recent tears.

"Hi, Elana ... erm ... I didn't expect to see you here. Are you ... erm ... okay?"

I feel like grabbing Blake in a tight embrace, right here at the door. Only people of a kind nature, truly kind, ask after others when their own world has fallen to pieces around them.

"I'm fine, Blake. I just wanted to see you ... to make sure that you're okay after what happened with your father. Is ... is he ...?" I become lost for words. My depressing facial expression finishes off the sentence for me.

"I visited him during the night at the hospital. My mother and sisters are there with him now. Come in, Elana, we can talk more inside."

Blake pours us both some water and then sits down in the lounge area. He keeps looking towards the window.

Waiting for his mother and sisters, probably? I can't imagine what it would feel like to be hoping for news about something as terrible as this. Poor Blake.

"The news reports haven't released any details yet. Did you ... you ... find out anything? I mean, about how it happened?" I ask.

Blake shakes his head. "My father didn't want to discuss it much. He was really tired and only spoke briefly. The hospital had to give him a high dose of pain medication. The ... the surgeon told us ... told us all ..." He takes a deep breath. "My father is almost certain to lose the leg. The damage is too extensive."

I nearly drop the glass of water. "Oh, Blake. I'm so sorry!" I say, steadying my drink with both hands.

Blake closes his eyes. It is a method used to compose himself - within seconds he is fine again - sipping his own water and thinking with a positive attitude. "It could have been a lot worse. My father wasn't in the building, just near to it, so ... we all have a lot to be thankful for ... You have to look at it in a certain way ..."

He's staying positive and so strong! I nod then smile. I'm not feeling uncomfortable, just slightly awkward, as if all the words I want to say need to be scanned first, to make sure they don't upset my friend. "Erm ... will he be home soon?"

Blake stands up and walks towards the rectangular lounge window. He crosses his arms and looks out at the street. "Do you ever wonder, Elana ... wonder what it's like out there? Outside of the community?"

The question is unexpected and an unusual shift in

the topic, so I can't answer straight away. I have absolutely no idea what to say in reply anyway.

A loud bang on the outside of the unit startles me. Blake doesn't move much, just a blink of the eyes and a slight frown.

His mother and sisters? He must have seen them arriving home. I should leave ... they definitely won't want me here at a time like this. But ... wouldn't they have a set of keys?

Blake's body suddenly tightens. His eyes open wider and his strong hands keep clenching to fists. It looks as if he is preparing for a fight. I can almost feel his strength growing throughout the room.

"Elana." He whispers my name as he walks slowly to the kitchen area, being very quiet with his steps. He kneels down on the floor and pushes a panel. "Sorry, it's just ... it's too big a lie for me, Elana ... I'm so sorry."

What's he doing with the floor? What's he talking about?

The panel moves to the side as Blake, very carefully and in complete silence, lifts it away. He nods towards the hole, now open to the small space above the concrete ground underneath his living unit.

I point at myself with confusion and disbelief, just as two more loud bangs hammer on the metal door. *What? He wants me to climb down there?*

"GO!" whispers Blake. His gritted teeth and bloodshot eyes hold such a definitive authority over me. I have no choice but to climb down through the rectangle gap.

This is getting scary now! What is happening? No answers come to me as my body slips underneath the metal. I stare at Blake but he is looking towards his front door.

I move myself down on the cold concrete as the panel slides back in place over my head. It is dark here, yet a small amount of natural sunlight creeps in around the edges. I see many pairs of boots in front of me, outside the main door of the unit - boots belonging to Community Guards. The only exception - a very expensive pair of black shoes, polished to perfection.

I try to imagine what could possibly have made Blake so paranoid and tense. *Why didn't he just open the door with me there? Why did I have to hide?*

"Sorry, it's just ... it's too big a lie for me, Elana ... I'm so sorry."

I try to explain Blake's previous words. I try to connect dots that aren't even there, but they won't make any sense for me.

Voices begin talking and I freeze. I'm not going to move because I will be heard by the Community Guards. There is no other choice but to stay quiet, stay hidden, and listen.

"Blake Wright. I need to speak with you. May I come in?"

"Mayor Hartner? Of course, sir, of course," says Blake.

The mayor? Oh, I hope he hasn't come by to deliver bad news? Perhaps something happened at the hospital?

I am thinking terrible and upsetting thoughts as the heavy boots of Community Guards follow Mayor Hartner inside. Even though my view is limited by the dim light, it looks as if more have arrived outside. *Why are there so many here?*

"Now, Blake, don't worry yourself. Your father is well and I've been told that the surgery was a success. He will be fitted with a prosthetic limb tomorrow, then begin physiotherapy shortly afterwards."

I've become too conscious of my own breathing, worried that if I can hear it, they can hear it. Being discovered in this makeshift hiding place will not end well for me.

"So," continues Mayor Hartner, "the only loose end we need to discuss is the conversation with your father during the night. We must have it settled. You understand that, don't you? The seriousness of it?"

It is strange how the mayor's tone of voice changes so quickly, so harshly. It could be a different person speaking altogether. Blake is being warned, that's what it sounds like to me.

"I don't know how I'm supposed to settle it, sir."

Blake seems to have an edge to his voice as well and I grow even more nervous.

I turn my head as far around as it will go, wondering if I can slide myself backwards, away from this troubling situation.

I can't get out that way! Thick concrete blocks and foundation pillars supporting the unit constrict my movements in most directions.

There is a certain feel to everything, as if it might escalate in a very short space of time. A dark and angry blanket has wrapped itself around every single word.

"Blake, I've listened to an audio recording of the complete conversation. I am fully aware of what you two discussed. So, again, we must have it settled. Your father won't go beyond his boundaries any more, not after the explosion. That only leaves yourself, doesn't it? To settle this, you have to tell me, right now, that it will go no further."

Silence follows and I hold my breath.

"Do you know, Blake, how difficult it is? I mean, think of the bigger picture for me. Actually try and comprehend it, just for a few seconds. It's taken us four generations to get to where we are today ... four generations! Think of what it was like for your grand-parents? Can you do that?" The mayor pauses briefly but it isn't long enough for an answer, he has more to say. "It doesn't matter if you can

imagine it or not, to be honest. I'll tell you what it was like …
horrific! The conditioning, the subtle manipulation of thought
… it didn't take very well. We have a greater success ratio
now … less resistance to the truth."

What is the mayor talking about? I think about
everything that has happened to me over the previous day.
The fact none of it makes sense terrifies me more by the
second. Why is the mayor, a normally jovial, likeable man,
becoming more and more irate with every word that he
speaks?

"I don't … don't know, sir … if I can … live with the
truth."

The mayor waits to reply. I hold my breath again
because I hear the clunk of heavy boots above my head on the
metal floor panels - the guards are moving about inside and
are close to me - only a couple of feet away.

Have they heard me? Do they know I'm here?

"A small part of the truth, Blake, just a small glimpse,
nothing else. And it can all end here, right now. I just need
you to choose, that's all. Which path are you going to take?"

Again, Blake and Hartner face off without words.

"Follow your father's example, boy! I'm becoming
impatient, as you can see. Why are you dragging this out?"

Blake finally finds his voice. "I'm … I'm sorry, sir …
it's just a lot for me to take in … for me to understand … it
changes everything! Everything I have ever been taught … it
turns all that to lies!"

The mayor seems to calm himself. "Yes, of course it
is, of course it is. I do understand, Blake, I do. I was young
once, like yourself, but I can't give you any more time with
this, you see that too, don't you?"

I hear footsteps moving about again, but not heavy
boots. They click like spiders running along a wall. I can only
assume Mayor Hartner is now pacing about, evaluating the
situation.

"We have ways of controlling such things, Blake, as you might have already guessed. It might not have worked on your father, not completely, but we can try other methods. Every adult has to keep certain secrets, every single one of them ... but they are gradually introduced to them. He knows I'm here with you today, in itself, that should be enough of an incentive."

"Or a threat."

I can't believe Blake has just spoken to the mayor with such an insolent, forceful tone. *What are you doing? Why are you so aggressive?*

"What did you say? What did you just say to me? I'm not threatening you, or your father! I'm giving you a choice! I didn't have to, did I? No, I didn't!"

Hartner reaches a personal limit and his patience snaps. It is as if a button has been pushed, switching on an anger, a deeply hidden rage. I hear him move again, picturing in my mind that he is standing close to Blake, face to face, intimidating him with furious eyes.

"Listen to me carefully ... you stubborn, stupid, boy! Choose, now! It's irrelevant that your father saw a couple of slaves killed! They shouldn't have escaped, should they?"

Did the mayor just say ... slaves? Slaves were killed? What does that mean?

"But ... it's wrong, sir! There shouldn't be any slaves in the first place! And why aren't any of us told about it? Why don't we know? Why aren't we told what it's like ... out there? Outside of the community?"

I remember the words. Blake said them to me when we were inside together. *Is that for me to hear? He wanted me to listen to all of this?*

A long pause drags out between Blake and Hartner. I hear footsteps move about above me - the mayor and the guards.

"This is exactly why, Blake. Because of how you're

acting at this very moment. Because you haven't had any conditioning yet … because, without that, you are not willing to accept it."

Accept it? Accept what? What does he mean by conditioning?

I dread whatever the next words will be, although none are spoken. More silence, more terrible silence. To me, time seems to pass slower than it should before a loud *CLUNK!* hums against the metal walls above me.

CLUNK!
CLUNK!
CLUNK! CLUNK! CLUNK!

Was th … that … gunshots?

I want to scream. I want to claw myself out from under the living unit and run as far away as possible. I know even the slightest noise: a loud breath, a sudden scrape of my body against the cold concrete floor … they will all lead to terrible consequences.

I have no option but to wait and watch as a drop of blood seeps through the floor panels a foot away from my face. For a cruel length of time, it clings to the metal girders, unwilling to let go.

Blake?

The drop of blood splashes gently in front of me on the cold and grey concrete.

Chapter four

The heavy boots thud around on the metal panels above me, like beats on a steel drum. They do not rush and carry no urgency. These guards above me ... *these killers* ... they are organised and efficient, following their orders precisely. They move like the cogs and gears of a single machine, working together.

Within a couple of minutes, I see two lines of Community Guards form outside Blake's home. The expensive shoes belonging to Mayor Hartner walk away from the scene, surrounded and concealed between them.

He ... he murdered Blake? Have I ... have I witnessed a ... murder? The air in my lungs disappears as I try to breathe. *I need to get out of here!*

I know I have to move - need to - and I have to do it straight away. My eyes look to the right, then the left. *I can crawl out near one of the other living units ... I'll walk away as if I haven't seen anything!*

I move as quietly as possible, using the noise from the guards to my advantage, while trying to keep the descending haze - the one that wants to swim over my mind and eyes - at bay. *Don't lose it now! I'm not safe here! I have to get away!*

I keep an eye on the heavy boots only yards in front of me, watching closely for a pattern or any sign they are leaving. The guards either stand still watching the doorway, or they move away towards the path. None of them venture further along the residential line and I see the thin opportunity I so desperately need. I can't crawl backwards so there isn't any other choice for me to take.

It takes me five minutes to get to the safest position, maybe more, and another minute to find some well needed courage. I am directly next to a gap in the residential line, two units away from Blake's, one-hundred and fifty feet from the nearest guard.

Do it! Do it ... NOW!

I check everywhere one last time, push my body sideways, then quickly stand up. *If any of the guards see me, I'll tell them that I am out, walking. They won't know I have been at Blake's ... will they? Hopefully, they'll believe the excuse and order me away from the scene ...*

I notice that other residents are peering out of their lounge windows, no doubt wondering why the Community Guards are out in such high numbers, and so close to their houses. They won't dare come outside to try and gain a better view, though, because of policing interference laws. If anyone dared to ask questions, they would be arrested for obstructing guard duties.

I hope none of them have seen me. They'll all be too interested in what is happening at Blake's ... won't they?

I turn and walk away from the scene with my heart racing and a feeling of sickness growing inside of my stomach.

••

I sit on the steps of the Town Hall with my hands shaking. I am sweating as well and fighting off the strong desire to scream out loud. It takes every ounce of self control and emotional strength to keep my thoughts locked away. I am an explosion. I am shattering glass. I am lightning as it crawls across the dark skies.

Blake's been murdered! Help me! Please, somebody ... HELP ME!

The insignia for Central Government appears on the screen in front of me. It fades away while a solemn musical tone plays gently in the background ... a composition in cello or double bass.

A woman appears: mid-twenties in age, with black hair styled in a neat ponytail. Her blue eyes are soft, comforting and show a tender nature. In any other circumstances, at any other moment, her demeanour may have worked on me.

Residents, today I must bring you unfortunate news.
As you are all aware from our ongoing bulletins, an explosion occurred last night at the steel processing plant in sector 1. A member of staff, John Wright, was injured in the blast.
He was taken to the nearest hospital, yet, sadly, despite all the efforts of the surgical team treating his injuries, he passed away earlier this morning.

My eyes widen with shock. "But ... but ... he survived? The mayor said that he had ... the mayor said ..."

His family - a wife and three children - are being comforted by grief specialists, and have chosen to leave the Essex Community Safe Zone, immediately. They will be relocated with the full assistance of Central Government. Our thoughts go with them.

I stare at the screen on the side of the Town Hall

building. A consuming disbelief stabs at me from the inside, as if it has gained a physical form. It is trying to escape the confines of my skin and voice itself. *Blake didn't agree with Mayor Hartner's plan ... so his father was killed as well? No! None of this is true! It ... it can't be!*

The woman gazes down to take a few moments of polite and respectful silence, then her eyes come back to the screen. She has changed her expression ... there is a more vibrant feel to her body language.

In other news, Central Government is pleased to announce that there has been excellent production and harvesting results over the previous quarter. This is predominantly in the grain mills and fish farms that supply local communities. Every food ration delivery will reflect this in the coming weeks. We thank our staff and their continual hard work.

'There will be an announcement soon that will make every resident feel that Central Government is rewarding them' ... I remember part of another prediction from the note. After everything which has happened this morning, I'd almost forgotten about it, folded underneath my mattress at home. How could something so mundane, so innocent as a piece of paper, hold such incredible power? From the moment it appeared in my life, I have been ... cursed ... my life entwined with an evil path that I do not wish to travel.

She didn't predict Blake's death ... maybe she didn't know about it? Perhaps the whole truth wasn't discovered, only parts of it?

I have to compose myself, and I have to be quick about it, there are Community Guards patrolling in small teams through the streets. I can't see my reflection but I know without any doubt that I look visibly ill, angry, and confused - all of which could bring unneeded questions.

What do I do now? Shall I contact the guards? No!

They were there too ... they were involved in it!

My parents will expect help very soon with the household chores, but I don't want to be around any other people, even my own mother and father. For reasons unknown to me, I don't feel as if I can talk to them about this hideous crime either.

Mayor Hartner is a trusted and respected official ... and the guards are supposed to be here to protect me ... to protect every resident! If I can't speak to them, what can I do? What can ... I ... My thoughts pause for a millisecond. In that time, they manage to evolve and become unrecognisable to me. *I can run! Just run away! I need to get out of here! I can't ... breathe!*

I think my body is starting to shut down. I recall my daydream from yesterday evening - running towards an unknown place with Jackson. The desire to keep going, no matter where it might take me ... it has returned, much stronger this time, more primal, more of a basic survival instinct.

Just go, Elana ... go and don't stop ... The manic idea plays out as my legs stand me up and push me along the street, speeding my body away from the Town Hall. Speeding me towards the perimeter.

••

"Halt! You are entering a dangerous area!" shouts a Community Guard. He moves swiftly to stand in front of me, shifting the weight in his legs to a defensive position.

"HALT!"

His stance shifts once more when I don't stop - offensive. Two others patrolling the perimeter close to him also stand in an identical manner.

I really don't care for this show of brute force. The incident with Blake has finally hit me with all its ferocity ...

It was murder, wasn't it? They killed him because he discovered some terrible truth? Did Mayor Hartner actually tell them to shoot ... or did he pull the trigger himself?

I am filled with a fear, a numbness that I wear like a second skin. It clings to my muscles and bones with sharp claws that refuse to let go. Mayor Hartner's words as well - too many were spoken that I don't understand ... that I don't want to even *try* and understand.

"... It's irrelevant that your father saw a couple of slaves killed! They shouldn't have escaped, should they? ..."

"... The conditioning, the subtle manipulation of thought ... it didn't take very well. We have a greater success ratio now ... less resistance to the truth ..."

"... It might not have worked on your father, not completely, but we can try other methods. Every adult has to keep certain secrets, every single one of them ... but they are gradually introduced to them ..."

"STOP!"

I suddenly see the guards aiming at me with their guns. *How did I get here? Have I really run this far away from the Town Hall?*

I feel exactly the same as when I wake up from a vivid dream or nightmare. Too many details flood my mind like a tidal wave of imagery ... hundreds of questions form ... a single, prominent thought pushes its way forward, then disintegrates instantly.

I grab the single thought this time and hold it tightly: *What am I doing?*

A gloved hand strikes out with trained strength and accuracy, hitting me directly in the base of the skull. I fly forward, carried by the gained momentum of my sprint, allowing a scream of pain and shock to escape from my throat.

My hands reach for the ground, yet as soon as my broken fingers push too hard, my arm shoots backwards with a relentless stabbing pain, sending my body down on the left shoulder. Underfoot, this part of the Community Zone has been covered in a loose gravel, layered with sand, over hard mud. I scream again as it shreds through my tunic and rapidly stops my fall. My legs whip up in the air, correct themselves, then pound back to the ground.

I stare across the gravel, still with a part of me wondering where exactly I was trying to run to. The expanse of explosives buried under the surface of the earth would only have ended in my death. This didn't cross my mind, not once. As soon as the news report had finished, a cloud of anger, fear … of uncertainty and confusion, it covered my eyes and controlled me completely. This, and nothing else, sent me running.

I gag, then choke. My lungs hurt and sting because I pushed myself to the limit. I kept on running, sprinting forward, despite the pains in my legs and stomach screaming at me to stop.

I push myself up to a kneeling position, seeing deep scratches on my shoulder and down the top of my left arm. My right hand is shaking and my face also feels hot, stinging with the same sharpness already cutting at my injured fingers.

A Community Guard walks in front of me, looking down at my face through the tinted visor of the helmet.

"I'm … I'm sorry," I begin, "… but … I … just had to run … calm myself down … I'm … I'm not feeling very well."

I hold out my right hand, expecting some assistance in getting back on my feet, yet it never appears.

"Up! Slowly," says the guard.

At that moment, an unexpected and terrible reality strikes me with force: at least three guns are pointing directly at my head. Others, unseen snipers housed in towers, will no doubt raise the number.

Why did I run? Why did I do that? Will I be punished for this?

A shadow covers me ... someone standing behind. A millisecond of sharp pain follows, right in the back of my neck. I want to reach up but a sensation has grabbed my attention, unwilling to let go. It begins as a warmth around my neck, a pleasant and soothing flow. It spreads down my shoulders within seconds, as if a thousand little fingers are crawling across my skin, tickling and massaging their way along. My arms are next, my torso, then my legs as well. The world has been painted with a glow, making everything seem brighter, more distinct, more interesting.

I stand up, as instructed. *That's ... amazing ... all the pain ... it's gone ... nothing hurts now ...*

Bright lights appear, now pulsing around the Community Guard in front of me - the sun bouncing off of the uniform. I follow them with wide eyes.

"I'm standing ... what do I do next?" I ask in a withdrawn tone. All I can think about is how warm I feel ... the sensation flowing through me makes everything I see so colourful and captivating.

Whatever the guard has injected me with has calmed me ... changed me. I'm now a docile girl who will pose no more threat. I'll obey all instructions and orders without a second thought.

I am not an explosion, I am flowing water. I am not shattering glass, I am smooth silk. I am not lightning as it crawls across the dark skies, I am warm sunlight.

••

Within less than a minute, I've been marched to the nearest Community Guard station and restrained. My arms, crossed in front of me, are locked in position with steel bindings. I have retreated to a dazed, quiet state of mind, of which there is little to no chance of escape. Self-control, and the ability to make or act on decisions, have both been inhibited due to the potency of the chemicals floating around inside my body.

Another vague amount of time passes. I'm now sitting inside a tram that has been commandeered by the Community Guards. The windows have been purposely tinted as well. I realise I have never seen this before and focus my limited attention on them, supposing that they were activated by a button in the front control booth.

The journey could have lasted for another fifteen minutes, thirty, perhaps even an hour … I don't know, or care. An understandable sense of time has left me, replaced by the dim light of the tram's interior, the constant hum that irritates my ears as it moves along, and the controlled silence of the six Community Guards sitting with me. It feels as if I am invisible, floating along unseen, an ethereal passenger watching my own life play out.

I can't move my hands or arms because of the restraints, and their weight. They pull my body forward and cause my back to hunch over. I have to keep straightening my spine in an effort to compensate.

"Stand up." One of the Community Guards, a woman judging by her voice and finer jaw line, grabs the top of my right arm and directs me towards the automatic doors.

"Yes, of course," I say, slightly slurring my words.

I have no idea where we've travelled to, or how long it has actually taken, yet this part of the silent journey is finally over. The automatic doors open to more dim lighting and a tight corridor. It is grey, as per usual, rising high before meeting the ceiling. It feels as if the walls could cave in on themselves at any given moment because of their weight and height. They are the colossal hands of a giant, able to crush any who walk between them.

I don't recognise my surroundings. They look familiar because of the uniform design that I am accustomed to from the Community Zones, yet something else is present here … a greater depth, a darker atmosphere … and …

Is this a hospital? The thought comes to me as I catch the odour of a strong antiseptic in the air. I can also pick out sterile cleaning formula, bleaches - a standard of hygiene has obviously been adhered to over a lengthy period of time.

"… The conditioning, the subtle manipulation of thought … it didn't take very well. We have a greater success ratio now … less resistance to the truth …"

Mayor Hartner's words. They fly to the front of my mind - so does his face. It sends immediate panic through my veins, increasing my heart rate and causing a thin cover of sweat to break just by my hairline. I desperately want to scratch there, but the heavy restraints won't allow it. My arms and shoulders briefly fight, then, more warmth floods in again like a strong ocean wave. It soothes any fears and eliminates my anxiety completely.

Where … where am … am I? I ask myself, yet the consistent glow from the lights overhead hypnotises me within a few seconds. My eyes trace around them, watching the colours float and change.

"Move."

The Community Guards surround me and march forward. I feel no hesitation to go with them, my body is too weak to resist, and my mind doesn't care to fight against their powerful flow either.

Claustrophobia, both mental and physical, screams and squashes at my chest as the guards and corridors give me no space to move in any direction for another ten minutes. It is ignored because all I want to do is follow the whirling, floating lights and extravagant colours they offer.

Eventually, the guards stop. I am taken inside a room and lifted on to the top of a metal framed bed which has a hard mattress and grey sheets. The restraints are left locked around my arms, pushing constantly on my chest.

My eyes shift left and right, or towards the ceiling. "Where am I?" I whisper, but the Community Guards walk away without giving me another second of their time. Whatever is about to happen to me, whatever path has been chosen, their part in it is over now.

I look about again, although not really interested. My mind only wants to find more lights to focus on, more swirls of the spectrum, from red through to purple, merging so beautifully.

The room itself is square, painted a light-grey colour. The bed on which I have been placed is pushed up against one of the walls. A large television screen is fixed with strong and thick brackets to the one opposite me. The door to my left disappears when shut … there is only a feint line of light running vertically on the wall to indicate its position or existence. The wall to my right contains another metal door, yet nothing else. There are no windows here, just a strip light in the ceiling. It pulses for me when I stare at it, beating along with the rhythm of my own heartbeat, sending beams outwards.

A new light shoots across my eyes - the door opening. It sends multiple streaks in from the corridor. I blink a few times before a content smile forms across my face. The hypnotic colours have multiplied for me to watch, pleasing my dazed mind.

Someone looks down at my face, silhouetted by the ceiling light. They stare for a while and I can feel my skin being prodded and my eyelids being pulled open even more than they already are. A new warmth flows, so much stronger than before, like a fast river along my body. *It's amazing … I'm free … warm … I never want it to end …*

My world fades from view as I flutter and stumble towards a deep unconsciousness. Images of my parents,

Jackson, and Blake all run to the front of my mind, demanding my complete attention, wishing to be remembered and thought of. They have their reasons and something important to say.

The dream that follows hasn't replayed in my mind for a long time. I must have been so saddened, so shocked by the real events that created it, there wasn't any other choice for me but to push it away somewhere. I hid it, never wanting to see that time in my life again. Up until now, it's proven to be a successful method. With opiates dancing in my central nervous system, the dream finds a way to resurface, never truly lost forever.

It happened at the beginning of December, about three weeks after I celebrated turning seven years of age. I find myself walking through the community with my father, for no other reason than to spend some time together. We are both wearing the coats provided by Central Government, and we're glad to have them too because of the cold wind punching its way in strong gusts through the streets.

Thick clouds cover all of the sky and a silence pulses from them ... not many wish to be outside in such weather.

Although it is a dream, I begin to ask myself questions about it. I find details previously unnoticed, uncared for, or that my younger self may not have asked.

"Where is my mother? When did that building change? It looks much larger now. Why does my father look so worried?"

We continue through the community streets, despite the cold, yet don't speak to each other. I can't remember why there were no words.

We see the Town Hall building, the school that I attended, and some of the estate housing. My father waves at the windows and balconies of the residential units when he catches the sight of a friend or colleague.

This continues for another ten or so minutes, until we reach the Plaza area, where we sit on one of the benches. A group of Community Guards walk by - ten of them - arranged in two lines of five. A tram moves along its rails, blocking the view for a few seconds.

As it trundles away, I feel shocked because the ten guards are now running in a different direction, responding to a call, or an emergency situation.

"I hope nobody is hurt, Father."

He doesn't reply. He stands up and walks in the same direction. I eagerly follow, even though I am slightly nervous about doing so, scared at what might be ahead.

The perimeter grows closer and closer. I can see something ... no, someone ... a person. They are heading out across the gravel.

"Who is that, Father? I can see a man. Isn't that dangerous?"

Once again, my father chooses silence over conversation. He has obviously seen the man as well because he moves deliberately to gain a better view.

"Stop here, Elana. No closer." These are the first words to leave his mouth for the entire dream.

I watch the guards chasing the man. He isn't responding to their calls for him to stop. He knows that the mine field is in front of him as well.

Another question arises: "Why would anyone do that? The explosives are buried out there!" Strangely, I answer myself. "You did. You just wanted to run ... you needed to escape ... Blake ... you remember Blake?"

I reach my hand up and grab my father's. My seven year old self is scared now ... scared of every possible outcome.

Still the man heads on ... still he surges forward ... never looking back ... only thinking to continue, despite the dangers of the mine field ...

I look up at my father to see whether or not he looks scared, but his face is solid and unreadable. A loud explosion sounds moments later.

"Father?"

My hand grips tighter as I watch the Community Guards stop and form in a line. Smoke and gravel shoots high above their heads, coiling like a macabre firework in front of the cloud covered sky.

I open my eyes. I am still in the grey room, feeling the warmth trickle around my body, smiling with a pleasure that has no boundaries or limits.

It takes all of five minutes for me to look forward at the screen and hear the voice too, amazed by how amplified both are. All the words spoken are crisp and sharp. Every inch of the screen is vibrant and alive with motion.

Residents,

Elana Mayne, a sixteen year old from the South Quarter, has unfortunately been classified as a fifty-fifty and removed from the Community Zone. She displayed irrefutable symptoms and has a troubled mind.

She was apprehended a week ago, attempting to flee, yet Community Guards caught her before she reached the perimeter mines. Her parents have been relocated, at their own request.

Our thoughts go with her, and them. This is never easy news to hear, or live with.

"That's me ... that's my name ... I'm Elana Mayne ... me ... my name ...," I mumble, unaware that many aspects of my situation have changed. My clothes are now a light-grey top and trousers, I wear no shoes, and an intravenous line has been inserted in each arm, attached to a cannula. One carries a clear liquid, one a lilac concoction. Neither of them have identification labels on the front of the transparent bags they feed from, hanging on hooks behind the bed.

Another voice speaks, coming from the corner to my left, by the main doorway - a man. "Let's watch something else, shall we? I like this one … very dramatic!"

I don't move my head away from the screen. I see a picture of myself, then it changes to show one of the metal living units that are so familiar in all the communities. My eyes widen and the warmth inside me drops some of its grip.

Blake?

I blink at the screen and look at my surroundings. Questions and fear are creating themselves and feeding off of each other.

"You were picked up by the CCTV network sneaking out of your little hiding place. So clever of John to create it, really. His promotion at the steel plant, although short lived, was obviously warranted."

I still don't feel any urgency to speak. It is surreal to be watching myself on the screen. I look so small as I crawl out from underneath one of the units, desperate for help. I stand for a few seconds like a lost child, wanting to cry for my parents to come and save me. I walk away, out of the camera's range. The screen flickers and then replays the footage again from the beginning.

"Curiosity killed the cat … or something like that. I don't hold much stock in those old world phrases myself. Why make up something that sounds so … so … innocent? Most of them are warnings anyway, so make them sound like warnings. Don't you agree?" asks the man.

I continue to watch myself on the screen. I realise then how thirsty I feel and wonder if there is any water nearby. There is a noise, like liquid flowing, or a tap dripping

... it's coming from somewhere behind the bed. My need for a drink disappears straight afterwards.

"For example ... stick your nose in business that doesn't concern you, and there will be serious trouble!"

"Can you tell me where I am?" I ask and turn to see Mayor Hartner standing in the corner of the room. I should scream, I should jump off of the bed and panic, yet the only reaction is a slight dilation of my pupils.

I've seen Mayor Hartner, and his family as well, on a few occasions at the social events in the Community Zone. He looks the same to me: late forties in age, six feet tall, brown hair parted on one side, green eyes, well built yet with a plump stomach.

"Listening in on private conversations can get you hurt ... or worse! Yes, that's much more to the point ... much easier to understand."

The heat returns to my body. It is welcomed too because the fearful thoughts and needed answers are getting louder, more persistent. The final images I see on the screen are the faces of my parents, before another bout of colourful dreams wrapped themselves around me.

••

"Think of something, Elana. Keep saying your name ... constantly remind yourself of *who you are!* Quote a line from your favourite book, an equation ... walk yourself from your house to college. Look at every detail of every residence, every building ... *find something to focus on!*"

I hear the whispered voice echo all around me. It's coming from somewhere in the room, somewhere close. For the briefest of moments, it sounds almost familiar. *The woman on the train platform? Is she here?*

I try to ignore the warmth floating across my skin but I'm too content to stay there, in my colourful world. I don't want to think about anything. All of my unnecessary thoughts stop the various sensations and make me feel normal again.

This calm, chemically induced state, has kept me firmly held for just over three weeks in total now, yet I have no memory of it. My sense of time has disappeared after running towards the perimeter mines and it has never returned. The screen in front of me has also been showing brief recordings of the sun rising and setting, yet at reversed or predetermined time slots. There have been recordings added in: noises, static, capitalised words - OBEDIENCE, GUILT, REMORSE, LOYALTY ... all followed by a designated dose of varying neurotransmitters, created to make me feel a certain way, to create a new memory and link it with a specific state of mind.

The light shoots across my eyes again as the door opens and shuffling footsteps enter the room, moving about slowly from corner to corner. It sounds as if small wheels, like those on a trolley, are trundling along as well.

"Is everything prepared?" a male voice asks. It is low, determined, purposeful. The kind of voice that sends a chill running down your spine.

"Yes, doctor," answers a woman.

That voice ... it sounds so much like her ...

"EM562. Low level subservience assigned. Let's begin," says the man, the doctor, the purposeful and chilling voice.

All the lights I have grown to love and depend upon disappear so suddenly, as if a fast moving train has stopped, flinging my body forward, crashing me through a wall. My body aches ... every muscle cries out for help.

The metallic bed hums as it tilts forward, bringing me to an upright position. Restraints around my ankles, wrists and torso stop my body from falling.

*"... Think of something, Elana. Keep saying your name ... constantly remind yourself of **who you are**! Quote a*

*line from your favourite book, an equation ... walk yourself
from your house to college. Look at every detail of every
residence, every building ... **find something to focus on!** ... "*

I stare at the large screen. All the questions, fears, and
lost weeks of reality - either dampened down or stolen from
me - are now cascading like boulders falling down a
mountain, bombarding my weakened mind. The instant
headache they produce is enough to make me feel physically
sick. My eyes pump and throb as the light in the ceiling
intensifies.

"Where ... am ..."

I can't complete my sentence because an image of a
smiling woman flashes up in front of me on the large screen.
There is an immediate reward, although not in the same dose,
of the drug that has been my companion, my comforting
friend, for so long.
As quickly as it is administered, it is countered with the
complete opposite. I feel cold, immobile, scared. Fear stabs
its cruel claws in and shreds away at me. *What's ...
happening ...?*

The image on the screen changes. The woman is now
angry. Her face shows ... DISAPPOINTMENT ... flashes on
the screen in large letters. Another image ... a man, pleased
expression ... I am rewarded ... the word LOYALTY ...
another ... a woman looking suspicious ... I'm plunged to the
depths of fear ... the word DISTRUST.

A tear falls down my cheek. My mind whirls and
thumps and screams.

*Where am I? What happened? Where are my
parents? Why are they letting this happen? I wish I could see
them ... I wish I could talk to them ... they'd help me! ... NO!
Elana, they won't! You disappointed your parents because
you didn't obey the rules! It's your fault! ... Blake died
because of you! NO! NO! NO! ... YES! You are wrong! You
are to blame! ... NO! NO! YES! NO! ... I ... I ... I ... wake up*

in the morning, at seven-thirty ... NO! ... YES! ... I ... I wake up in the morning at seven-thirty. I wash. I eat my breakfast ... I clean my teeth ...

The session with the chilling and purposeful doctor lasts for two hours. My screams fill the room and many tears fall, yet they are always ignored.

Chapter five

I dream with a cruel and vindictive twist. *I don't want to be here ...*

I am back at home with my parents, sitting in the lounge. We smile and laugh, yet the reasons behind such happiness and positive emotions have been omitted. Every part of it plays out like an edited film, with key frames and crucial information removed.

In one moment, I'm sitting opposite my parents, in the next, I'm standing in the kitchen area holding a glass of water. My mother and father's attitudes have also changed suddenly. They stare at me with shocked and upset expressions on their faces, as if I have admitted something terrible to them both.

"I'll be back, I promise. I have no choice but to sort this terrible mess out. Do you understand?" I ask. "I can't accept what has happened but I have to try."

"No, I don't understand," replies my mother. "How can I ever understand this?" she adds. There is so much worry on her face, it makes her seem older, as if a decade has been lived too quickly.

"That won't be easy, Elana," says my father. "You are in a lot of trouble. And don't forget that your mother and I only know so much. We've been told stories, moved away from our home and friends. What makes you think that you're capable of dealing with this? You say you're going to sort it all out, but can you? Impossible!" He rubs his hands together with frustration and avoids eye contact with me.

I don't agree with my father's tone but decide to keep quiet. His face distorts between anger and disappointment just as the dream shifts again. My mother has now moved and is standing directly next to me.

"I'm scared, Elana. I'm scared for you, and us as well. I wish there was an easy way out," she says with tears in her eyes.

"It's my choice. I'll have to *make* you both understand, if that's my only option. Does that sound like a good idea, Father?"

Another shift in the dream occurs before I receive an answer. I'm now standing at the front door. "Goodbye, Mother, Father. I'm so sorry about everything. I will come back to you, even if it takes me the rest of my life, I will find my way back to you."

My mother wipes a tear off of her cheek. "Be safe, Elana. You know we will always love you ... we'll always trust and believe you."

My father stands just behind her, emotional himself yet keeping his silent, stern exterior.

"I love you too, Mother ... and you, Father." I hold out my hand. I want to feel the touch of my parents one last time ... know their comfort ...

The hallway darkens. I see my parents standing hundreds of feet away, unreachable ... then the darkness swallows everything like an insatiable beast.

••

I open my blurry eyes and know immediately that I have been crying in my sleep. The familiar room focuses a few seconds later.

I sit up on the bed after a couple of minutes to rest my chin on the top of my knees, staring at the blank television screen in front of me.

I wake up in the morning. I wake up in the morning at seven-thirty. I wash. I eat my breakfast. I clean my teeth. I get dressed. I prepare myself for college. I study many subjects at college ... The Pythagorean theorem is named after the Greek mathematician Pythagoras ... a squared plus b squared equals c squared ...

I quieten my rushed thoughts, taking an emotional pause. My mind has become my greatest ally, my strongest weapon. *I'm sorry ... I will find my way back to you. Goodbye, for now ...*

For the next ten minutes, I sit motionless on the metal bed, continuously repeating self taught mantras to myself. Even though I struggle to stay lucid because of the injections somedays, I try to carry out this routine once I am awake.

The light that usually covers my eyes when the door opens doesn't touch my face this time. It cuts a glowing line behind me, across the grey sheets and down the wall to my right. It isn't the nurse or the doctor because they always talk to each other before entering.

"Up. Get dressed. We leave in ten minutes," says a male Community Guard as he places a dark-grey tunic on the end of the bed.

Where am I going?

He drops a pair of black plimsolls on the floor, then walks out of the room.

I flex the fingers on my left hand, unable to remember when they healed. *I study many subjects at college ...*

Exactly ten minutes later, the same Community Guard re-enters the room and collects me. We start walking through the high and grey corridors, turning right, left, straight ahead, another right turn ...

A memory floats by, caused by this part of the building. I remember being brought in here, wherever *here* is. *When was that? How long have I been here? When did I see Blake murdered?*

I keep concentrating, almost certain that a train and tram station lay ahead, just around the next corner. *Straight ahead and turn right ... I came in that way ...*

The Community Guard decides to turn left instead, continuing on through the labyrinth of grey walls. I walk closely behind him, playing a game inside my head: match my footsteps exactly with his - left, right, left, right.

Ten or more turns and long corridors follow, then a set of steps that spiral down. I count to seventy-six before losing my train of thought and quitting this new game. If the amount of time we have spent on the stairs - continually heading lower and lower - is anything to go by, the step count ends somewhere close to four hundred.

I notice two more Community Guards standing at the end of a corridor that feeds off of the stairway, on either side of a set of large steel doors. Despite their size and weight, they open very quietly and quickly. I hear a slight hissing sound and guess that some sort of pneumatic system is in place to control and lock them when required.

"Inside," says my escorting guard.

The doors slide shut behind me and I need to take a couple of deep breaths to steady myself. I'm now standing inside a large hall with an incredibly high ceiling, surrounded by a thousand ... two-thousand ... it is impossible to count, truly impossible, because of their sheer number ... I am surrounded by teenagers just like me.

They are all dressed in the same style of clothes as well. A mass of dark-grey cloth, utterly silent, standing and staring towards the far wall. Not one of them speaks and they hardly move either - an occasional sway to the side, or shuffle of their feet being the only indication that they are alive and not lifeless mannequins. They all just stand, obedient and silent, waiting for orders.

I walk forward and position myself behind a younger and shorter girl with black hair. *She only looks about fourteen years old! And that boy over there is even younger!*

"Listen carefully!" bellows a voice. It must be amplified and distributed by a speaker system because it echoes around the large hall with clarity. "The doors at the far end will now open. File out, collecting your backpacks along the way. Once you have your travel kit, you will be placed in the assigned group while outside on the platform. Follow your Community Guards as you begin the journey to your designated areas."

A loud noise - a grinding whirr - begins. Metal drags against metal somewhere in the hall, then a thin strip of light runs vertically in the distance. It looks as if someone is cutting the walls open with an invisible knife made of sunlight. Being inside for so long, away from any windows, has taken its toll on our eyesight. We all need to blink a few times to refocus.

I try to remember the last time I saw it - natural sunlight. A shake of my head follows, as well as clenched fists, used specifically to push a memory away.

I move step by step, closer to the light. A large and heavy backpack is soon placed in my arms by a Community Guard. It has a red Central Government insignia attached. Step, step, step … closer to the light … step, step, step … closer, closer, closer … all of us. We are skin covered automatons, we are controllable life, a conveyor belt of bodies, flowing forward.

Outside, I try to gain a sense of direction, possible location, and even the time of year. Unfortunately, none prove easy. The sun is blaring above me and the perfect blue sky is only marred by a dark thunder cloud, accompanied by a few crashes far away in the distance.

I turn around, risking the anger of the Community Guards, yet I have to stand in awe of this giant building - the building that I've been imprisoned in for an unknown amount of time.

It is hundreds of feet - maybe even a thousand feet - tall. Layers of thick concrete placed on top of one another. After each floor the layers reduce in size, creating a jagged pyramid shape. At the top, a large cylinder rises skywards. Train tracks sprout off in different directions a short height above, like branches - metal branches sprouting and growing from a cold tree trunk made of thick stone.

I realise that I have disrupted the line and its flow of movement. A teenage boy in front of me stands eerily still, waiting for it to continue. The expression on his face is that of confusion and a growing fear, at least that is how I interpret it. The boy wants me to move so that he can as well. Somewhere in his mind, a punishment is coming. I quickly turn around and rejoin the others … step, step, step …

The platform outside is an area that has been constructed, again of the usual grey concrete, running around the entire building. There are stone stairways leading off of it in different directions and I count ten of them in total.

More monotonous steps follow as all the teenagers shuffle along in different directions, finding their Community Guard group.

I see mine - red - easily with fifty guards in control, all with the CG insignia on their uniforms. I head towards them and within a couple of minutes, I'm one of three-hundred teenagers ready to leave.

The guards take everyone down the nearest stairway to the beginning of a concrete path, running directly underneath the train tracks. It cuts through the columns of steel and stone that raise them high in the air.

Thoughts enter my head. Verbal equations are assessed and calculated at unprecedented speeds. My heart begins to race and I feel sick because I have no idea of where this part of my life will take me. *Mayor Hartner's words to Blake ... before he ... he ... was murdered ... all I've suffered here since the guards brought me to that room.*

"This way! Move!" shouts a guard.

An hour passes and everyone is ordered to stop for a short break. We take a welcoming drink from a water bottle that is included in all our backpacks. It is extremely hot and the sun is directly above my group. *Noon, somewhere in the world, somewhere unknown to me.* Flat land as far as the eye can see ... an ocean of concrete.

I think about the photographs I've studied in college, those showing the old world. I wonder what might have been under my feet back then - who would have stood where I do now.

After the virus, and once the basis for Community Zones had been designed - and internationally agreed upon - vast areas of land were reduced to rubble. They were cleared of all that wasn't necessary, flattened, then new foundations were poured on the ground - foundations for the future - that locked the past underneath, forever.

Certain reminders still exist around the globe: mountain ranges, deserts, forests, lakes ... none of which were destroyed, or altered, unless deemed absolutely necessary.

Another hour drifts by with silent footsteps. Everyone stops for more water and we are permitted to eat a couple of tasteless biscuits. The Community Guards either mutter to each other, always being careful to keep their voices low, or respond to radio communications being fed through the earpieces in their helmets.

I haven't noticed many birds in the sky since starting

Elana Mayne

this long and tiring walk. I gaze as far as possible, hoping to catch a glimpse of one in the distance. I wish to see something innocent and free. Instead, a whole part of the sky shimmers, grabbing my attention and causing me to stare. It is a long way ahead, close to what looks like a crossroads or junction in the path and overlying train tracks.

What is ...? I think of my past and a memory stirs - one of the visits to the London Community Safe Zone.

Shortly after stepping off of the train, I had seen bright streaks of light, like crystals or white fire, shooting out of the ground. Our class wasn't close, yet their incredible size and isolated location made them visible. I was truly astounded by the enigmatic beauty of the light for a few minutes, as were a lot of the other children on the same trip. We were all unable to understand what could cause such a phenomenon. Our tutor explained, once he had noticed the interest and distraction, that it was named 'The Solar City'. Fifty buildings were erected after the virus, covered entirely in solar panels. They provide a percentage of the energy which powers the south of the country, feeding the communities. It is just one of the many that now power the globe. Central Government uses every feasible method that it can to harness the power of natural energy: wind farms, hydro-turbines, even lightning towers.

We are moving east ... north-east ... but we must still be near to London, right? I think to myself, still desperate to pinpoint my location.

The rest of the first day continues with exactly the same routine: walk in silence, stop to drink, walk in silence, stop to drink and eat. I calculate we have covered an approximate distance of twenty miles.

As everyone tries to get comfortable on the hard ground to sleep, using their backpacks as uncomfortable pillows, I listen to the sounds of the night. They are so much different to those I have grown up with. In the residential lines of my Community Zone, it is nearly always peaceful. The hum of a train or tram moving around, people talking to each as they walk outside, the marching of boots as guards patrol. Now, I can hear owls, insects scuttling about, foxes and other animals calling to each other.

Where do they all live? There's nothing but concrete and metal out here.

Day two is a longer and much more tiring day. We wake not long after sunrise and continue through to sunset. My feet and legs are aching. I don't know how the other children in my group feel because it is so difficult to read their faces, and nobody speaks. Nobody ever speaks.

At close to noon on day three, while everyone stops for water and more tasteless biscuits, I look ahead with a hidden sadness. A very thin boy, aged about sixteen with black hair, falls to the floor. Two Community Guards drag him away from the crowd. They force some more water inside his mouth and sit him up, talking to him loudly. No real urgency or care presents in their voices or demeanour. Every action they perform looks unmotivated … 'Because I have to', instead of, 'Because I need to'.

The boy stands again five minutes later and the walking recommences. This episode of excitement, or non-excitement for all the brainwashed young minds, is over.

The landscape changes twenty minutes later. I control my facial expressions because all I want to do is smile. A line of trees grows not far ahead … hundreds of tall trees. Life, nature, vibrancy … not endless concrete. I can hear them rustling in the breeze and even notice the air changing its aroma - cleaner and fresher. The greens and yellows jump off of everything else visible, giving it a new energy, a new sense of life glowing and escaping from the blank grey.

The train tracks above are obviously high, raised over the canopy line, and I can see that it veers off to the right shortly after.

Is it a forest or a wood? Are we going to walk through? Please ... let me see this ... let me step inside ...

My thoughts are answered when I see the leading group of Community Guards, four of them, head between the tree trunks. The children at the front of the group follow closely, even though none of them share my concealed excitement. I am placed halfway along the line, so eager, yet so unable, to increase my pace.

I allow my eyes to follow the distinct line of the concrete path in front and to the side of me. It stops perfectly, so straight a boundary housing this new and exciting area. It is as if the forest has cut an area out of the ground and lowered itself inside.

I wonder if it's the outer perimeter for one of the Inhabitable, or Wild Zones? I can't tell if it's natural or man-made.

A cry of desperation breaks through my state of excitement. A girl with brown hair has stopped walking and is looking about with sharp turns of her head.

"Mother! Father! I know I live near the trees! There are trees ... near my community! There are ... I've seen them beyond the perimeter moat ... there are trees! Mother! Father! I want to go home to my parents! Please, take me home!" she cries.

The closest Community Guards react to the unexpected outburst - they turn around to assess the situation - when the girl starts to run.

No ... don't run! Don't run! My mind screams the warning. I feel my heart sink but I don't react ... I *can't* react.

The girl hurtles away through the tree trunks, certain she is close to her home community, certain she will be able to meet with her parents somewhere soon. I can hear her calling for them and remembering the trees near her home again. My heart aches for her and the broken mind she now possesses.

Three Community Guards give chase, splitting off in a formation that appears so fluid, it can only have come from months of intense training.

"Stop here! Wait for further orders!" shouts a guard.

My solemn group of silent bodies stops walking within a second of the call.

Don't run! Why did you have to run? I try to stop thinking about what will happen next to the girl with the brown hair. The confused girl who rediscovered a dampened memory at the worst possible time, now chasing unreachable dreams.

Four noises - *Gunshots! NO! Why did you run?* They fly through the branches and leaves, wrap around tree trunks, warping and merging together to form a singular echo. All the beauty I initially immersed myself in on seeing the forest disappears once the prolonged noise reaches my ears. I can almost see the colour and life around me drain away, imagining a grey forest instead. One to dread instead of one to enjoy. Tainted now and forever by blood and death.

A flock of birds flap out of the leaf canopy in the distance, scared from their branch perches by the commotion. *I'll try and remember you, I'll try.*

I fight off all the emotions that have surfaced. I know the girl with the brown hair will not return with the three guards. The image of her running through the trees will be the last memory I will carry.

I sigh as I look around, making a mental note of the layout for this part of the forest, trying to assign a specific tree or bush to memory. I don't want to forget her, the girl, not ever, or where she died either.

"Forward!" calls a female guard. The group continues to walk … and we walk with one less number.

..

A crescent moon pokes through the tree branches above as I feign sleep on the leaf and earth covered ground, clutching at my water bottle. Everything glows with a silvery edge as the moonlight swims through and across the forest. There are guards awake while others sleep - a basic rota system - they walk along the line every now and then to check on us.

An unexpected sound catches my ear. *Thunder.* It rumbles for a few seconds and then fades, followed by a tapping sound. These grow louder, faster and closer.

And now the rain ...

A sudden downpour falls from the sky, crashing its way to the ground. I open the top of my water bottle and watch it fill as a couple of minutes tick by and more thunder smashes loudly in the sky.

The nearest guard stands two-hundred feet away, ignoring the weather. She doesn't move in an attempt to find shelter underneath the thick cover of leaves from the branches above her head.

It should happen any second now ... I'll wait for the next one ... I will find my way back to you ... find my way ...

I hear another rumble. It slowly builds up with occasional loud crashes ... then rocks the sky with a deafening sound.

... back to you ...

I roll away from my backpack, clutching at the water bottle, moving under the cover of the rain smashing on the leaves, and the precious seconds that the thunder has provided.

I lodge my body against a large tree trunk and listen for specific sounds. There are no pounding boots, no calls or orders between the guards ... just the rain and my thumping heart.

Don't stop! Go!

I jolt forward, keeping the trees between me and the group as much as possible, concealing my body from any eyes that will inevitably look in this direction. I know that time is against me. It will only be a minute, possibly less, before a guard notices that I'm not by my backpack.

A hissing noise cuts through everything else ... then another. I turn my head as I run to my left and jump behind a tree. The red streak of a flare flies by me, only twenty feet away. One has also been shot in the air and is already descending back towards the ground. It starts to cover everything with its searching red glow, creating shadows, finding that which wants to hide ... *me.*

Where did the other one go? Did it burn out in the rain? I calculate my situation, wondering how it is possible that I haven't been seen yet.

I can't see where the flare fired straight through the trees landed, yet there is a red tint to the leaves that confuses me. *It looks like it is below the trees ... how is that even possible?*

My mind races with questions and self directed orders, my body surging with fear ... I have to make a move ... I have to do something ... *Go! You can't stand still ... GO!*

I run forward again, darting between and behind the trees, pushing myself to an unknown limit. *If I can just stay out of view for a little while longer, get to a darker part of the forest, maybe hide underneath a large pile of leaves?*

I cry with shock as the ground disappears from under my feet for a second. I lurch forward, still with my legs and arms moving ... instinct throws my hands out in front of me.

My body smacks on the wet ground, flipping me over. I have built up quite a speed while running, and now something else has been added ... it is driving me along ... no, not driving me ... pulling me down ... I am falling down a hill or muddy cliff. I suddenly realise why the flare looked like it was underneath the trees.

I slide along the sodden ground, rolling over and over, smacking through bushes and fallen branches on the way. The world glows with red light, streaked with rain like drops of blood pouring from the sky.

"No! No!" A sharp pain in my leg causes another scream and I immediately feel sick. My dark world, painted by the eerie red light of the almost burnt out flare, is slipping away ... I'm afraid I am going to pass out ... there is no escape from the greyness that has started to creep over everything I can see.

I grit my teeth and try to claw my hands in the mud, but it is a pointless effort. I pull my arms over my head and try to get my legs thrust out too, hoping they'll get hooked on something that can slow me down ... again, pointless. I have no control, no way to stop the descent ... *Please ... don't let it end here ...*

Then, as suddenly as it started, my body slows. I've reached the bottom, falling no longer.

Run! Elana, run! The guards will be after you ... the guards ... Stay awake! You need to run!

My inner cries become nothing more than whispers. I don't have the strength to continue, or even get up. My attempt to flee has failed.

"There's no need for that. Lower your weapons. Now."

"STOP!"

I can't see who the voices belong to, both of them male. One is definitely a Community Guard ... but the other sounds much softer, younger ... non-threatening. I want to look but there are only moments left before I disappear towards an unconscious world. I am completely unable and unwilling to imagine what will be waiting for me when, or *if,* my eyes open again.

"I'll take her in. There'll be no deaths in my presence. Are we understood?" says the soft voice.

I hear no more words.

Chapter six

The following dream pulls me back to Blake's living unit, despite subconscious wishes for it to stop. I'm not crouching underneath this time, though, I am resting inside on the sofa, watching Mayor Hartner. He moves around as blurry and unnatural seconds pass. He sits in the lounge or paces across the room as his face distorts with anger. His features change beyond their normal shape, shocking me: bulging eyes, gritted teeth that are sharp like a growling animal, and pale skin.

Blake stands up and looks directly at me. "Elana, I need to move your leg to clean away some of the mud. I'm sorry if it hurts," he says. His voice sounds so different.

He walks over to me and lifts my leg up. "Sorry," he says, again, as a vague sensation … a numb pain, passes through my thigh.

Mayor Hartner stands by the front door, watching us. His face carries a wide smile that pulls his lips open too far. "Curiosity killed the cat, Elana," he says while rubbing his hands together.

I slowly open my eyes, unsure whether I am still dreaming or tasting reality. I can see a window to the right and feel the warm coat of sunlight on my face. It's an amazing yet very brief return to the world, reminding me of normality. How I used to wake up every day before my life changed.

A strong hand touches my forehead as the soft voice follows. Some words are spoken that sound like 'rest' and 'safety'. I can't really hear them properly, so I let the sun be my last sight before sleep welcomes itself again, cloaking me in its soothing grasp.

A shadow floats across the window. The strong hand returns, as does the gentle voice. "Don't worry, you're going to recover, I promise," he whispers.

Am I in hospital? I think. *The Community Guards! They caught me at the bottom of that cliff! I'm back in the building ... they took me back!*

"I'm just going to change your bandages, then you can sleep again," floats the voice.

••

I see a light-grey sky as I open my eyes. I feel different ... focused and energetic. *There aren't any windows in the building ... If I can see the sky, I must be ... somewhere else?*

A gentle breeze flutters across my body, causing it to tingle. It is the first real chance I've had to look at my surroundings, instead of drifting between bouts of clarity and a dream state. I am in a bedroom, easily three times the size of my own. *How did I get here? Is this where I've been when I wake up and hear that voice?*

This bedroom is not like any other I have seen before. In the Community Zone they are painted white, the furniture is a light-brown or grey tone, and it is only built with functionality in mind.

Beautiful.

The walls are painted in a maroon shade and edged with wooden skirting boards and patterned coving. Colourful curtains and venetian blinds, both in shades of cream, are suspended from the top of the window.

Ornate furniture - a wardrobe, bedside cabinets, a chair - they are all constructed from a dark, reddish wood. They glint and shine as the sunlight breaks through the light clouds. The bed sheets under my skin are soft and plush, carrying on the theme of maroon and cream, completed by the two-tone carpet.

This can't be right! I ... I ... am I still dreaming? I may be surrounded by a level of beauty and decadence that surprises me, yet it also scares me. I get out of bed and a stab of pain shoots through my left thigh, as if sharp nails are digging at my skin.

What's wrong with my leg? I grit my teeth, let out a growl of pain, then steady myself. My grey tunic has been ripped in various places, and it is dirty with stains from dry mud. A lot must have been washed or rubbed away because I can smell antiseptic soap on my clothes and hands.

My leg ... I notice there is a scar running up my thigh, about three inches in length. It raises slightly because it is still fresh and raw, surrounded by bruising. Somehow, the stitches look as if they were created by a semi-professional hand.

On the side of the tall wardrobe, I notice a mirror and hesitate to move. *When ... when did I last see myself?*

A further push of courage moves me forward two more steps. *Is that ... really me?*

I see a girl. She is scared and tired, with pale bruises on her legs, staring back at me from the mirror. I look so different because my hair is longer by a few inches, and I have lost a couple of pounds in weight.

I search around in the bedroom some more. Small bottles of medicine and antibiotics - ones that I recognise - sit on top of one of the bedside cabinets: painkillers, infection treatments, sterile ointments. There are also bandages, some scissors, and my ID card, also stained with mud. *That bottle ... the lilac liquid ... I saw that in the building ...*

"What is this place? Who could have brought me here?"

A floorboard creaks behind the door to my right. *Someone is outside!*

My hand grabs the pair of scissors as I step back, starting to panic. A shadow spreads underneath and across the carpet, like ink crawling and seeping closer to me.

"May I come in?" a male voice asks. I don't know how, yet it is a familiar one. I search my memory, knowing it is in there somewhere, knowing somehow that it isn't a threat.

"Who ... who are you?" I demand in a loud voice. I grip the handle of the scissors tighter and point them at the closed door, ready for whoever might walk through.

"Can I open the door? Please?"

I think carefully about my next move. *Climb out of the window? Rush by him? Use the scissors, Elana! Use them if you have to!*

The shadows move slightly. Their inky darkness moulds together, reaching for me. I watch as the door-handle turns. My heart races at an incalculable speed and I fear my consciousness will fail me.

He's coming in! I back up another few steps and hold my breath as the door opens.

"Good afternoon, Elana," says a young man. Seeing me awake and walking about brings a smile to his face.

Who are you?

He looks to be seventeen years old and is about six-feet in height. I am drawn to his innocent, dark-brown eyes. They are the same colour as his hair - cut and styled in a short and neat fashion. He is wearing black trousers, a blue shirt, and black boots - they are definitely not normal government issue.

*I've never seen anyone dressed in such clothes ...
especially someone of our age ...*

He holds up his hands to show, and hopefully prove, that he isn't a threat. "See? It's just me. No guns, no weapons of any kind ... nothing ... only me."

I wave the scissors out in front of my body. I want to try and look courageous but it doesn't quite work. I'm a defenceless little girl because my hands are shaking too much for it to be impressive or threatening.

"I'm just going to reach down here, by the door, okay? I've brought some food for you to eat. It's here on the floor, I promise."

He waits for a second or two but doesn't get a definitive answer from me - he doesn't get a reply at all - so slowly bends down anyway. "It's soup. I made it for you."

Oh, that smells delicious! I'm so hungry!

The young man walks inside the room a few steps further, carrying a tray with a bowl on it and a glass of water.

I snap myself back from the tempting thought of food. "Where am I? Who ... who are you?"

Before replying, he puts the tray down on the bed. "My name is Brin. We're ... in a safe place. Will that be a good enough answer for now?"

"No, it won't!" I snap back. The scissors wave left and right with sharp swings.

Brin retreats by a few steps. By the look on his face, my loud outburst and offensive attitude has caused an unexpected shock.

"Why did you help me? Did the Community Guards bring me here? Is that it? Now that I'm awake, you're going to contact them straight away and send me back to them?" I ask. I'm having trouble getting my mouth to work fast enough because the words are pouring out.

Brin looks at me. "No ... nothing like that is going to happen."

I tense my arm and manage to hold the scissors steady. I need a few seconds to assess and plot the next action to take. Something comes back to me … trees glowing red … the forest … mud and pain …

"I heard a voice … there were voices … the guards had found me … they did, I remember hearing them!"

Brin stays still. "Yes, that's correct, you did hear them. Do you remember hearing me speak as well?"

I'm not sure if I do. All the voices spoke at exactly the same time that I fell unconscious. "You work for them or something like that? You're a guard, or training to be one? Why help me? I don't understand any of this!"

I let the unfamiliarity of my surroundings, gaps in my memory, and this young man, grow the fear inside me at an uncontrollable rate. *How can I trust you, Brin? You're a complete stranger.*

I need to stay calm, at least try to, and focus on the present moment. At any second I could find myself running again. "Just stand still, Brin, while I think … okay?"

Brin smiles back at me. He freezes in a comical pose, making himself laugh in the process. "Look at me, Elana. I'm only seventeen, I can't be a guard yet, can I? I'm only just old enough to start their military training. Is this okay, or do you want me to move?"

He's making jokes? "This isn't funny, Brin!"

"Sorry. Can I move, though? I need to get something else from outside the door. Please?"

"No!" I reply with venom coating my voice.

"Please? Or, can you get it for me? It's just a cane … outside the door. I need it sometimes. It rained last night and was quite cold … plus I've been up and down those stairs a few times today."

"No! Stay where you are!" I ignore his request and continue with my memories, pulling every detail out, checking if it makes any sense to me.

I decide to return to the last definite point in my mind, the one that couldn't have been corrupted by my dreams. "I was in the forest ... there were flares ... I fell ..."

Brin slowly sits down, always keeping his eyes on me. He rubs at his left knee, looking glad that I haven't run forward with the scissors to force him to stand up again, or attack him.

"I fell for ages ... I fell down some sort of cliff? My leg hurt ... I must have cut it?" I speak quietly, asking myself more than Brin.

Brin nods towards the window. "Don't get too close, there are eyes everywhere ... so to speak. And yes, you had a nasty cut on your leg. I cleaned it up and closed the wound as best as I could. I'm quite proud of it ... there was a lot of blood."

I reach down and feel the new scar on my leg, then, step slowly sideways, never taking my eyes off of Brin. His overly helpful nature is distorted, making me cautious instead.

"I won't move. You can trust me."

"That's not as easy as it sounds," I say and peak out of the window for a split second. There are trees, exactly like those I walked by recently with my slave group, green grass, and a high fence next to a steep bank. *Is that where I passed out?*

"You found me? Out there?" I ask, pointing the scissors at the window.

"Yes." Brin nods. "By the fence."

My memory stops at that point and nothing but a haze of dreams flutter by afterwards. Mayor Hartner and Blake ... sunlight through the large window. *The voices ... why did the guards leave me alone?*

"I heard people, Brin ... guards shouting? Someone talking? Was that you? You're either brave or stupid. Nobody stops Community Guards from carrying out their duties," I say. With every sentence, I add another piece to the puzzle, or try to.

"Do you remember what was said?"

"No, and that's exactly my point. I *need* to know how I survived. While I was in the forest … a girl tried to run … the guards chased her down … I saw them …" I didn't want the image of the girl with the brown hair being hunted to reappear. I see her terrified face and hear her cries. She never returned to the group. Another memory merges … a large screen showing images of my melancholy parents.

No … I can't see you … soon … soon. I shut my eyes, tightly, and clench my free hand to form a fist. "They don't hesitate to shoot, Brin, you know that, don't you? And, well, you don't look strong enough to take out a group of armed guards. No offence."

"Loads taken," he replies.

"So?"

Brin stands up, rubs his leg and stretches it out a bit, then sits back down. "Listen, Elana, swear to me that you'll listen. Don't do anything, or think anything, stupid, okay?"

I don't respond straight away and let a few seconds tick by. "I can't agree to anything … not right now," I say. I don't feel in total control of my emotions or behaviour.

Brin waits for a few seconds before conceding. "I … erm … I told them to. I told the guards to leave you alone." He looks at the floor, almost as if he is reluctant to explain, embarrassed even.

Told them to? That can't be true! I move a step closer towards Brin and the bedroom door. Rushing out of here is growing more tempting with every word he speaks, and maybe the only course of action I can follow next. "I just said to you that nothing gets in the way of a trained guard. Impossible!"

Brin doesn't falter with his explanation. "It is possible. I'm … erm … well, I'm more important than they are. In certain situations, I technically outrank them, and this turned out to be one of those situations."

I run his words through my mind but they won't connect properly. There are too many gaps, too much missing information.

"My family … we own some land. This house for example," he adds.

My knuckles turn white as the grip on the scissors grows tighter. "You work for Central Government? Someone in your family does?"

"Yes," replies Brin.

I return to my thoughts, joining images with voices, adding in Brin's version of events as well. *Okay, I'm at the bottom of the cliff. I am covered in mud, bleeding, injured … I hear the guards, I hear a soft voice too … was that Brin speaking? Why was he out there? Why be out in the rain and thunder? Did he hear me scream, or see the flares? It's just possibilities, nothing else …*

My grip loosens on the scissors. "How long have I been here, Brin?"

"I'll answer that question, but not until after you eat. This soup is still warm. You need to eat, Elana … you need to get your strength back to normal." Brin picks up the tray and holds it out in front of him.

Something explodes inside my mind, like a volcanic eruption. All the time I spent under sedation with the doctor has smothered and replaced my true feelings. I'm angry and fearful. *You are shattering glass!*

I possess a hatred towards everything I've discovered, and nothing in particular as well. "Brin, how can you stay so bloody calm all the time? I don't need to eat! I need to work out what I'm going to do next! First of all I'm ripped out of my home by the guards, taken away from my parents, my friends …"

I pause because I can picture my mother and father,

Jackson as well. I hold back any tears that are trying to fall. "I have to find my parents … I have to try and sort this mess out … I must try!"

Brin stays relaxed and level-headed, ignoring my outburst. "Elana, please, eat. It will help you feel better. I know you have a lot of questions and we can sit down and work them out, together. At least you're safe here, for now."

I take some deep breaths as I stare at Brin, especially his eyes. I can see an expression on his face although it is impossible to read. I know it shows, somehow, that he is trying to help.

"Thank you. I am … am very hungry," I say.

The bowl of soup has filled the room with a savoury aroma. I grab it as I sit down, unable to resist the unbearable hunger any longer. I place it on my lap yet manage to keep the scissors pointing at Brin. He gets up and moves across the room, without me saying a word to him, choosing instead to stand by the wardrobe, a safe distance away. I take it as a display of politeness and another invitation to trust him.

"This tastes amazing!" I feel better with every spoonful. It is thick and full of vegetables.

"Thanks. I have more downstairs. I'm quite proud of my soup skills."

I'm already running my finger around the bowl, licking it and relishing every single drop. I almost think about the last time my mother served soup, for lunch, or a dinner, then repeat a physics equation to myself instead, clouding the memory away.

Brin looks at my face as if he is searching for something in my expression.

What are you looking at? Why are you staring at me? I think as I look back at him, then blink a few times. I feel very safe, just for a second, even though it isn't warranted.

"You realise that you are in danger, Elana? I am too, because I've helped you. It's rare that any psychological conditioning techniques are resisted, and you haven't fully overcome them either, that's almost impossible, but they don't allow for mistakes. You saw how the guards chased you. They can't have any escapees."

Why do I feel ... warm? It's like ... the room ... in the building ... but ... I'm not in there now ... I'm here with Brin ... I'm not in that room ... nobody can make me feel that warmth here ...

I have a frightening idea. "Brin ... what did ... did you do? Did you drug my soup ... my delicious, lovely, soup?" I ask in an airy voice. I stare at my reflection in the spoon, distorting my face up and down.

Brin laughs. "Thanks for the compliment. Listen, Elana, it's just a small dose, nothing else. You're still safe. I knew that there would be a lot of questions when you finally woke up. I didn't want you running about, screaming ... it could attract unnecessary attention. I hope you understand, but I thought it best ... for both of us. You're just relaxed, nothing else," he explains.

"Ahh, clever ... and quite good with soup as well," I say. I believe him, which is strange because there isn't any reason to. "I knew there had to be more to the story. I knew you had more to tell me."

"Not really. Everything I've told you so far has been the truth. After I told the guards to leave, I carried you straight here and started working on your injuries. The cut on your leg was very deep. I have a fully stocked medicine cabinet here, and my mother taught me to sew ... don't laugh."

I do. A lot. "You stitched me up? You ... you stitched me up! Ha!" I run my finger along the scar on my thigh as I try to control an episode of laughter. "How long have I been here, Brin? Tell me, please?"

"Six days. Today is the twenty-second of June. I had to use a strong anaesthetic, and some sedation tablets as well.

You were running a temperature for a few days." He ignores my drug aided amusement, although I do notice a wide smile.

"Six days? Near the end of June? But ... that ... can't be right?" I count the days on my fingers but give up at four and study my fingertips instead.

"Why not? I've no reason to lie about the date."

I think about the girl in the forest again. Once her memories returned, she was defective, no use to them any longer. She lasted less than five minutes before the Community Guards found her ... found her and ... *You have to think the word, Elana ... think it ... they killed her, murdered her!*

"I assure you, Elana, it has been nearly a week."

After everything that has happened to me ... how have I managed to even survive for six hours? I shouldn't have woken up after I fell down the cliff! I'm ... I'm defective ... a useless slave.

"Brin, even though you stopped the guards from taking me, or shutting me up for good, it doesn't change the fact that they know I'm here! You keep saying I'm safe, but I can't be, not when Central Government could arrive here at any minute!" I shriek. The drug is losing its power ... reality is fighting it, and winning.

Brin ignores me deliberately as he walks a couple of steps across the bedroom. He eventually turns to face me. The look on his face is a mixture of accomplishment and concern, plus something else - defiance - although that part seems distant, aimed at another, not me. "Listen to me. I can guarantee that Central Government will not come here."

I am growing tired of Brin's continuous empty promises. *He lives in a different world! His family has privileges, government standing ... what does he know?*

"You can't be sure, Brin! You can't be! Do you understand that? I need to get out of here ... I need to get away and think about what to do next!" I stand up, having to place one hand on the wall for a second to steady myself and feel balanced.

"Elana! The reason I keep saying you're safe is ..."

"Well? Why?" I ask as I look about on the floor for some plimsolls.

No reply.

"Brin? How can I be safe?"

"Because ... as far as the guards know ... you're dead."

Chapter seven

The words sink in at an agonising pace, as if Brin is repeating them in slow motion. *I'm ... dead?*

I sit back down on the bed. My legs simply give way underneath me and lose all their strength after Brin confesses. The room blurs and I feel as if someone is pushing on my chest, restricting my lungs. "I'm ... dead? You ... you actually told people ... *I am lightning as it crawls across the dark skies* ... that I'm dead!?"

Brin grows apologetic with only his eyes. He obviously regrets his decision, even though, in his opinion, it was the only course of action possible. "I reported that you died of your injuries, yes. As far as the Community Guards know, or care, you are no longer a problem, or a relevant threat."

The low dose of whatever drug Brin has added to the soup vanishes completely. I am furious. I've never known rage like this before and have no way to control it. I'm furious at Brin and the hidden lies, furious at Mayor Hartner, at Central Government.

"Why would you do that!" I scream and launch the soup bowl across the room. It smashes on the wall next to him.

Brin peeks out of the window before he picks up the pieces of the shattered bowl. "Elana, calm down, please! It was an impulsive decision, okay? Why would I save you from … well, they'd have executed you, we both know that … and then waste all that effort by leaving a trail for them to follow? I bought you some time … to heal … to think. I'm not sure where you were headed with the Community Guards, but this has to be a better option … it has to be."

Run! I need to get out of here … now! Find my parents … tell them the truth! I think, but ignore the loud inner warnings, needing instead to slow down my mind. Brin's intentions sound genuine, yet there always seems to be more in his eyes.

"It's only those in power, Elana, nobody else! The ones who control the … people like you. Everyone else will only know, and believe, that which they have been told. You were exiled to the Uninhabitable Zone because of infection from the virus …"

Think about it … you're safe … for the moment.

I see my parents in my mind - at least they won't be devastated by grief on hearing of my death. *Don't believe anything, please. I know you both hold a hope that you'll see me again, one day, as I do you … don't let go of that hope …*

"Do you know about it, Brin?" I ask. As soon as I've spoken, my memory returns to Blake's death. I have to watch the drop of blood fall again.

"Do I know about what? I just told you, I had no idea where the guards were taking you," he defends, placing the shards from the broken bowl on the tray.

"No, that's not what I meant. Regardless of where I would have ended up, do you know *why* I was with them? Do you know what they tried to do to me in that building? What they were trying to create?"

Brin stays very quiet as he rubs his knee. He looks at me before replying in a quiet tone. "Yes, I know … I'm sorry," he says, apologising for all my pain, even though he isn't responsible.

"They tried to change me, Brin … in that building … to change me so that I would become a servant … a slave! The whole reason I am here is because I overheard a conversation! I heard someone talking about slaves being killed!"

Brin stands, horrified. His actions, his noble actions, have caused me terrible torment. It would have been impossible for him to guess how I would react. I expect he had an idea, yet he could not have predicted the extent of my behaviour after I woke up.

Is this it? Is this how the world really works? So many secrets, lies … and what happens now? Will I end up as Brin's servant?

I remember sitting on the steps at the Town Hall, after Blake's murder. I focus specifically on the shock that consumed me, knowing that it is on the verge of appearing once again. Irrational thoughts taunt me, clawing at my skin like a wild animal.

I wake up … I wake up in the morning … Calm down … calm down! Now is not the time to chase speculation and assumptions, especially when I don't truly believe them. Brin hasn't treated me badly … *not yet.*

Mayor Hartner's words return once again, haunting me as if he is following, always close behind, always near. A spectre from my old life. The life he decided to rip away from me.

"This is exactly why, Blake. Because of how you're acting at this very moment. Because you haven't had any conditioning yet … because, without that, you are not willing to accept it."

Brin finds his voice again. "Certain people, more than you will be able to comprehend at the moment, know about this, Elana. It depends on your position in society, your place in the bigger picture ... your career placement. I mean, some people go to work every day and, to them, you are just numbers on a screen ... variations in a large equation, nothing else. The power has changed so many ... in a ... a sickening way."

I can't understand any of this, I can't ... I won't. *I WON'T! How many lies are there? Just how much has been hidden from me? From everyone?*

"Elana, are you ... you going to be okay?"

"No, Brin ... no, I am not ..." I turn away, hiding my face. *I'll find my way back to you ... I'll make all the lies disappear ...*

I am utterly lost. I am walking at the bottom of a deep ocean, blinded and crushed by the pressure of the dark water that smothers me.

I drop the scissors, fall to my knees and cry without shame or regret.

••

I soak myself in a warm bath as the tears flow freely down my face. It is impossible for me to stop them any longer, and I don't want to either. There are reasons to cry, so many of them.

Brin noticed my changing emotional state and respected it in his own way. He ran me a hot bath so I could clean myself up and change clothes, then excused himself to eat downstairs.

From the short time I've been with Brin, I can sense that he feels guilty, and useless as well. He joked with me in an attempt to lighten the mood, promising not to drug my food again the next time we eat together. I didn't laugh. I didn't even manage a smile.

As my body tries to relax in the warm, scented water, I see Mayor Hartner in my mind.

Who can make decisions like that? To order the death ... the murder ... of a teenager ... so easily? Would Blake still be alive if he had agreed to stay quiet about everything?

My thoughts shift to that of my parents, the main cause of the tears. *What do you see now when you think of me, when you think of your daughter? Is there a part of you that doesn't believe everything they told you? There has to be ...*

My mind travels back to *that* room in the large building. I watch a news report ... one I've seen before ... they played it to me so many times.

Residents,
Elana Mayne, a sixteen year old from the South Quarter, has unfortunately been classified as a fifty-fifty and removed from the Community Zone. She displayed irrefutable symptoms and has a troubled mind.
She was apprehended a week ago, attempting to flee, yet Community Guards caught her before she reached the perimeter mines. Her parents have been relocated, at their own request.
Our thoughts go with her, and them. This is never easy news to hear, or live with.

A couple of unexpected knocks on the bathroom door bring me away from the searing emotional pain. The bath is helping slightly, embracing me with warmth and a floral aroma. "I'm ... I'm nearly finished," I say, although it's untrue. "I'll be getting out in a minute."

"Elana, listen, I'm really sorry. Every single thing you hate at the moment ... it's my fault. I don't know how to change that fact, but I know I want to. If you need to take it out on me - I mean your anger, your fears - that's allowed. I deserve it ... but ... I couldn't just let you die out there ... I couldn't let the guards do that ..."

It is obvious to me from Brin's voice and shuffling footsteps outside the door that he means every word. Feeling helpless and responsible, guilty as well, it is all upsetting for him. *I don't want to focus my hatred on Brin. He saved my life ... I should be treating him so much better.*

I slowly dry and dress in the clean tunic which Brin left out for me in the bathroom. It isn't as painful as I had expected it to be either - only the skin on my leg tightens around the scar. "Thank you, Brin ... for saving me. I haven't said that yet ... and I should have."

Silence hangs in the air for a second before Brin responds. "It was the least that I could do. I ... don't agree with it, Elana ... any of it, I never have. Just because my family know certain secrets, it doesn't mean I walk the same path."

The footsteps behind the bathroom door shuffle away before I can speak again.

I hope he believes me. I am thankful for his help ... I am.

••

Feeling less emotional and invigorated after the bath, I walk to the bedroom door a few minutes later. As I reach for the door handle, my heart speeds up and I am suddenly apprehensive of speaking. I am sure Brin is the only other person inside with me, however, I've been shouting since waking up. In my mind, someone outside could have heard me and grown suspicious. *What did he say to me before? Something about 'eyes being everywhere'. What does that actually mean?*

"Brin?" I say, suppressing the fear that 'eyes being everywhere' doesn't mean armed guards. It is somewhere between a whisper and my normal voice. *Where is he?*

A lot of paranoid thoughts spark all at once: betrayal,

imprisonment in a different form … a different type of cell … Brin's secret about saving me has been discovered?

I decide to look around, despite all the concerns I now hold. I reach to grab the scissors, just in case the need to protect myself arises, and notice a handwritten note on the bed.

Elana,

I had to leave for a few hours and I'm afraid it couldn't be avoided. I know I keep saying it, but you will be safe here. I'll return later and bring dinner, or cook for us both. Feel free to look around, just stay away from the windows and don't go outside!
If you get hungry, help yourself to food from the kitchen. Thanks for trusting me … or trying to, at least.
Brin.

I put the scissors in my trouser pocket and walk out of the bedroom, hesitant with every step. Fortunately, the house is light and doesn't provide many shadow filled corners … ones a group of Community Guards could hide in, waiting to ambush me.

This house has been built in a square design and seems quite small too. The maroon and cream décor has been used throughout as far as I can see, making everywhere feel light and safe.

I wonder if there's anything here I can use? Perhaps a map of the area? A knife? … Anything that might be useful in the days ahead?

I see only one door on the other side of the hall and try it. "Locked," I whisper.

Another bedroom? Brin's? Who is he, really? I don't understand how he can have this house to live in, by himself, at such a young age.

The stairs begin at the end of the hall yet my feet

refuse to move very quickly. Every single step is followed by a lengthy silence as I listen for noises downstairs. My imagination haunts me as it plays out hundreds of scenarios, all containing Community Guards waiting for me. *I'll be gripped in the arm bindings again ... they'll take me back to that building ... shoot me on sight for escaping ... I can't be allowed any freedom, not now.*

I shake my head with strong defiance as I make my way to the downstairs hall, seeing another three internal doors, plus the main front door. I wish to open it and run to the outside world ... run all the way to my parents ... *Stop it, Elana! Stop it!*

The first door opens to a bathroom, exactly the same in design as the one that joins with the bedroom I am using. The second leads to the lounge at the front of the house. I remind myself about staying away from the windows, yet it is so difficult. I see the clouds from earlier today have completely disappeared, allowing glorious sunshine to burst in. My eyes dance across green grass and the sprinklings of glorious flowers. Every detail enhances the invitation to rush out and immerse myself in this new world.

The lounge is a minimally furnished space: a cream sofa and two armchairs, a large screen sat on a table, a desk in the corner with stacks of paper and pens scattered across the top of it. The main features, though, are several bookcases and shelves that cover two entire walls. It looks to be a very personal library, possibly Brin's. It's definitely a place of peace and focus to study or work.

I look at the spines on some of the books. I can tell from the titles that most of them are political or historical works.

As I don't discover anything of use from my brief search here, I walk back to the other door in the hall, finding the kitchen, and another door to the tempting outside world. My desire to run is growing to a level that is almost uncontrollable. A set of keys sit on the kitchen worktop, almost calling my name ... goading me to give in and let my instincts take over. The door could be opened so easily ... *No ... I can't ...*

I grab a couple of biscuits, a few slices of dried bread and some water. Then, my eyes stop on something else ... a sharp knife. Without questioning my own actions or motives, I snatch it then return to the bedroom, locking the door behind me. *Are you doing that to keep people out, or keep yourself in?*

••

By the time a beautiful sunset has painted itself across the sky for a while, subsequently replaced a few hours later by the dark of night and a thousand stars, I am in a state of panic - Brin has not returned.

Where is he? Has something happened, something terrible?

Even though brief periods of anxious sleep do come to me over the next couple of hours, they are full of nightmares. In one of them, I'm back amongst the trees, being chased by the Community Guards. I try to hide as the red flares float and glow around my body, always showing my position. I run between the shadows, or crouch down near fallen branches and bushes. One of the guards discovers me, yet, when he removes the helmet, Mayor Hartner's face stares back at me, smiling sickly and laughing. *"Curiosity killed ... Elana!"* he says.

My body shoots upright in bed. I'm covered in sweat which makes the tunic stick to my skin, feeling tight and constrictive, like I am bound inside my own body.

"What am I doing!?" I say, noticing the knife from the kitchen is in my hand. I hold it out in front of me as the thoughts in my mind are replaced with reality.

Being alone in the bedroom doesn't help. I'm scared by the slightest noise and always wondering about Brin. *He's changed his mind ... he contacted the Community Guards! They'll be here soon to get me! No, Elana, no ... you're not thinking straight ... he wouldn't do that ... he wouldn't! Would he?*

"I can't do this! I can't stay here like this! ... I need to get out of here!" I cry through gritted teeth. My fear is in total control as I put on my plimsolls, grab the knife and head down the stairs. My goal is firmly set on the door in the kitchen ... and the keys near to it.

I open the cupboards to search for essential items and supplies. "Water ... food ... it took me three days to get here ... but ... I don't even know where I'm going to go!"

A deep breath comes next, a tear is wiped away, then I find a small backpack. I shove in a couple of bottles of water, some tins of beans and a large handful of biscuits.

That'll do, Elana! Just go! ... No, wait ... wait! My finger runs up the scar on my thigh, speaking to the pain of my past injury with touch alone.

I hurry back upstairs to the bedroom and grab a bottle of painkiller tablets and two bottles of medicine from the bedside cabinet. *Go, now!*

Back in the kitchen, I snatch the keys off of the side. It takes me four attempts to find the correct one that unlocks the door because my hands are shaking so much. Then ... *click!* ... it is open ...

I can almost hear Brin speaking to me. *"You're safe here, I promise."*

I stand, just for a second, looking out at the darkness, wondering where the next step might lead. I hope that Brin will walk in and actually say the words to my face. He will apologise for being so late and stop me from leaving. I give myself another five seconds, yet this daydream never happens.

I know this is wrong ... why can't I stop myself? I peek my head around the door frame, just an inch or two. In the limited light, there seems to be a few bushes dotted about. *That looks like the best route ... I can use them as I head toward to the fence ...*

One of my feet steps forward, then snaps back in hesitation, as if I am crossing a dangerous barrier like the minefield back home. *Do it, Elana! Do it now!*

I run and crouch down behind the nearest bush, always expecting to be grabbed at any second, or hear Brin running out of the house because he has returned and can't find me.

Another bush, then another. I'm getting closer to the raised bank and forest with every burst of energy and movement.

As I crouch again, concealed behind thick leaves, I hear a couple of familiar sounds. Although they are on grass, they're unmistakable. It is all I can do to hold the screams inside my throat. My hand flies across my mouth, my heart races ... the thud of heavy boots ... the scream wants to fly ... THUD! THUD!

What do I do? WHAT DO I DO?

"Perimeter area four is secure," says the voice of a Community Guard.

The thudding boots march away as the guard continues his duty.

It takes me a few minutes to breathe properly again before I dare to move away from this concealed location, always expecting more guards to appear. I keep looking back towards the house, wanting someone ... *Brin. You want Brin to rescue you again ...* to talk me out of this idea, but the small building soon disappears in the darkness, becoming just another shadow among many. Another unrecognisable dark shape that I have no choice but to fear.

The fence ... I saw it when in the bedroom, but it

looked a lot different then - smaller, less intimidating. Now that I am up close, reality hits and dents my already low confidence. It is made of thick steel posts, all standing at least eight feet tall, joined by horizontal bars which have been welded together. A difficult obstacle, physically and mentally, to overcome.

This was a mistake! Go back, Elana ... can you go back? Get back in the house and think this idea through ... you aren't safe out here! You can never be safe out here ...

I look behind me, yet don't even know where the house is any longer. I am lost in the night, living through and battling against the consequences of my own actions.

What's that noise? Is it ... thunder? No, it's more ... like a machine ... what is it?

Bright lights cut through the bars of the fence, the tree trunks and branches as well, casting lengthy shadows across the grass. The noise grows louder and closer to me, roaring sporadically. There are two lights - circles of white - floating at about the height of my chest, always getting brighter.

Carefully, I move my body as low as possible to the ground, laying flat under the bush, waiting ... *It's getting closer!*

A large object creaks out of the darkness, like an enormous animal defending its territory, scouring its lair. My confusion fades briefly and I recognise the source of the noise and lights. Whilst in college, learning history, I saw images and short videos that showed different methods of travel in the old world: aeroplanes, different types of vehicles, motorised bikes. I've never seen one of these up close ... until this moment. What I know used to be called a truck moves along the ground, rolling on thick tyres with deep ridges moulded across them. I wasn't aware the Community Guards even used this type of transport. They are powered by an engine, but don't use electricity or electro-magnetism, like the tram and train networks.

The truck looks as if two metal cubes have been welded to form one. I catch sight of two guards sitting inside behind a sheet of glass or plastic at the front of it. There are two doors, one on each side.

It stops moving thirty feet away from my position. One door opens and a guard steps out, then walks to the fence. A beep sounds, then a grinding noise fills my ears. It is terrible to endure, as if a mechanical beast is howling. It makes my teeth clench and my spine tingle.

What's going on?

The guard gets back in the truck, there are a couple of roars from its engine, then it moves away towards ...

There's a gate! That's what the guard was doing! Opening a gate!

My heart jumps with pure excitement, fuelled by flowing adrenaline. I've been handed an opportunity that might never present itself again.

I wish I knew what the time was!

I know I want, *and need*, to be far away and hidden somewhere safe before sunrise. My eyes scan everything around me. It is a much easier task now because of the powerful lights on the front of the truck.

That bush ... no, it's too small ... the larger one instead, then to the bank and the thick tree trunks ... you can do this ... you have to do this!

I stay low with my head darting left and right. I use such sudden and sharp flicks that my neck muscles start to sting in retaliation.

I move as fast as the crouched stance will allow, running through the gate, staying away from the line of light the truck shoots through the darkness.

I stop behind a tree stump, take a breath and check my surroundings again.

Quickly, Elana! You're nearly free ... you've made it

this far ...

I dash forward, finding a tree trunk much wider than my own body. It is the perfect starting point, hiding me from any eyes that might be looking in this direction. The guards in the truck are facing the opposite direction. *I hope they can't see me ...*

The truck's engine roars again as it moves away. I assume that its main purpose is to patrol the forest, and other areas that are inaccessible by foot. I wonder if they are Brin's personal security, necessary because of his family's government position.

I've ... I've done it ... I'm ... free ... I expected different emotions to flood through me: elation, possibly relief, a sense of pride. None of these surface. Instead, I feel alone and sick. *I brush my teeth ... Sometimes I take a tram to college, sometimes I take a train ...*

With a dread in my heart and no conviction other than to survive, I take a small sip of water and begin walking up the leaf covered bank.

Chapter eight

The forest proves to be a daunting place of contrasts for me in the first hour of 'freedom'. I'm surrounded by natural beauty in many of its forms, yet there are also a plethora of fears to contend with. All the noises shrouded in darkness dance around me: branches snapping, the shrill cry of foxes and other animals, leaves rustling nearby. They all slow down my pace because every single one forces me to hide behind the nearest tree trunk, anticipating discovery.

It had been so much easier, so much safer, when I was accompanied by the Community Guards. My captors - cruel, trained to kill, strict and without remorse - also carried the role of protectors.

I'm worried because I still don't have a set plan of any kind, apart from surviving for as long as possible. My legs are moving, though, so I know that I haven't given up yet in either a mental or a physical sense.

I'll find my way back ... I'll find a way back to you. All I can do is keep telling myself to continue.

A couple of hours pass by and the sun eventually rises, granting the forest a beautiful colour, a new life. Most of the terrifying thoughts are banished once the shadows disappear. Fleeting birdsong becomes my background music as I move in a south-easterly direction, indicated by the sun's position above me in the sky.

"If I can find a landmark, an old building I recognise from college photos … anything … I'll have an idea which direction I'm heading in … but … I don't even know where I am to begin with!" I mutter to myself, with severe disappointment, as I kick at the leaves on the ground.

The sun climbs higher as my levels of stamina are tested. I ignore everything and push my aching body on.

It must be three or four hours since I left Brin's, at least? I'm hoping I have managed to walk for a sizeable distance.

I sink to the floor against a fallen tree stretched thirty feet across the forest. It's covered in moss and tiny clumps of grass and flowers. I decide to eat a couple of biscuits, drink some water and reward myself with a couple of minutes rest.

Do I need medicine? I don't feel any pain in my leg. I'm tired, that's all.

A few squirrels spiral around a tree nearby, causing an innocent smile to form on my lips. *At this rate, I'll end up like you … living in the forest!* I think, making myself laugh.

I take the bottles of medication out of my pocket due to curiosity and focus my attention on the lilac coloured one. *Is this what I was given in that building? I'm certain it was hanging up behind my bed?*

The purpose and dosage instructions are printed on a transparent label: *Liquid anaesthesia. 0.5ml per pipette volume. Anaesthetic suggestion ~ 3.5ml minimum, depending on subject BMI. DO NOT EXCEED 10ml per 24 hour period.*

"Anaesthetic suggestion?" I decide to put the bottles away and let my legs rest the natural way. I think I've had enough chemicals pumped through my body recently.

Where am I going to sleep? I'll have to do it out here, the same as when I was with the Community Guard group, I suppose? … Sleep … I am very tired … shall I sleep now? I could shut my eyes for ten minutes ... sleep ...

I quickly force my body back up and pour some of the water in my cupped hand.

NO! Wake up! my thoughts shout as I throw it on my face. I check ahead of me and pick out a distant tree. It stands out from the others because it has leaves of a striking yellow colour.

"You can drink and eat ... once you reach that tree," I say as another handful of water is thrown on my skin.

The new routine is set, despite my incredible fatigue, and it continues for a couple of hours. Tree after tree. New goal after new goal.

••

Although the leaf canopy provides some cover, and I drink regular sips of water, it is incredibly hot. As the sweat covers my forehead and my feet turn to blocks of heavy, dragged concrete, I eventually decide that enough is enough. I need to find a concealed area with full shade where it will be possible to sit down, rest for a lengthy period of time, and decide on my options. I know they are limited and this fact worries me constantly. Somehow, it is being ignored with a defiance and denial that I didn't know existed inside me.

On first impressions, a ring of nearby trees behind some thick and high growing bushes looks perfect. I move myself in, making sure that the leaves are covering every angle of sight possible. Immediately, the light-grey of my tunic contrasts against the dark-brown of the bark. I almost peal it off due to the sweat layering my arms, scrape it across the dirt and then put it back on. I don't want to but I rub my face and hands as well, making my skin less conspicuous. The sun isn't directly above me, although not far off, so I guess the time to be between eleven in the morning and noon. *I should be proud of myself ... I've managed to walk a long*

113

way today ... so far. I have to reach somewhere different soon, don't I?

A smoky aroma drifts near to me, mixed with a glorious sweetness. *What's that? Food? Out here?* I think as I sniff at the air.

It proves to be a terrible idea as hunger instantly rips at my stomach. I salivate as luscious thoughts of roast meat dinners that my mother cooked once a month return to me. This is different, though, more succulent somehow, more enticing.

A sudden laugh, distant but unmistakable, sounds from my left, then another straight after. *Is that a man and a woman? I must be close to ... what could possibly be out here?*

Every part of my mind screams at me. *No! Stay by the trees, you need to stay hidden!*

I ignore every single one of the warnings and start to walk in the direction of the laughter. I don't know why but I need to see these people. These cruel people ... who are nothing like me, who are so different.

How can they flaunt their happiness? How dare they laugh when I'm so close by, scared for my very life? I think, unaware that my hands have clenched and become powerful fists.

It takes only a few minutes before I see a tall concrete wall ahead of me. It is covered in thick ivy of varying greens, yet brickwork is still visible when I get close enough. The voices have grown louder as well, but I still can't make any words out. They are nothing more than a jumble of noises now, constantly annoying me, constantly provoking me. I don't actually care what is being said and feel an uncharacteristic hatred towards them. It is raw and threatening to control me. I don't understand why and my disdain won't allow for any time to find the answer.

A few of the trees nearby have thick branches

crossing and twisting over each other. I remember physical education lessons at school and college, and how I was capable on a climbing frame set up. I see the trees differently because of this as they have now formed suitable beams to stand on, courtesy of my imagination.

My balance isn't in question, however, heights are not a strong point. My mind always tells me it is *all* about feeling safe without the ground under your feet. Once the fear sets in, it is very difficult for me to shake it off.

That one will do ... I can start there, go up two branches, move along to the end. As long as I find a decent foothold, I should be able to see over the top of the wall. It's eight feet high, or thereabouts.

I wonder what I might see. *Are there other houses around here, like the one Brin lives in?* I ask myself with a spiking urgency. *I need to see what's happening!*

The aroma of food, the voices, the sense of jealousy over their freedom ... they are all pulling me closer, drawing me in like siren song.

I begin to navigate the branches with calculated moves. I have to be certain my hands are gripping firmly before I climb further up, or change the position of my feet.

SNAP!

What was that?

"Perimeter search continuing. Section three is secure," says a voice. More twigs break. The sound is close, too close.

I freeze and inhale, keeping the breath inside my lungs. The words I heard feel as if they have found me and are wrapped around my neck, squeezing tight.

My grip loosens, as does any focus and, more crucially, my balance wavers. I lunge forward, wrapping an arm around the tree for safety. The ground looks a lot further away than it actually is - about six feet - and I have to blink so my vision stops swirling.

Hold it together! Hold it together! If you make a noise now, the guards will definitely hear you! Stop looking down ... stop!

I keep my eyes shut for a few seconds and try to steady my body. The thick branch under my feet helps a lot because it feels solid and secure.

Lift your head ... look forward ... you won't fall ...

I open my eyes with conviction, staring straight ahead and not at the ground below. I can see four guards walking through the forest, carrying automatic weapons in their hands. They are parallel with the line of the concrete wall. If I hadn't moved to investigate the laughter and delicious aroma of food, they would have seen me, I'm positive of that. Their area of interest is only yards away from the ring of trees I'd chosen to hide in.

There isn't any ... urgency ... they are just patrolling this part of the forest. They don't know that I am here ... not yet ...

One of the guards stops to study the ground and bushes where I rubbed my clothes in the dirt. They stay still for a few seconds, examining leaves and broken twigs.

The guard's hand suddenly flies up in the air. "Over here! It looks like recent activity to me!" she shouts.

That's it! They'll track me here, to the tree ... what do I do? Run? Yes! Jump and run!

I prepare myself for another frantic escape attempt through the forest. The daylight both hinders and helps because even though I can see better, so can the guards. For a moment, the bedroom at Brin's seems like such a safe and welcoming place.

Why didn't I just stay there? Why did I let myself become so frightened?

I move away from the tree trunk and place one of my feet across the branch, positioning myself to drop down on the hidden side of the tree. It should give me valuable seconds to run as fast as I can.

My head starts spinning, vision blurs, and my hands are damp with sweat.

Is that ...? It sounds like another truck, like the one near Brin's house ... have they called for reinforcements already?

I sit down on the branch. I am ready to hold my breath and push ... *Drop, sprint, get as far away as possible* ... but a vehicle appears between the trees, stopping me. It isn't a truck like I saw during the night near to Brin's. It still has thick tyres, yet it looks newer, definitely more expensive, and reminds me of the photographs I studied at college that showed other vehicles. This type was commonplace, used mostly by families to travel, called a car.
The metal bodywork has a shiny finish in maroon, glistening in the sunlight. I ignore the splendour, threatened instead by this mechanized animal as it moves closer to my current place of safety.

Don't stop there! No! NO! I stand back up, readjusting my body for balance. I feel cornered, totally trapped, and my lungs are tightening. My heart is already racing, and now, with the vehicle directly underneath me, I'll have to rethink any possible escape route from the beginning ... *if* there even is a chance to get away any longer.

The door of the car opens and the driver steps out. He wears black trousers, a red shirt, and black boots.

Brin? I can't believe my eyes. *What is he doing here?*

Brin is seen by the guards straight away. He simply waves in a friendly manner and stays by the vehicle.

They don't scare him at all. He holds a power over them that I wish I could use.

"Drop down and get in the back. Lay down below the seats and stay quiet, this isn't over yet," says Brin without looking up. "As soon as I start talking to the guards, make your move, Elana. Don't hesitate."

117

What? He knows I'm up here? How?

I can't think of an answer to my questions at this very moment. I need to get down from the tree, hide inside the vehicle and wait.

Brin walks away, looking off to the left. He stops a couple of times, as if something has caught his attention and it warrants further study. The guards see this and copy his actions, forgetting their search in and around the thick bushes.

When do I go? Now?

Brin walks further away, joining the group of guards. I can't hear him, though. I watch as he points his finger in the direction of trees and bushes in the distance ... away from me ... drawing the eyes of the guards with him ...

NOW!

I drop to the branch below, then the next. I allow myself one quick look over my shoulder ... *still safe*.

I grip tightly and swing my legs down, landing on the ground as quietly as possible. The leaves rustle, not much thankfully, as I jam my back against the tree, letting a moment of inaction prepare me for the next step.

How do I get in? Are the doors on these vehicles like trams and trains? Are they automatic, or do I need to open them myself?

I move slowly and silently around to the side of the car - the one the guards can't see - and grab at the handle. *Come on! Come on ... open!*

It clicks and I pull the door a little bit towards me. It isn't easy squeezing and moving my body through a tiny gap.

Brin told me to stay below the seats, I think with relief, so I crouch low and wait.

I am cornered prey. I am a fly, dangerously close to the spider's web. Once again, my life is in Brin's hands.

••

"I've taken a different route back to the house, but there's still a steep drop coming up. Stay where you are, you'll be fine," suggests Brin.

I don't answer. Brin has been back in the car for fifteen minutes and it is the first time he's spoken. I know he is angry with me, disappointed too.

I need to trust him ... or try to, like he said. There have been chances to hand me over to the Community Guards ... quite a few chances, and he hasn't. He has always protected me ... but ... how can I trust anyone?

The journey lasts for another quiet ten minutes. Brin stops the car and turns off the engine. He sits for another minute, then turns around in his seat. "We're back. How ... erm ... how do you feel?"

I look up at the windows and bricks of the house. I can see half a smile on Brin's face and a sincere tint in his eyes. "Better ... erm ... thank you ... and I'm sorry ... really sorry ..."

"Any idea where you were going?"

I lift my head and body up a little, but stay beneath the level of the window. "Not really," I reply and think about the aroma of food and the laughing people. I had directed and channelled such a strong rage towards them. "Where did I end up? I heard people nearby ... talking and laughing?"

"You've been to a barbecue, Elana, right?" asks Brin.

"Yes, quite a long time ago. It was a social event in the summer, arranged by Central Government, although I can't remember why. I was only eight ... or nine years old."

"That's what you heard. There are other houses close to where I found you. They were preparing for one."

I'm a little bit intrigued by this. "Oh, so, it's a special occasion for them today?"

"No. The sun is out, Elana, and they felt like it. Nothing more."

"Oh, I see. That's ... well, that's very different to the

119

Community Zones," I say with disappointment.

I know why I felt so much hate for the laughing people. Their freedom. Their freedom and the very lives they are allowed to live, so different from my own.

Brin changes the subject finally and lets his frustration out. "You realise how dangerous that was, don't you? I mean, you were so close to the guards. They could have seen you ... then ... well, then what would have happened?"

"You didn't come back to the house, Brin ... I panicked, it's as simple as that. I ... I don't know ... I had to get out!"

"Luckily for you, my mother is a protective woman, and I'm the son of an important government official," starts Brin.

"What does that mean?"

"It means my spare keys have a tracking device on them. Once I worked out what you had done, I just needed to find you. I checked around the house first to make sure you weren't close by ... I thought maybe you'd changed your mind but didn't want to risk running back inside," explains Brin.

"That's not far from what actually happened," I say, remembering crouching by bushes, regretting my decisions.

"We all act out of character sometimes, Elana, especially when scared."

I had forgotten all about the keys I took with me in the backpack. They must have been shoved in after I unlocked the door. That entire portion of the evening is now a blurred mess in my memory.

"I'm going to reverse up near the front door of the house, then I'll open it. You can go straight in after, okay? I expect you're hungry and tired too?"

"Yes, I'm both." I nod my head while answering. "Sorry, Brin. I ... it's difficult for me ... you know? I have nightmares after my time in that building … every thought gets worse and I can't … can't stop them. It feels … feels like I'm trapped, no matter where I am …"

Brin doesn't speak but his face answers. He knows exactly what I'm trying to say. He doesn't understand it on the same level as I do, but he knows.

Brin prepares a delicious lunch for us both: vegetable soup, thick bread, and some sliced beef as well. He keeps quiet mostly, only speaking to check whether or not I'm enjoying the food, or to offer me more. There are a few other similar questions and polite small-talk.

After eating, I take a bath and change my dirty tunic and trousers. It isn't a lot, yet I manage a couple of hours in bed, resting and grabbing bouts of sleep. The knife stays underneath my pillow at all times, close enough to make me feel safe.

When I return to the lounge, I find Brin sitting at the desk, reading.

"Hi."

"Hi."

"Sorry I took so long, Brin. I guess I was very tired," I say.

Brin closes the book and puts it next to him on the desk. "Can I ask you a question, Elana?"

"Of course."

"Who's Blake?"

"What?" I snap. I become defensive at the very mention of his name. My eyes widen with anger. "What do you know about Blake?"

Brin continues, despite the confrontational tone he's met with. "Listen, I treated your injuries for nearly a week, remember? During that time, and just now while you slept, you said the name Blake. I'm curious, that's all."

I clench my hands a couple of times, making strong

fists, then turn away towards the window. "He … he died," I say.

"I'm … I'm very sorry to hear that. Were you two close friends?" asks Brin.

"Not really, no. He … everything that has happened to me … it's all connected to him … every thought, every nightmare … it's all linked."

I move to the sofa and sit down. I don't want to ever forget Blake, or what happened, I only want the memories to stop causing me such crippling emotional pain.

Brin's eyes grab me in a stare, akin to Miss Collins during my progression interview. "Maybe if we talked about it, that might help?" He sits forward, inviting me to answer.

I feel too apprehensive to consider the offer. "I'm … not good with trust at the moment, Brin. Do you understand that?"

"Yes, I understand."

"Do you, though? I mean, how can you?" No reply comes so I continue. "Let's just say that my life changed, completely, after Blake's death."

Brin pushes for more information. "You told me before that you overheard something? Because of that they tried to change you? I'm only trying to help, Elana. If I can understand how you feel … I don't know … it will help *me* to understand *you*. It might also give us a direction to go in … what happens next, you see what I mean?"

I think for a short time, realising that he has a strong case. "Okay … okay. I … witnessed … his murder."

"Murder? Blake was murdered?" asks Brin, shocked.

I nod and force myself not to cry. I look away again, finding a strange point in the room to focus on: the brass door handle. It's polished, like a lot of the furniture and stylish fixings in the house, reflecting the light with a golden tint.

"Why?"

"He found out that slaves had been killed … well, his

father saw it happen, then he told Blake about it. The mayor of my community, Hartner, he came to see Blake ..." I pause to rid my mind of *that* drop of blood. I see it so clearly, as if I am back underneath the metal panels of Blake's home. "The mayor gave Blake a choice, accept it ... or ..."

Brin stands up. He paces away and turns so that I can't see his face. "And the father?"

"While I listened to Hartner and Blake talking, the mayor definitely said that he had recovered after the explosion. But then I saw a news report saying that he had died because of his injuries."

"Explosion?" asks Brin. He is piecing together bits of information as well, much like I had attempted to do after Blake's murder.

"Yeah ... erm ... he worked at a steel processing plant in my community. I think he saw the slaves killed there, or at least that's what I guess happened. He lost a leg in the explosion ... a warning ... they hurt him as a warning so that he would keep quiet. Then, as I just told you, after Blake ... died ... that's when I heard that his father had died as well. I ... I had to run ... I didn't care where I was going, I needed to get away ... that's all I could think about."

Brin crosses his arms, obviously thinking on my words. "The explosion could have been an accident?" he asks, tapping his chin with his forefinger. "These things happen sometimes. They're horrible when they do, and tragic, yes, but they do happen."

"No ... because the note told me it was going to happen ..." I stop speaking. I'm not quite sure if mentioning the note I received is actually a good idea.

"What? A note told you? What do you mean?"

I worry and wonder if I have revealed too much. I curse myself inaudibly through gritted teeth before continuing. "I found a note, handwritten, hidden inside my tunic. It told me about things that *would* happen. The explosion was predicted on there. I … I thought it was just a Rogue woman, spreading lies, like all Rogues do … but …"

"But?" asks Brin. He paces again. It obviously helps him to think.

"Well, it happened!" I say with an unnecessary tone. I sound defensive for some reason.

Brin sits back down. "So many lies, just not from the places you expected."

As I watch his studious behaviour, I can't decide if Brin does understand me. He has grown up knowing details that others aren't allowed to. He sees the lies and secrets from a different perspective … he stands on the other side of the line. *He said to me before,* 'I … don't agree with it, Elana … any of it, I never have. '*But ... how can he be who he is ... in a powerful and political family, and think like that?*

"Can you help me?" I ask. "You're the only person who can at the moment."

"How?" Brin is surprised by my request. He's used to offering his support, not being asked for it. "What can I do, apart from hide you away?"

"To see through it all? I want to know … everything … I … I don't care how many lies there are, I don't care how much it hurts me … I … want to know." I make sure that I have Brin's eyes firmly locked with my own. "I need to know."

Brin doesn't like this idea at all, his face shows it without hesitation. "That could be dangerous, Elana. Look at how you are now, after your time in the Tower."

"The what? The Tower?"

"Yeah … I mean the hospital building, where they … erm …" Brin pauses, wanting to be careful with his words. He knows how fragile and upset I can be. "It's nickname is the Tower."

"That's a perfect example, Brin. How would I ever discover that, without your help? It doesn't have to be all at once … just a detail here and there … that way I won't overload and lose my mind … I hope …"

Brin ponders this offer for less than a second. "Okay. I'll do it."

"You will?"

"Yes."

"I thought you'd disagree with me. You think it's a good idea, then?" I'm definitely shocked. I had expected Brin to abruptly end the conversation, or he would find an excuse to delay it. He's lied about saving my life and is secretly harbouring me from Central Government. There are more than enough reasons for caution and pessimism.

"No. But it'll help you. I promised to do that."

"Why?"

"Sorry, what?"

"Why, Brin? Why do you do it? Start at that point. If you want me to trust you, start there. Explain to me why you walked out of this house in the pouring rain, confronted armed guards … and saved my life."

Brin walks again, hiding his face.

"I'm a … slave, Brin. Why does my life matter to you? That's what I'm having trouble with." I have to wipe my eyes after speaking. Calling myself a slave, admitting that I have been altered in such a way, grips my heart.

When he turns, Brin's expression shows an anger that troubles me. He looks so intimidating, so strong. His eyes are piercing.

What have I done, or said, to upset him so much?
"We … erm … don't have to do this now. Maybe later?"

Brin ignores me as he lifts his left foot up, placing it on the sofa. He rolls up his trouser leg so that it sits above the knee. "See that?"

I look, unsure where I've taken him with my questions. There is a circular scar on the skin by his kneecap, almost central, about an inch in diameter.

The day I met Brin ... he asked for his cane to help him walk ... and I ignored him!

"On my twelfth birthday, a ... slave ... a girl of about your age ... she dropped a plate of food on the floor during the family dinner. Hannah, that was her name. My father was furious ... so angry ... he ... started shouting at her, inches from her face. He called her useless, a waste of space ..." Brin moves to stand normally again and rolls his trouser leg back down. "What you have to understand, Elana, is that my father is a strong man, very strong, but it's ... corrupted him. He has no limits, no restraint. He's a narcissist, he's obsessed with his own power, and he's not afraid to use it either."

"I don't know anybody like that, Brin ... I don't know what to say." I can see how painful it is for him to speak of this incident and regret my persistence. *If I hadn't pushed for his help, he wouldn't be like this.*

"He shoved her, this girl, Hannah ... still yelling about how stupid and useless she was. I hated it, every second of it, but my father wouldn't stop. My family were shocked too, but scared enough to keep them from getting up and intervening. All the time, my father is growing angrier. She wasn't answering him at all, Hannah ... but then, she had been *programmed* not to ... it annoyed him more. He wanted a confrontation, a proper argument, but her silence provoked him."

"So ... what happened?"

"I begged him to calm down, stood in front of him, crying. I asked him to stop, to leave her alone. I think I even got down and started tidying up the food myself ... but ... that's when he pulled out a gun."

"A gun? What?" I ask in disbelief as my eyes widen.

"He just ... right there, by the dinner table ... and this girl ... she didn't even seem scared. I guess her brain was so broken by that time ... but I thought she would at least scream or cry, anything really. Instead ... she ... she dropped to the floor like a … like a crumbling statue. There was a patch of blood on her tunic, here." Brin points to his right lung. "And then I shouted at my father again. I jumped in front of him, screaming at him, telling him to stop and sit down, that he'd ruined my birthday … then he … he pulled the trigger again."

It takes me a few seconds to connect all the images and parts of the story in my head. Suddenly, I gasp and my mouth drops opens with genuine shock.

"Your father … he … he shot you? He did that to your leg?" Asking the question rips at my heart. I can almost sense my own father placing a comforting arm around me.

Brin blinks a tear away. He looks so much older, so much more mature and wise to the true darkness of the world. I fear this unknown path. The entity of truth surrounds me like a thick fog.

"And that's why I helped you, Elana, and can never agree with any of these secrets. That's the reason I couldn't leave you out there near the forest … the reason that I don't agree with how those in power use it. Because I tried before and I failed … because I failed … and Hannah died."

Chapter nine

I sit on the edge of the bed, alone, watching a flock of distant birds fly above the forest. Their swift movements are graceful and magical as they soar effortlessly, twist themselves in the air, or glide high above the green world beneath.

Brin decided to sit in his bedroom a short time after the emotional confession concerning his father. He needed to retreat and I didn't try to stop him. He needs some time alone, which I understand so well, especially since arriving at the house after being rescued.

Has he ever been able to talk about it before? Who would he go to? Are there others out there who know about Hannah ... the girl he couldn't save?

Other questions keep rolling about in my head as well, over and over, begging to be answered. They are important questions about where my life will be in a week, or a month. *I shouldn't imagine so far ahead ... I can't.*

I whisper them, think them as well, resort to asking my own reflection, but, regardless of the method, no answers ever come.

I sit in silence for another ten minutes, playing out many ideas, seeing where they might take me. I even get up and walk about in the bedroom, borrowing Brin's pacing skills. It is for no other reason than to be moving, keeping myself active … doing *something*. However, the realization that no course of action will follow, none whatsoever, has already set in.

"What can I do? I can't fight these people. I can't defeat them!" I say in a dejected and angry voice. "I suppose living free … resisting the manipulation in the Tower, that is revenge in itself, isn't it?"

I sigh at my own words. It *is* an answer, but not good enough. I need more, much more. Bold thoughts keep crying out so they are heard and revenge seems to be an idea - a dangerous and dark path - which I cannot ignore.

"How would I take revenge? Am I even capable of it? If I am, if I can push myself to be *that* person, where does it all begin? I can't just walk back to the Community Zone and confront Mayor Hartner!"

The mirror on the wardrobe shows me an unfamiliar reflection once again. Such a different girl … stronger, wiser … yet it has been forced on me. *I have been forced to change. Forced against my will.*

Sadness creeps in, caused by loneliness and a need to see my parents. I hold a crushing need inside me that never fades. It is heartbreaking to even imagine their faces.

I reach down and feel at my thigh, specifically the scar underneath the trousers. "If I am capable of revenge …"

The reflection changes, almost as if it is a different Elana looking back. This one is angry, powerful, full of disgust. "… *When* I take my revenge, I shall change them too. I shall take all that they hold close away from them. All that they love …"

I open the door, walk across to the other bedroom and knock on it a couple of times. "Brin! Brin! Can we talk?"

Shuffled footsteps sound before he opens the door. "Hi."

"Are you … you feeling better now?" I ask.

Brin nods. "Yeah, I've been reading, that's all. I thought you might have fallen asleep again, so I didn't want to disturb you. What's wrong?"

I peek through as much as possible, trying to see what his bedroom looks like. From my limited viewpoint in the hallway, it doesn't appear to be much different from the one I use. Next to Brin's bed, I notice a pile of photograph frames stacked up, which I think is odd. They are all face down so none of them can be seen. *Actually, there aren't any photographs in the house. I wonder why?*

"Nothing, I'm fine … I just wondered if we could talk some more? I … know the face of my enemy now, Brin … and I want to do something about that. Can you help me?"

Brin raises his eyebrows. "Come in and sit down, Elana. This isn't a good idea, okay? Please, trust me on that."

I knew I wouldn't get a positive response. I stay quiet as I sit on a chair in Brin's room, thinking carefully about my upcoming words. They need to be perfect. I want answers, information, details that will help. Brin could possibly provide all of these for me.

"Revenge, I'm guessing? I understand that, Elana. What did you have in mind?" Brin stands by the door with a searching expression planted on his face.

"Oh … erm … I …" I stumble with my words. I did not expect Brin to want to hear my ideas at this very moment.

"Best to have a plan first, eh?" says Brin. "And, I take it that this enemy you speak of, the one you've managed to give a face to, it's one person? You're targeting an individual?"

"Yes, I am."

Brin crosses his arms. "The mayor of your Community Zone? Hartner?"

I don't know exactly what I expected Brin to do, but it wasn't stand by the bedroom door, asking me question after question.

"Yes, Mayor Hartner. Is that wrong? What should I do, then? My only other option, right now, is to stay here, but we both know that isn't going to last forever."

Brin sits down in another chair opposite me. Before he has a chance to open his mouth, I continue. I have a feeling I know what he is going to say anyway.

"And don't promise me that I can live here, or that I'll be safe. It won't stay that way. It can't. Okay, I have a kind of freedom, thanks entirely to you." I smile to hopefully let Brin know how grateful I am. "But it isn't the way I want it. I can't carry on like this, it isn't possible."

Brin stands up but he doesn't say anything, and I don't expect him to either. I know he will see this conversation as a lot of ridiculous and futile words. I'm acting on impulse with pure anger as my closest ally.

"Come downstairs with me, Elana. I want to show you something. But …"

"I have a terrible feeling I'm not going to like the next part of your sentence," I say.

Brin gives me another questioning stare.

"I know it won't always be that way, but it's to be expected. You've a lot to tell me that I won't like to hear," I add, trying to explain my sharp tone.

"Then you're prepared for it. Good. You're going to hate this one … there's no other way for me to put it. I'm sorry for that, really I am. But … erm … try and prepare yourself."

I follow Brin to the lounge, dreading whatever is about to happen or be discussed. He scans a finger along the shelf and then takes a couple of large and heavy books in his hands.

"What are those?"

"More lies, I'm sorry to say."

I watch as Brin opens each book to a specific page. They contain illustrations … topographic and thematic maps.

"Where is that?" I ask.

Brin doesn't answer straight away. He looks at both maps carefully, then turns the page in one of the books. "Come and look at this, Elana ... but ..."

"I know, I'm going to hate it. You've already mentioned that." I honestly don't mean to sound so sarcastic, it just happens.

"I simply want to show you that your enemy doesn't always have one face."

"One face? What does that mean?" I ask, confused. Brin sometimes speaks in an enigmatic manner, weaving clues instead of blurting out harsh truths.

"What do you see? And, crucially, what *don't* you see?" he asks, pointing to both illustrations.

What is he talking about? I study the pages as I have been instructed to do. I'm not familiar with the exact areas on display, and they haven't been marked or labelled on the maps either. The aerial view of a Community Zone stands out immediately. It looks so much like the insignia of Central Government when viewed this way. "Is that deliberate? Someone designed it that way?"

"Yes. The perimeter, the Community Guard posts, residential areas, the barracks, and the jurisdiction bureau."

"I don't know what I'm missing here, Brin," I snap with frustration. "I can't see anything out of the ordinary."

"What is situated directly outside of your community?" pushes Brin. He is so apprehensive to speak but covers it well. "I mean beyond the perimeter. What is there?"

"Outside mine? There is an Uninhabitable Zone. It stretches for twenty miles, then another community perimeter begins ... one of the smaller London zones."

Brin continues to look at the two books. He doesn't want to make eye contact with me whatsoever, deliberately keeping his head turned away because he is afraid and guilty - even apologetic to do so.

Then, a few differences click in my head. One of the maps has the initials UZ printed on it. I presume it stands for Uninhabitable Zone, the other doesn't ... and the perimeter lines have arrows drawn inside them, pointing in different directions. On one they faced inwards, the other outwards.

"Do the arrows indicate the different types of perimeter, Brin? Is that what it is ... mines, electrified fence, and so on?"

Brin sighs. "What is the perimeter for, Elana?"

"To keep us all safe, of course. The zones need something to stop fifty-fifties, or wild animals, from getting in. The communities and residents need to be protected."

The fact that Brin is asking such an obvious question worries me.

Brin moves his finger to the arrows pointing inwards, then he slides it across to the ones pointing outwards. "Or ...?"

"Or?"

Brin taps on the book a couple of times. My mind clicks again. It causes my heart to completely skip a fast beat, as if he has reached in and squeezed it. *NO!*

I don't want to say the words out loud. *He said I would hate it ...*

They start anyway, my words, and Brin joins in with me, so that we speak at exactly the same time. "To keep everyone inside!"

Brin continues the sentence on his own as I let the weight of this latest discovery sink in. "To keep every single resident, in every single Community Zone, all over the world ... trapped inside. Then, you are all *exactly* where those in power want you to be. Under their control, on their terms. You are all prisoners, without even knowing it. You go to sleep safe, you wake up safe, and you thank Central Government for keeping it that way."

I need to sit down. I feel sick and it is growing worse

133

by the second. Sweat forms on my brow and the palms of my hands.

"Elana, I keep saying it, but I'm so sorry. One man … Hartner … is not your only enemy. It's much larger than that."

Brin is about to place his hand on my shoulder for comfort, but I push it out of the way and run to the kitchen sink.

••

I hurry back to the bedroom to clean myself up. I selfishly ignored Brin when I heard him say there were other things I had to know.
I feel terrible after vomiting in the kitchen, and embarrassed as well. I don't want to speak to him any longer either, not at this moment. *He warned me! He warned me that I'd hate knowing!*

As I brush my teeth and throw water over my face, connections start forming all by themselves. Before now - before the truth - I had needed Brin's secret knowledge to light the way ahead. Now, links are showing up by their own power and will. Paths are weaving their way through the cloud of lies, spreading like roots in the ground.

I move to the bed, sit down and wipe a few tears from my eyes. *Central Government telling everyone to stay inside their zones wouldn't be enough … there would still be a temptation, or a … a choice … I never wanted to venture away from the community, the safety, because of the infected areas. But …*

Darker questions spark as I pause. Every moment angers, confuses, and shocks me. I feel sick again. It never really left me, lingering around inside my stomach and chest. *What if those were lies as well? No, they can't be! Can they? If it hadn't been for Brin and the truth, I couldn't even begin to think this way ... now, though, I can't tell one from the other ...*

I sip some water from a glass on the bedside cabinet. I want to go back downstairs and hear Brin say the words, not my own inner voice. *Create a threat so perfect, so complete, that it can never be questioned. If you do, you are labelled a Rogue. If you continue, you are displaying symptoms of the virus and banished as a fifty-fifty! I was thrown out and taken to that building because of what I had seen!*

I stand up and pace across the bedroom, asking myself if it all fits together. I can't think like Brin because I haven't had his upbringing. *So, it's a lose-lose scenario ... the perfect threat? Behave, listen to Central Government ... say one word out of line and they'll ...*

The girl in the forest runs for her parents. A cruel memory that pokes through, giving me a message. ... *they'll banish you ... take you to the forest? The Tower? One pull of the trigger and all the questions go away, forever ...*

I hurry back to the bathroom and drop to the floor, holding my stomach. I need to try and stop it cramping and whirling about. All the thoughts are too much to accept, even *try* to accept. My entire life is crumbling around me, as if the walls are cracking and the floor has become a violent whirlpool. There is no way I can stop it happening.

"Elana ... can I come in?"

Brin! I can't talk to him now, I just can't!

"Are you hungry? Thirsty? Erm ... we can talk some more, if you want to?"

Stay grounded ... stay grounded ...

"Or ... sit together and say nothing. I don't think you should be ... alone," offers Brin. His words are coated with a helpless guilt.

"Don't blame yourself, Brin," I say as loudly as possible. I don't want him to hear my emotions or sense my physical state. "None of this is your fault. Just ... just give me a bit of space … I'll talk soon, I promise."

Footsteps shuffle outside the bedroom door. "Okay. I … think I have an idea." Brin's words are fast, as if he's been granted a moment of pure clarity. "I need to go out, but I'll return within half an hour. I think it will be good for you."

I am about to question Brin's mysterious sentence but I need to wash my face again and try to cool down. *I take the tram from near my house to the college. I study many subjects. I enjoy science … I wake up. I get dressed …*

Hurried footsteps disappear down the stairs.

What was he talking about? What will be good for me?

I hear the sound of the front door closing as it echoes through the house.

••

My dream puts me back in the progression interview. I stand in the large hall, waiting for the unpleasant Miss Collins to appear and pick out all of my invisible faults. There aren't any others here in the separated sections this time, though. I am alone and much more scared.

I don't understand any of this!

I hear footsteps behind me. I try to turn but fear stops me from moving.

"Blake?" I ask, not expecting to see him. He is wearing a dark-grey suit and carrying files in his hands, the same as Miss Collins when I met her.

"Hi," says Blake, smiling. "Ready?"

"What are you doing here?" I ask. "Ready for what?"

"Interviewing you, Elana. Why else would I be here?"

"Oh, right. Of course."

I am confused by this dream. Everything about it is vivid to the point of exaggeration. The location, Blake, the familiarity … it is all *too* real.

"So, Elana, where do we go from here?" asks Blake in a blunt tone.

"Go? What do you mean?"

"Indecisive still, I see?" Blake proceeds to scribble something in the file he is carrying.

"That's not fair, Blake! How am I supposed to react when every new day, every new hour, brings up more and more lies! I only came to your house to see how you were! I didn't want any of this!"

"But you have it, don't you, Elana? You have to decide what to do with it, that's what happens next. That's what is important." Blake grabs my upper right arm and squeezes it.

"Hey! What are you doing?"

He sighs and makes more notes. "Still not military worthy. Shame."

I frown. "Do with it? There's nothing I can do with it, Blake!"

"Stop thinking of yourself as weak and outnumbered. Think of yourself as a dangerous threat."

"Blake, you're not making any sense."

"I am. You just can't see it yet." Blake scribbles once more, sighing with disappointment. "Elana seems unable to process ideas from given information … demonstrates a confused and unfocused attitude."

"Do you have to write this all down? Is it really necessary?" I ask, wishing for Blake's pen to disintegrate between his fingers.

"Yes. This *is* an interview. You are here to prove yourself capable."

"Of what?"

"You know what to do, Elana. You spoke of it earlier."

"I did?"

"You'll remember. And make sure you remember this dream as well, it'll help you."

I'm about to ask more questions when I hear a front door slam shut. I turn to look behind me as the room blurs and moulds back to reality.

"Blake?" I mumble, not fully awake. "Oh, I must have dozed off."

A female voice from downstairs - a *new* voice - causes my eyes to spring open. She sounds young, yet strong and upset.

Who is she? Why is she here!? I grab the knife from underneath the pillow.

Brin's voice joins in with the female but I can't make out the words properly. It is definitely a conversation … not heated, but sharp.

"You did what?" cries the female.

I hear her so clearly this time because it is impossible not to. Whatever Brin said, it's shocked her.

I need to hide! I need to run! I think, deciding there can be only one reason for the female's reaction: She knows about me. *I thought Brin was going to keep the fact that I'm here a secret?*

I swing my eyes around the bedroom, calculating the options … the very limited options. I ignore the panic building inside and my trembling hands with rapid gulps of air. *Hide? I've got the knife and scissors … I can fight my way out? Maybe I can get downstairs and sneak by them both?*

Footsteps on the stairs.

The window! Climb out and drop to the ground … I can run!

I move across the bedroom and open the window, realising I am desperately unprepared for yet another escape attempt. The bag I filled with water, basic food, and the various medications … *It's in the bathroom!*

Footsteps outside the door.

It's too late. There isn't any time left for me to think. I start to see everything as a series of rushed images, my mind flipping through them at high speed like a handful of photographs.

I grab the chair from near the end of the bed and move it quietly so that it is underneath the window. Then, I tip-toe back to the bathroom, slipping myself in behind the gap between the open door and the wall.

This isn't going to work!

"Elana?" says Brin as he stands outside the bedroom.

If I stay quiet, he'll think I'm asleep and leave me alone ...

"Elana? Can I come in?"

At least a minute ticks by before the door handle turns. I hold my breath and tense my muscles to keep every part of my body still. I can just about peek through the gap but my area of vision is limited. I only see a few feet of the room and some of the bed.

"Elana? Where are you?"

Brin walks to the bathroom and looks inside. He is inches away from me on the other side of the door. "Where is she?"

I expect the door to swing open at any second. Instead, Brin takes the bait and walks across the room to the open window.

"She must have climbed out! Hearing you must have scared her! I need to find her, she can't have gone far!"

He hurries out of the bedroom. I don't hear any other footsteps move with his, though. The female ... the other voice ... *Where are you? Did you stay outside the door?*

I breathe as quietly as I can, letting my mind tick away. I need to find out why Brin has brought another person to the house.

"I used to find places like that when Brin and I were

growing up. Hide-and-seek was *always* my favourite game."

She's still here? In the bedroom! My heart accelerates in a split second, causing my legs to shudder.

"I'm not a threat to you, Elana. My name is Violet. I'm Brin's sister … we're twins. He asked me to come here but he didn't say why until five minutes ago, when we walked through the front door. Apparently, so he told me, there's a problem that needs a 'feminine touch'. By that, I'm guessing he was referring to you."

I have no choice but to push the door and show myself. I feel stupid standing behind here now that it is no longer a useful place to hide.

"Hi," says a girl with straight black hair, a couple of inches longer than mine. She has dark-brown eyes, black-rimmed glasses, and her face carries an innocent expression. She's five-four in height, wearing a white blouse, cream trousers, and white, flat, shoes.

I look at Violet in front of me, unsure what either of us will do next.

"Erm … hi," she says.

My hand drifts over the pocket where I keep the knife. *I don't feel threatened … Violet doesn't scare me … Should I stay here, or run now that I have a chance to?*

Violet smiles, raises her hand and waves awkwardly, then smiles even wider. "Erm … You wait here while I go and find Brin, okay? He's already freaking out about you disappearing. It's best if I get him back in the house before his behaviour raises questions. Patrol guards could see him out there."

"Sorry … I … I didn't know what to do! I heard you and …"

Violet smiles again. "Relax, we'll talk in a little while. Stay here," she says and runs off out of the bedroom.

He brought his sister to talk to me? Another person to trust … well try to … and … and how can she help me?

The dream about Blake chooses to return and I replay everything ... all the words and details from the beginning. I know it is all inside my head, and all the questions and answers are there as well. I wish I could make sense of them.

Blake said to me: *"You know what to do, Elana. You spoke of it earlier."*

"Am I talking about revenge? Is that what I need to plan for?"

"Stop thinking of yourself as weak and outnumbered. Think of yourself as a dangerous threat."

I let Blake's words - my own subconscious words, spoken by him - play out again. I sit on the bed, trying to listen to them, hoping for a plan to present itself ... hoping for Blake's memory to guide me along the correct path, the path I haven't seen yet.

"Elana!" Brin runs back in the bedroom with a look of relief on his face. "Will you stop doing that to me? Please?"

Violet follows, smiling. "Relax, Brin. She's here. You're here. I'm here. Stress isn't invited."

I laugh a little bit but stop myself when I realise how much it has scared him. "Sorry, Brin. But, strictly speaking, I didn't do anything. You just couldn't find me." I look at Violet with a childish smile.

"What an interesting little problem we have here." Violet moves towards the window in the room and stares outside. "And what exactly am I going to do to help, Brin?"

"I asked myself the same question," I say, with a slight sarcasm.

"Aww, we can't blame Brin. He's not very ... comfortable around girls, Elana. He gets all shy and doesn't know what to say. It's so sweet."

Brin looks at his sister, then me. The look in his eyes is one of pure embarrassment and his cheeks flush red. "Yeah, shall we stop that? Right now, please? There are more important matters to deal with here."

I giggle at Brin's awkward behaviour, as does Violet: his eyes are down towards the floor, he doesn't know where to look and he crosses his arms.

"Elana, you need to stop running off, or making me believe that you have, okay?" Brin turns his eyes to me and stares with renewed confidence. "Violet, I know you'll keep quiet about this. I need you here because we've reached a stalemate and the next step is proving difficult to find. I thought maybe a fresh perspective would help provide the answer."

I move to the wardrobe and check my reflection, gazing at my own eyes. I imagine an ethereal version of Blake over my shoulder, nodding his head. "It isn't difficult to find, Brin. It's simple."

"It is?"

"Yes. Revenge. Like we both mentioned earlier. I want Mayor Hartner … I want him to lose everything!"

Brin and Violet don't speak. They look at me with surprise.

"He took everything from me … everything! My family, my home … he even tried to take my mind! And … he can't have that power, it isn't right, none of it is right! I listened to him threatening Blake … he decided to kill him without a second thought!"

"Okay, Elana … calm down, please!" says Brin. He isn't sure where my new vigour has appeared from, or how to act now that he is faced with it.

"I'm sorry, I didn't mean to get angry … but …"

"I'll help you," adds Violet.

"What?" cries Brin.

Violet looks at her brother with a sadness clouding her eyes. "Brin, do you know that I still wake up in the middle of the night because I've dreamt about … *it*? I replay that day sometimes, calling myself a coward because I stayed at the dinner table and didn't help you ... all because of fear. I've said sorry to you thousands of times over the years, but do you know what I actually felt like, after father shot you? I mean, you know how upset I was, but I've never been able to show you *exactly* how it made me feel! How sick? How angry?"

When Brin was shot! She would have seen it all! How did she deal with something like that?

Brin seems surprised at Violet's remarks. He shakes his head and avoids looking at her eyes. Seeing her this way obviously hurts him.

"That's how I felt! Like that!" Violet points directly at me. "You saved her, Brin. Okay? This is your chance to help ... your second chance." Violet takes Brin's hands. "This time, we can do it together ... and this time, we can do it right."

Chapter ten

Downstairs in the lounge, I sit in silence with Violet while
Brin is in the kitchen. He is preparing hot drinks and some
sandwiches with the sliced beef leftover from our lunch.

I have allowed a nervous and unwanted tension to fill
me. *Come on, Brin … hurry up! I'm not comfortable in here
with your sister … I've only just met her.*

I don't want to feel this way, yet my lack of trust stays
firm, despite their family connection.

"When I stopped Brin searching for you outside
earlier, he told me a few details …," says Violet with a shaky
voice. "I'm sorry, Elana. I can't even begin to imagine what
you are going through … it must be terrifying." She smiles
and genuine sympathy radiates off of her.

"It … is … and thank you."

"I can see why you've decided that Mayor Hartner
should fall. I've met him a few times and he is exactly like
everyone else … hungry for power, and he abuses that which
he already has." Violet pauses for a second. "They all do."

"Maybe that is our answer?" I suggest. "We could
start there and plan around that fact … the power hungry
behaviour?"

"What do you mean?" asks Violet. She adjusts her

glasses and moves across the sofa, closer to me.

"Take his power, take it away from him … something like that? If that is the one thing which he desires and needs, it could just as easily be his weakness as well."

Violet purses her lips in thought. "We'll work it out. It has to change, it has to."

Brin walks in with the food and drinks on a tray. He places it on the desk and sits down next to Violet. "I don't like this idea of yours, Elana, but I must be able to help. With all the knowledge and privileges that Violet and I have, there has to be a plan in it all somewhere."

I want to check my earlier fears before I carry on. If they are true, it could make any upcoming plans or ideas change. "Brin, after you told me about the Uninhabitable Zones, I had some ideas of my own," I say. *Am I ready for more of the truth?*

"Really? Such as?"

"Rogues and fifty-fifties … the Uninhabitable Zones … they're …" I take a deep breath. "… they're lies as well?"

"Are you going to be sick in my kitchen sink again after I answer?"

I blush, a lot. Violet smacks Brin on the arm. "Don't be so nasty!" She is half serious, half messing about.

"Sorry about that," I mumble, apologetically.

"Yes and no," answers Violet.

"Yes and no?"

"People do discover secrets, Elana, or have a moment of morality … their conscious wins out. Then, it's up to them to decide how they act. Look at you … strictly speaking, you're now a Rogue. You're questioning everything Central Government has ever said to you."

I understand Violet's explanation. It makes me think of the incident in the college library, the announcement about the Rogue man, the woman on the train platform … *Could it really have been the same woman in the Tower? The one helping me to overcome the conditioning?*

"And the others? Fifty-fifties?"

Brin and Violet look at each other. Brin speaks first. "The virus has been under a level of control for many years now, Elana. There are isolated incidents, but nothing on the scale that people in the Community Zones are led to believe. If my memory serves me correctly, the last fatality was eight years ago. It is just another method they use so that nobody questions ... disappearances, or relocations. Don't get me wrong, some relocations are valid due to career placement, yet ... most are not."

That happened to my parents! No! Don't think like that!

I throw my sandwich back on the plate. "I've lost my appetite, sorry Brin."

"I understand, it's okay. Are you going to be sick now?"

Violet hits Brin again, harder this time. "Stop it!" she growls.

I ignore the sarcasm because I am unravelling the world I've grown up in, dissecting it piece by piece. "So, instead of being sent to live in the Uninhabitable Zones, which don't even exist, what really happens?" I ask. To be honest, I think I already know the answer, or at least I fear as much. It is easier to see the next step now that my mind is focusing clearly on the depths and layers of deception.

"The Tower ... or ... execution ... some are sent to laboratories as subjects. The conditioning is always being improved and adapted, but ... the scientists need minds to work on. It isn't like people will volunteer for such things."

I wanted to follow a career in science. It worries me that I might have ended up like the purposeful doctor ... the one I remember from my time in that room.

"I wake up in the morning, I eat breakfast, I brush my teeth ...," I murmur as I shut my eyes, battling the negative

146

thoughts. I am controlling them to the best of my ability, fearing they will grow stronger, untameable.

"What are you doing?" asks Violet. She seems bewildered at this behaviour. Brin has stopped eating his sandwich mid-bite, also intrigued.

"Oh, sorry, I didn't realise I was actually speaking those words out loud," I explain. I am a little embarrassed to have both Brin and Violet witness me performing such a strange technique. "While I was in the Tower, a voice spoke to me, a woman. It was really weird because she sounded exactly like the one who spoke to me on the train platform … who must have given me the note I told you about, Brin. She said I had to focus my mind, think of anything I could to concentrate on, then keep repeating it. I don't know if it was only that, or there are other reasons, but I *did* resist their attempts to change me … break and mould my mind … it's helped a lot ever since I escaped."

Brin and Violet are fascinated by this information. It seems that although they know the truth, there are details that can still surprise them both.

"Then …," starts Violet. She stands up and walks towards the lounge window, pursing her lips again. "… if there are people out there … in the communities, or working in their decided career … Rogues who haven't been discovered yet … can we use them as well?"

"Oh, stop it, Violet!" snaps Brin. "Sit down so that we can concentrate on Mayor Hartner."

"What?" Violet looks totally dejected. The corners of her mouth lower and she scrunches her eyebrows. "It's just a thought. We aren't experts at this sort of thing, are we?"

"We're helping Elana, remember. That's what we agreed to do. You need to focus, not just start throwing crazy and grand ideas about."

"Why not, Brin? I've been here and known about Elana for a lot less time than you have, and I can already see that action is needed … a clear way to move forward. Sometimes the best plans are created from gut instinct, or an idea that sounds impossible."

I sit, totally silent. I hope the bickering will end here because it is making me feel awkward. I can see the difference in their personalities so clearly, though. It hadn't been evident with Brin until now, with the contrast of his sister joining the equation. Violet is impulsive and thinks of the larger scheme, whereas Brin is methodical and patient. I feel drawn to Violet's attitude so much more, as if she is the flame and I am the moth.

"So … erm … Mayor Hartner …," I say, quietly, guiding Brin and Violet back to the subject at hand. "What do we know about him? Anything we can find out will be helpful. Anything at all."

"We have access to databases and such, but they won't give us any information about him … not as a person, not his character. His schedule will be useful, I'm sure of that. What we need to do is learn about the man behind the title. If we can see what the power has done to him, how it's changed him, then we may have something to work with."

I completely agree with Brin. Having details about where Mayor Hartner will be, and when, opens up opportunities for other actions.

"How, though? I mean, how can we find that out?" I ask, trying to find the missing details.

"Well," starts Violet as she walks across the room, "we could always … watch him. You know, his daily habits?"

"Can we do that?" I am not sure how all of us will achieve this. Mayor Hartner is an important individual, protected at all times.

Brin crosses his arms. I hope it means he is giving the idea some serious thought.

"That isn't a bad idea. At the very least, it's a starting

point. If he's going to show his true personality, he'll do it in the privacy of his own home, where he believes it to be safe."

A noise, like some sort of horn or muted klaxon breaks through the silence outside. It sounds in bursts of a few seconds, causing Brin and Violet to rush towards the window.

"You've got to be kidding me!" moans Brin as his face drops. He looks angry, shocked and panicked.

What's wrong? What is it? Are the Community Guards on their way?

"Get her hidden, Brin! Upstairs ... quickly!" orders Violet. She grabs my food plate and cup, then heads for the kitchen.

Brin doesn't question Violet's demands and pulls at my arm, almost dragging me out of the lounge and up the stairs. He reaches to open my bedroom door, then stops. "Sorry, I'll explain later. Someone's coming to the house and they can't see you. It wouldn't end well, trust me on that."

What does that mean?

Brin walks to his bedroom door instead and unlocks it with a key from a bunch in his pocket. "Elana, sit in my room, stay quiet, and I'll lock the door behind you, okay? I need to clear some stuff from your room and hide it. Stay in here and wait for me. Remember, completely silent. If you hear me outside ... I'll make a noise ... yeah, I'll cough a few times ... if you hear that, get yourself hidden ... under the bed, in the wardrobe ... drop out of the window if necessary and crouch behind the bushes ..."

"Brin!" I am so close to having a panic attack, it's shooting horrendous bolts of pain through my chest. The last couple of minutes have shaken my resolve to its limit. "What's wrong? Why has that noise freaked you out so much? Who's coming here?"

"I'll explain later. Get in and stay quiet!" Brin pushes me through the doorway.

Okay, okay ... I brush my teeth. I get dressed ...

I do exactly as he has asked, even though my trembling legs and body make walking a single step challenging. *I get dressed ... I check the knife ... I che ... wait ...* I think about the new line in my calming mantra, wondering when a weapon had been added. It doesn't worry me as much as it should - it makes me feel safe and stronger.

"Stay quiet," says Brin once again. His apologetic voice seeps through from the other side of the locked door. The words wrap themselves around me, taking much of the fear away. Then, I hear him walk down the stairs.

Maybe I can see out of the window? As long as I'm careful, I won't be noticed by ... whoever is here? I walk with slow and silent steps, but can't see anything, or anyone. The sound of an engine approaching outside roars for a few seconds before silence returns.

Guards?

A female voice calls out, strong and loud. Whoever she is, she is laughing and calling for Brin and Violet. Next, bangs on the front door, more laughing … then, muffled conversation.

A friend, maybe? They seem so worried though ... but that has to be because I'm here, right?

I sit on the bed, hoping I will see Brin and Violet soon, and they will explain everything to me.

••

The clear night sky flickers with bright stars as I stare out of Brin's bedroom window. I'm standing a safe distance away, still listening as best as I can to what is happening downstairs. It has been a lively few hours, if the excited voice of the female and her occasional song outbursts - ones that I don't recognise - are anything to go by. She is very loud, energetic, and her footsteps thump a lot of the time.

I did think about going to sleep, but I need to stay awake. Brin might return and signal for me to hide. I considered reading to pass the time, but all the books in his room are based on government legislations and how they differ from those of the old world. I should be interested after everything that has happened to me, yet I'm not.

Why would he stack all those photographs in here? I wonder to myself.

I don't want to invade Brin's privacy, yet it strikes me as unusual, again, that there aren't any in this house either, not anywhere. Even in the grey and white community housing, family photographs are displayed. It is a welcome addition to the bland walls, reminding us all again how important family values are.

Another burst of shrieking laughter rises up from the lounge below. I sit on the floor and pick up the top frame, seeing Brin and Violet standing together. He is wearing a suit and blue shirt while she decided on a knee-length dress in the same colour. They look like loving siblings and the smiles are not forced for the camera, as far as I can tell.

Why does he suddenly look familiar? The next two show Brin on his own.

I've been here with him for quite a while now and I'm only just realising it? Maybe he reminds me of someone else?

I look at the first photo again, scanning Violet's face as well. *What is it that I've seen before? There is something about both of them, not just Brin. I'm sure of it.*

I pick up the next frame to see a family portrait … *Oh … no! It … it can't be?*

I cannot believe my exhausted eyes. The memory returns, the one that explains why Brin and Violet are all of a sudden so familiar to me. The casual clothes they wear, being so close to them in person, the psychological conditioning I received in the Tower, it has all thrown me off, until this moment.

In the centre of the photograph stands a husband and wife. Their three children are seated in front of them, smiling. Brin and Violet are next to the mother and the elder sister sits next to the father.

I remember Brin told me something, not long after I regained consciousness. *"My family ... we own some land. This house for example."*

Some land? Some land is an understatement! I don't know if I should panic or laugh, the shock is that confusing for me. I recall a specific lesson in college covering government and political studies, realising it is where I recognise the family from.

Am I correct? I haven't made a mistake, have I? No, I'm certain that I haven't! My mood hovers somewhere between disbelief and anger. The family in these photographs are extremely well known. They are reclusive, by choice, and nobody ever questions it. They don't want their faces on the information screens placed around the Community Zones, overlaid with government messages of encouragement.

Brin ... Violet ... and that must be Saskia ... is she downstairs now? My nerves spark a powerful warning through me although I'm not able to pinpoint the cause.

Brin said that if she discovered me here, it wouldn't end well. Saskia looks a lot like her father ... is there more, though? Does she resemble him in personality as well? Is that why Brin and Violet are so worried?

Brin and Violet, my current friends and only means of safety, belong to the Dencourt family. His full name is actually Brinleigh. His father, Marcus Dencourt, does not own *some* land, as I believed before seeing this family photograph. He owns, and controls, the *entire* country.

Why didn't you tell me this, Brin?

Loud footsteps sound on the stairs.

I realise that I am actually a fugitive, an unwanted

problem, and I'm being harboured by the son of the most powerful man in the United Kingdom. One of the most powerful people in the world. His correct title is First Administrator - every country has one. It means, in very basic terms, that every single government official, mayor, Community Guard ... every single person is in his grip of power.

The footsteps reach the top of the stairs. A loud laugh. *Saskia?*

I wait for Brin to cough, our prearranged signal of imminent danger. It never happens, though, only more laughing and shrieks of excitement.

Stay calm, Elana. You aren't in danger ... not yet.

Loud noises follow for at least half a minute. It sounds as if someone is stumbling about. During my time in Brin's room, I've heard a lot of forbidden language from Saskia. She curses, a lot. She curses at Brin, at the door that won't open quick enough ... at the fact that she is hungry or *needs* another drink. I can't hear her at the moment.

After another minute or so, the noises stop and I hear Brin walk across the hall. He unlocks the door but I stay on the bed. He hasn't coughed to signal otherwise.

"You okay in here?"

"I'm fine," I reply.

Brin doesn't seem to notice anything in my words or tone.

"I'm sorry about all that. It's over now, well, for a little while at least, but we are going to have to change our plans."

I have a lot to say. *Am I annoyed with him about this?*

I decide to start directly and explain what has irritated me the most. "So, what shall I call you? I mean, I can't just keep calling you Brin, can I?"

Brin stands near the door, confused. "What? I don't understand."

"It should be sir, shouldn't it? No, I'll call you …
Brinleigh … or Master Dencourt. How's that? Is it acceptable
to you?" I ask and know my blatant sarcasm is on show. I
really don't care. Brin isn't a threat in my eyes any longer,
even now, after uncovering the truth. *Do I trust him despite
his family name? Have I finally allowed it to happen?*

"Damn photographs! I knew I should have locked
them away." Brin rolls his eyes and looks disappointed with
himself.

I cross my arms to demonstrate my disappointment,
and the many other emotions I feel as well. "Or, maybe, you
should have just told me the truth, when I first woke up?
How's that for a novel approach to trust?" I ask, resisting the
strong urge to snap at the end of every word.

"Point taken, Elana. I might not have gone about this
very well, but it could have worked against me. You might
have panicked even more than you did … and where would
we be then?" Brin moves and sits on the end of the bed.

I shrug my shoulders. I don't actually want an
argument, but I want Brin to know that his lies have, and will,
hurt me. "Is Saskia over there, in the other bedroom?" I
whisper.

"Yes. Fast asleep … well, she has had a lot to drink. I
doubt she'll wake up until after lunch."

"You mean alcohol? She's … she's drunk?"

"Yes. She missed us both while away on business.
Tonight was an impromptu reunion, a chance to catch up with
us and have some fun."

"Have you two been drinking as well? You do realise
that it is illegal until the age of twenty-one?"

"We've only had a glass of wine, Elana," defends
Brin.

I shrug my shoulders. "Oh, my mistake, *Mr.
Dencourt.*" The sarcasm I add is perhaps a little too much,
however, it is intentional.

"… And we watered it down with lemonade. Haven't you? At a birthday or a wedding?" he adds.

I've seen another gaping difference in our two worlds and it's proving difficult for me to let go. "No, Brin, I haven't, because it is illegal. I followed all the rules and obeyed all the laws. Remember?"

"Saskia is twenty-two and loves to enjoy herself. Violet and I get caught up in that … a lot. But I've been walking about with the same glass in my hand all evening. Saskia was too busy singing and dancing about to even realise."

Brin looks at the floor. He is obviously embarrassed again. "It isn't an excuse, Elana, but we couldn't say no to Saskia … not many people ever do. She'd wonder why and then keep pushing … probably until an argument broke out."

A pause follows. He speaks with a light-hearted tone of voice and forces a smile, yet there is a truth to his words as well.

Is he thinking about a specific memory? Has he really had fights with Saskia? Been pressured and pushed around by her?

I want to avoid Saskia and meet her at the same time, it is a strange, conflicting state of mind.

"Anyway," continues Brin, "Violet has already explained to her that we are going away for a few days to study in one of the other houses - we want to visit some Community Zones for political research. As soon as she believed there would be any type of education involved, she immediately lost interest. By the time she wakes up, we'll be miles away."

"We're leaving soon?" I ask.

It scares me to hear those words. It scares me to imagine being outside … outside where guards could see me. I believe in Brin and the safety he offers, however, I've experienced the power of Community Guards as well. They

155

often confront each other in my thoughts.

Brin must have noticed my concerns and reluctance. He reaches forward to touch my hand with a gentleness I crave. "You're leaving in a few minutes, with Violet. She's going to drive to her house, not far from here, while I pack a few things. I need to leave a message for my parents and clean the house of any evidence which could lead to you. I'm only covering my tracks, Elana. If we're about to start something, we need to be careful ... all of us do."

"Erm ... okay." I do not sound convinced.

"Don't worry, Elana. It's just unexpected that Saskia arrived back from Europe. She doesn't come down here much, but she never misses *anything.* She's too perceptive for that, I'm afraid to say. It is something that she inherited or learnt to master from our father."

"I'm ... scared, Brin. Promise me I'll be safe again ... please?"

Brin leans further to put his hand on my shoulder, but stops himself. "I promise that you'll be safe ... and guess what?"

"What?"

Brin smiles and holds his hand out for me to grab as I stand up. "I'm scared too. We can be scared together. Now, go with Violet. I'll see you as soon as I can."

••

I'm told the drive to Violet's house will take twenty minutes at the most. I can't see much of the surroundings because of the darkness, and I have to lay below the back seats of the car again, as I had to do when Brin tracked me to the forest.

"We're nearly there, Elana. My house is only a couple of minutes away," says Violet as she turns the steering wheel and slows the car down. "There won't be any patrols, so you can sit up now if you want to? How do you feel? You seem really quiet?"

"Am I?" I reply as I move my legs and body out of their cramped position. "Sorry … it's probably just nerves, I guess. And …"

"And?"

"Brin never told me who he really is … who you both are. I found family photographs in his room while you were downstairs with Saskia."

"Oh, right." Violet mumbles her words. "I … I hope we can still be friends, Elana … I don't want it to ruin that … please?"

Is she serious? She believes that I'll treat her differently because of who she is?

"Of course we're friends! I'm not annoyed about it, don't worry, and I understand why he chose to keep it a secret," I say. "But it has shocked me … a lot."

"I expect it would. You can still trust us, though. Well, I hope you can?" Violet stops the car outside a house that looks very similar to Brin's in size. It has ivy growing up the front and flowerpots outside. I wish to jump ahead several hours so I can be surrounded by sunshine and see the colours on the petals.

"You both have houses? Of your own? Don't you live with your parents?"

"Lots of questions?" Violet turns around to face me. "Yes, we have our own houses. They still belong to my father, though, all of them. He believes, as do a lot of the powerful people in the world, that this sort of gesture will prove how much they care … erm … there is also a main house. It's about twenty minutes away. We use it for official purposes … dinners, parties, birthdays … the rare occasions that we are all together in the same place."

I see a glint of tears in Violet's eyes. "So … where are we?" I ask, redirecting the conversation. "I have no idea … I haven't known, not for a very long time … not since I was … still at home."

Violet's eyes dry up as she turns away. It is a subconscious response to show how deeply ashamed she is, as if, somehow, there is a part of her that is responsible for all the terrible acts in the world, especially those that I have endured. "The nearest Community Zone to this house is Oxford … about an hour north-west of here."

I imagine a map and walk myself around it. I have been transported, and moved, many miles from my home. A thought of my parents sparks. *I wonder where you are now? I don't even know where you live … but I will find you …*

It is impossible to control my emotions after that. My own eyes fill with tears.

"Look at us two! We're so different … different upbringing … yet the world still makes us cry."

Violet gets out of the vehicle, rushes to her house and opens the front door. She waves her hand to indicate that I can go inside. "Quickly … up the stairs, it's the door on your left. I'll be back in less than five minutes."

••

The interior of the house is arranged much like Brin's, yet with lilac and silver décor. The wallpaper and paintwork enchant me on the stairway, but I carry on, reach the top and find the room I need.

Inside it is furnished much like the one I grew accustomed to at Brin's house. Seeing somewhere familiar helps with my anxiety straight away, so I sit on the bed and wait.

The front door clicks shut, footsteps sound on the stairs, then Violet walks in the room, smiling.

"Okay, now we wait for Brin. This is only a temporary stop, Elana. We will be back on the road in a matter of hours, I expect. Shall we eat? Sleep? I'm no expert at this sort of thing, as you can probably see." Violet fidgets for a short time before sitting in a chair. She keeps on flicking her eyes towards the window.

"I'm too … excited to sleep … or scared. My appetite is … I don't know … I know I'm not hungry, though. But …"

"But?"

"Don't … don't leave me alone?" I plead. I am embarrassed to ask, but this is not the time to lie about my fragility.

Violet smiles with a sympathy beyond her age. "We can stay together, I won't go anywhere, I promise."

"Brin does that a lot … I mean, he promises me that I'll be safe. Your kindness must run in the family."

"Me?" Violet asks.

I nod with a smile.

"Our mother and Brin … we do want to help others, but we can't. It isn't the correct behaviour for people like us. Saskia and my father don't hold the same values, unfortunately."

Violet has the look in her eyes that Brin displayed when I first met him … a distant defiance. It is becoming clear and easy to understand where, and to which family members, these are directed at.

"Where does Hartner live? I know he has a residence in the community, but does he have a house as well?"

"When Brin arrives, we'll work out the next move, Elana."

Violet stands and peers out of the window as the sound of an engine humming grows closer. "And here he is," she adds with a laugh.

"Is something funny?"

"I think he has packed the entire house from what I can tell. Honestly, he must have had trouble fitting it all in the car!"

Violet cleans her glasses on her blouse before heading out of the bedroom.

I laugh at her words. I don't risk looking out of the window to see for myself, then follow Violet down the stairs to the lounge.

There are just as many books as Brin has, although they are not from the same genre. These titles are all geographical or architectural.

The sound of the front door opening and closing, followed by heavy bags thumping on the floor, signals Brin's arrival.

"Hi. Any problems on the way?"

"No … we bonded, though … there were quite a few tears. It's a girl thing, Brin. One day, I'll try and explain it all to you."

Brin's face turns bright red.

"Bring enough stuff with you? Emptying your house is a *really* clever way to keep Saskia from suspecting anything."

Brin's face turns a brighter red. "You can stop picking on me now! I had to make sure we are covered, that's all. I brought the laptop computer too, so we can study the databases. I'll go and get it."

"Right, where were we?" asks Violet.

I am still trying to stop myself from laughing. I find the sibling banter far too entertaining. "Erm … Mayor Hartner? Where he lives, what he does on a daily basis?"

Brin returns. "If we're going to watch him, it will be better to use his private residence." He sits down but doesn't open the laptop. "Elana, are you sure you're ready to see the information?" he asks as his fingers tap on the top of it in a steady rhythm.

"Ready?"

"We're going to be close to your home, Elana … you're bound to experience … difficulties."

Will I react like the girl who remembered her parents? Will I try and get back to the Community Zone? "I'll worry about that *if* it happens." I mumble the words without any real conviction.

"And ... can you promise me that you won't do anything unexpected? For all I know, you'll see Hartner and rush forward to attack him," jokes Brin, although there is a genuine worry in his eyes. He knows better than to try and predict my behaviour.

I check the knife ... I check the knife ... "I'm not promising anything. Sorry, I just can't do that. I don't know how I'll react."

Violet joins in. She wants me to stay focused and not become upset again. "I have plenty of maps in here and I expect we'll need them soon. We can't even begin planning without them." She takes a large book down off a shelf and opens it on the coffee table in the middle of the room.

"This is Mayor Hartner's main house," says Brin, tapping at an illustration. "And we'll be over here. It's about ten minutes away by car, I'm not sure about the time on foot but we can work that out once we get there. A section of our land directly borders his and it'll be the perfect place to use. As long as we are careful, and I mean *careful*, there won't be any suspicion."

I move closer and study the layout in the book. "What's this large area over here? The one right next to Mayor Hartner's land?"

Brin doesn't answer. Violet smiles an apology.

I study again ... the letters *'CZ'* are placed in the centre of the large square. *Why are they being so quiet? What could upset ...* I see various words next to the buildings and illustrations: College, Town Hall, Plaza ... Train station.

... upset me ...

My mind blurs the room around me. I recognise the illustration and a breath empties out of my lungs. I'm back on

161

the streets where I used to live, I'm on the tram to the library, I'm with my parents.

... That's ... that's ... home ...

Chapter eleven

After we all enjoy a hot drink and some biscuits, Brin loads up the car with extra bags containing some of Violet's clothes. It takes him a couple of attempts to get them all inside, causing Violet to giggle and whisper, 'I told you so', continuously.

He doesn't speak to me very much, and neither does Violet. They both understand that returning to the Essex Community Safe Zone will not be easy for me to endure.

"Why don't you try and rest, Elana? Believe it or not, it's four in the morning. We can all blame Saskia's unexpected return for that. You must be exhausted?" says Brin as he starts to drive away from Violet's house. "We'll be travelling for a few hours, so it's your choice."

"I don't think I could sleep, even if I wanted to," I say.

"I know what you mean," agrees Violet.

A thought suddenly crosses my mind as Brin turns right. "Hang on, how will we get there, though? Where are all the roads? I've never seen anybody driving a car along one before … not in my entire life."

Brin stays quiet. He concentrates on driving across a grass field towards some tall trees. Once illuminated by the lights on the front of the car, they look as if they are forged from pure silver. We're moving through an unknown, metallic world.

Violet turns to him, hoping for, and expecting, the answer as well, yet he doesn't speak. "That's deliberate," she says, giving Brin a stern glare because he avoided the question.

"Deliberate? Why?" I ask. I try to work out the reason but come up blank.

Violet spins her body around in the front passenger seat so that she can talk to me face to face. "Okay … all the private houses, land, and everything else too … slaves being walked about … the roads and cars … they can never be seen by others … people like you. People who don't know the truth. Can you imagine the kind of questions that everyone would ask? Those in power decided a long time ago that their privacy was of the utmost importance, one of their most fundamental and basic rights. The train tracks are constructed in a very specific layout and route around the country … well, the world for that matter, to ensure that this remains the case."

I've been on the train many times before. Have I ever been near to a line of slaves, like the one I was in?

I ignore my first instinct and desire, which is to complain once again. I want to rant with venom about all the injustice in the world I have recently discovered. It is as if the familiar streets - those I have walked on for so many years - are only now being seen properly, with open eyes.

"Will I … see anything? Anything that will …?"

Brin knows exactly what I am to ask, so he cuts me off mid-sentence. "I hope not." The words are almost whispered with apprehension and guilt.

He didn't promise … he always promises …

Violet gives me the most reassuring smile that she can manage. It doesn't fully work, though. "A lot of the road network runs directly underneath the train tracks. It's the most logical place, if you think about it. Nobody travelling on a train at high speed will ever see them. We do need to go through some other areas as well, I'm afraid, and you may see …"

"See what?"

"Slaves, perhaps? How those in power treat others? Almost definitely. It's unavoidable, Elana, I'm sorry to say."

I remain quiet. I don't know how to deal with the thought of being around people like me … people who have been to the Tower as well. *What will happen when I see them? I could so easily have become like them … following orders … my mind taken from me!*

Brin drives along an empty road, concealed by tall trees on either side, for another twenty minutes. Nobody speaks until Violet notices that he is changing direction and heading towards a vast field. I only notice it because sunrise has begun to layer the sky with a blue glow, caressing the horizon.

"Brin, where are you going?" asks Violet.

"Slight detour, that's all."

Violet doesn't know what her brother is doing, or where he is going. I have a constant tingle of fear running throughout my body. It has been present ever since we left Brin's house and the safety those walls provided for me. Every mile further that we drive away, it hits harder.

"Don't worry, either of you. I thought a quick visit to the orchard would be a good idea. What do you think, Violet?"

"Yeah, great idea," replies Violet with a wry smile.

Orchard? "Why are we going to an orchard?"

Brin turns his head so that he can smile back at Violet. His eyes glance at me for a second. "All I seem to do is hurt you with the truth. I've made you see an unpleasant world ever since I saved you. I thought you might like to see something beautiful for a change."

"Oh ... erm ... thank you ... erm ..." I move across the seats so that I am directly behind Brin, hiding my red face and embarrassment.

Brin turns the car around a tight bend. The road disappears and grass returns underneath the car's thick tyres. I am still wondering what else to say, worried I'll fumble my words, when I suddenly see trees out of the window, all around me.

It's amazing ...

Hundreds - maybe thousands - of trees, running in lines I can't even see the end of, spread out in front and to both sides of me. Every possible shade of green imaginable floods my eyes as the sunrise skips across and through the leaves in sharp beams. They either light the trees directly or bathe them in deep shadows.

"Where are we?"

Brin stops the car and smiles. "I told you, it's an orchard. This one provides a lot of the fruit for the communities in this area. You've probably eaten a few apples from here, Elana."

"It's ... it's ..." I am utterly speechless.

"Come on, let's all have a quick walk around. We're almost guaranteed privacy for another hour or so. The guards, staff ... and ... erm ..." Brin paused.

Slaves ... he doesn't want to say the word ...

"They'll get here for about six," adds Brin.

"Are you sure?" asks Violet. "We don't need any unnecessary questions."

Brin grows impatient and directs it at Violet. "It'll be fine. Come on, usually you'd be the one suggesting something like this and I'd be calculating risks. Let's go!"

I notice the switch in personalities as well. Since I have met Brin, he's always been much more conservative in his nature, planning every move before carrying it out. This is unlike him.

"What if someone sees me?" I ask. My body stays firmly in the back of the car. I'm determined not to move until clear about all the possible dangers. Even something as simple as stepping out to breathe the open air sparks fear for me.

Brin sighs with disappointment. All he wanted to do was bring me to a magnificent place that I would enjoy, somewhere I could walk freely, outside. It isn't running as smoothly as he had planned, or hoped.

"If we sit here for ages, it *will* be too late," Brin says. His impatience weaves through every grumbled word.

"Brin, I said I was scared, remember? I'm not acting like this for any other reason. I know you understand."

Brin's eyes soften and he loses the defeat in his eyes. "Hang on." He opens my door, then, with a renewed light in his eyes, walks to the back of the car. It opens up and he rummages through one of the large backpacks.

"Here, put this on. I brought it with us just in case a situation arose. I think this is one of those situations," he says.

Another tunic? Why? "How will changing my clothes help me to calm down?" I ask.

"This one has a hood. It'll keep your face covered, and it is how ..."

"... how personal servants are supposed to dress ..." I finish Brin's sentence for him. I'm not actually sure how I know this information. I spoke the words without any real thought.

Violet stares at me, because of what I've said. "It's because of the Tower. You would have been ... erm ..." She rubs her forehead, as if it physically hurts her to explain. "... programmed, for want of a better word, with these details. Do you remember anything else? How to behave? Anything like that?"

I've repressed as much of my time in the Tower as

possible. I built a fierce wall of sanity inside my mind. It protected me from their torturous attempts to steal everything.

"I don't want to remember any of it!" I reply, angrily. "It was ... was the most terrifying time of my life. I could almost feel them changing me ... I mean, as if they were physically holding my personality, my memories ... holding them in their hands to remould as they wished."

Violet's eyes shut tightly, fighting the urge to shed a tear. "Brin, I'll help Elana change. You go and ... and ... stare at apples, or whatever. Just don't look through the window."

I'm pulled back to reality due to Violet and her sense of humour. *Has she used that over the years to help? Is that how she copes with the world ... her world?*

We both laugh once Brin has shut the car door and left us together.

Violet climbs through to the back seats. "It's simple. Keep the hood up and let your hair fall over your face a bit, if you need to. You'll only be spoken to if Brin or I tell you to do something. Just say yes and follow the order." Violet has an angry flash in her eyes - another distant emotion aimed at someone who isn't here. "... and ... if that should happen, pretend we both said please as well. You know we aren't really ordering you around."

I nod my head. I know all their actions are false, only carried out to protect me. "Why did he bring me here?"

"Oh, it's exactly as he said earlier. He wants to do something ... show you something ... that will be good for you. Okay, a large orchard is a bit of a strange choice, but it's better than hiding all of the time. You see?"

"Yes, I understand," I say with a beaming grin.

"There's a reason that Brin always plans ten steps ahead, Elana. When he does try spontaneity, it doesn't usually work ... it seems awkward. His heart is in the right place, though."

I look out of the window. Brin is still standing a few

yards away.

"Off you go. I'll drive behind you two. If we cross any guards, or the agricultural staff, act like I said. If I need to, I'll order you back in here."

"Okay."

"Oh, by the way, you see this blue button?" asks Violet, pointing to the panel near the steering wheel.

"Yes. What is it for?"

"It locks all the doors on the car from the inside. It might ... help you feel safer."

"Oh, right. I hope I'll never need to use it. Thanks, Violet."

"I ... erm ... should be thanking you, Elana."

"Me? Why?" *What have I done to deserve any gratitude? I've turned their lives upside down since Brin took me back to his house.*

"Isn't it obvious?"

I think about my answer but can't find a single reason. "Erm ... no, sorry. What am I missing?"

"You've given us both ... I don't know how to explain it. It's a chance to ... to prove them wrong. To prove to all of them, my father and everyone else in power, that we don't have to live as they do."

"I've brought you both nothing but trouble!"

Violet ignores me completely. She needs to speak and I doubt anything I say will be able to stop her. "It's so difficult to live with all of it, Elana. Once you reach a certain age and realise what is happening ... it gets inside you. It's pollution, as dangerous and corrupting as the power itself. You feel helpless, alone ... pressured. You argue with yourself all the time to accept it, let it happen ... just give in. I've lost count of the number of times that I have cried myself to sleep, or hidden away with my tears because I felt ... *different*. The day that happens, though, the day you stop being yourself, it's the day you change. You become that which you hate the most."

I can see years of pain, years of personal pain, in Violet's eyes. Her whole life is on show for me to view. How it has been lived, how it has been managed and endured.

I don't know what to say. How can anything I say take away that kind of sadness? She must trust me so much to talk to me ... I wish I could help her too ...

"Hurry up! It's only a tunic!" says Brin as he appears next to the car. He still has his back facing the window, though, showing politeness.

I launch myself forward and wrap my arms around Violet. "I better go before Brin loses it." I open the door while we are both still laughing.

"Let me guess? You two were talking ... probably about me?" asks Brin.

"No, not about you. Well, not *all* the time."

"My sister talks too much ... but she is ... amazing. I can't begin to imagine how I would have recovered after ... what happened to Hannah ... if it wasn't for her. I mean, my mother and Saskia were there too, and Saskia hasn't always been so ... understanding of the system. Violet is different, though."

"Twins do share a special bond. It is still studied in biology. The connections are fascinating," I say, regretting my words, wondering why I am suddenly having trouble thinking of something to say. *Science? Biology? There must be other things to talk about? Why am I so nervous all of a sudden?*

"So, you like it here? I know, it's a field full of apple trees, and it is a bit too early in the year to eat them, but, still, it's not a small bedroom, and you can try and feel free."

"I do like it, Brin, thank you. It doesn't really matter where I am, does it? The fact that I can do this is ... thank you ... *again.*"

"We have forty minutes, maybe a little less, before

others will arrive. It isn't enough time to see all that is grown here, though. This place has thousands of apple trees, pears too, and over this way are the strawberries, blackberries, tomatoes ... you name a fruit or vegetable, it probably grows here."

"And then it is sent to the communities?"

"The best of the crops go ... well, you know where they go, Elana, I don't need to tell you."

"No, you don't. I have a good idea about that already." *The best of everything will be reserved for those in control.*

"After all the select products have been reserved, a measured quantity is sent to communities. Remember when I told you that someone, somewhere, goes to work and sees all the residents as parts of an equation?" asks Brin.

"I think so."

"This is an example of that, well, one of them. The number of residents in a community are permitted a set amount of food for each particular week. It depends on the time of year, the age of a person, their build ... there are so many factors involved. Nutritionists decide it all, on your behalf. You are sent exactly the amount to sustain you, no more, no less."

"How kind of them," I say. "If I ever meet these people, remind me to say thank you."

Brin smiles at the sarcasm. "Then, they'll send that information to another department, and so on. Eventually, a neat little parcel of food is put on the train and delivered to your door."

I think for a moment about the ration deliveries that I used to unpack with my mother. Brin walks off to the right where the apple and pear trees start to thin out.

"Look at this, Elana." He stands at the border of a large field. A low wire fence has been placed around it but Brin steps over with ease. Hundreds of green lines - rows of bushes, plants, and leaves - ran away from them.

This place is unbelievable! It must be the size of my community ... maybe larger?

Brin kneels down near to one of the bushes and moves a few leaves about. He cups something in his hands before standing back up, then smiles widely. "Go on, my treat." He holds out a strawberry towards my lips.

I blush as I bite the succulent fruit. *Oh, that is so delicious!* "I've only had these a few times in my whole life, Brin. And now ... now I'm surrounded by them."

I look at the ground where Brin picked the strawberry from as the sweet taste lingers on my tongue. "Can I have another?"

Brin laughs. "Of course. Don't touch the green ones, though, they're not ripe yet."

I grab a few more in my hand as Brin walks along the fence line. I can hear the car close by, roaring gently between the trees.

"Brin, this is going to sound ... well, I don't know how it will sound, but I'm not sure I was ever unhappy with Central Government ... for the way they fed me, I mean. I never went hungry."

"No, you didn't," starts Brin, "but you never got a choice either, did you? Wouldn't it have been different if you could have decided for yourself what to eat ... not pick from the food they *told* you that you had to."

"I see your point. I suppose subtle control is still control."

"You've never tasted chocolate, eaten a double cheeseburger, salmon either. That's one of my favourites," says Brin.

I've heard of chocolate and salmon, but have absolutely no idea what a double cheeseburger is. "Yes, but they are luxury foods, Brin, and rare too. That's why I've never tried them."

"Rare! They're not rare! If we drive one-hundred miles in that direction, we'll arrive at one of the many hidden salmon farms in the world." Brin points behind us. "You could eat it every day for the rest of your life if you wanted to! They hide all this because the … slaves … they work in these places."

I remember Violet's words about the train tracks being purposely routed. *All I ever saw were fake Uninhabitable Zones, or Wild Zones … and there aren't any train tracks in sight here.*

"Maybe we can eat some double cheeseburgers, one day?" I say, hoping it will lighten Brin's mood.

"It's the first thing I'll do when this is all over," says Brin, but his voice deepens with anger. He decides there is still more to complain about. "And the clothes you *have* to wear … when to wake up, when to study … the progression interviews too, they are all monitored."

"Monitored? How?"

"Think about it. Someone goes in who is strong, athletic and physically fit …"

I immediately think of one name: *Jackson!*

"… as long as they aren't overly individual, they'll end up as a Community Guard or in the military. But even at that point, those who could cause a problem are sifted out. They might end up being watched afterwards."

"I'm not sure I understand you, Brin. Central Government will monitor children? Just in case they misbehave?"

"Yes … but it isn't that simple. Let's say someone has been in trouble. They are warned or punished, but it happens again. It is probably decided then, at that age in their life, that they will never progress in their career. Even if they are only fourteen years old! They'll be blacklisted from that moment. As far as Central Government are concerned, they don't listen to the rules and they can *never* be trusted."

"I can't believe the depths they go to, Brin. Or why they do it?"

"Why they do it?"

"I'm still trying to see it, Brin. It is still all so new for me, so … unbelievable at times. I have to try and think like they do."

"Why they do it is the simple … because they can! Greed rules them. They're not going to share what they believe is theirs and theirs alone. This has been the mindset for a very long time now, Elana. People grow up, like Violet and I did, being told that we *have* to act the same way."

I hear Mayor Hartner's voice inside my head. *It's taken us four generations to get to where we are today … four generations!*

A twig snaps nearby and I swing around, fearing that I'll see a Community Guard. *No, Violet would have warned me.*

Instead, a boy walks towards Brin. He is just over four feet in height, thin, with blonde hair and blue eyes. I guess that he is about twelve years old. *Why so young? Did something happen to his parents?*

Brin stands in front of me as the boy walks off in silence. "He's getting ready for work today, in the fields. We need to get back to the car, though. Community Guards and other staff will be here any minute now."

I look at the boy, wishing that I could take him in my arms. I want to be the rescuer, like Brin. *I could have so easily been standing where you are now. I do wonder, sometimes, if it would have been easier for me … if I was like you … if I knew nothing …*

••

"Elana, have you ever seen a giraffe?" asks Brin.
"Sorry, what did you say? A giraffe?"

"Yes. A giraffe. I want to know if you have ever seen one before?"

What a strange question! "Erm … well, in a photograph, yes."

Brin stops the car. We have been travelling for nearly an hour, driving mostly underneath more of the rail tracks. Now that we are entering private, secluded areas, the roads reappear and the train tracks veer away - ensuring privacy for those that need it.

"Look out of the window. It's much better than a photograph, trust me."

What is he talking about? I look right - nothing but an open field with a few trees planted across it. Then, as my head turns left, I see it.

This can't be real … I'm dreaming …

An adult giraffe stands behind a tall wire fence, only one hundred and fifty feet away. "Oh … that's … oh, Brin, it's so beautiful!"

"Come and have a closer look," says Brin through a large and wide smile. His eyes are beaming with excitement as he opens the car door. "I thought you'd like it." He is feeding his own emotions directly off of mine.

Violet grins too. "We're on the edge of a Wild Zone, Elana. Those aren't lies, although they aren't as wild as you're told. They're maintained by animal keepers and so forth. Do you know what a zoo is … well, do you know what a zoo *used* to be, in the old world?"

I do know this information because I studied the topic during my time in college. "Yes, they were protected areas, before the virus spread, housing wild animals. It was a form of entertainment for people to visit."

"Imagine that concept controlled by Central Government. Then, add in that some of these animals are rare … I mean *extremely* rare, and you soon have a desirable private collection. It's another chance for them to show off and prove how powerful they are ... but to see it like this ... you kind of ignore that because it is so stunning."

I half agree. I'm having trouble pointing my hate at Mayor Hartner, or the faceless people who control every aspect of life in the world, because of the majestic animal only yards away from me.

Brin touches my shoulder. "Look through the trees. I can just make out a herd of elephants ... over there. Do you see?"

I do see them, although I can't believe it. Approximately ten elephants stand together in the distance, swinging their trunks about, or lumbering a few steps with their giant legs.

"Hold on a moment," I start, remembering something from the illustrations at Violet's house. The initials 'WZ' were in an oval area next to Mayor Hartner's land. "... we're close, aren't we? The house that we're going to, and Hartner's?"

Brin hesitates for a second, although he knows there isn't any point in trying to lie or hide anything from me. "Yes, you're right. The house we are going to use isn't far away from here ... and his residence is off to the left. The outer fence of the Wild Zone is built a short distance after those elephants, a few hundred feet further back." He points a couple of times, indicating the direction.

He's close by? I can get to him ... I can reach him ... wait, what are you thinking? Why are you planning alone? They've helped you out more than you could have imagined, or asked for, and they didn't need to. You can't betray them, not now. Patience is crucial ... "Nearly there ... then we can find his weakness ... and use it ..." *I check the knife ...*

"I hope so," says Brin.

My eyes take in as much detail as they can. There are areas of swaying tall grass, others of dark green that have been mown short, and many tall trees. I suddenly catch fast movement away to the left and see smaller animals I also recognise: deer, antelope and gazelles spring up on their powerful legs. *Unbelievable! This has to be the most beau ...*

A loud crack rings through the air. A second ticks by, more straight after. I swing my head from left to right but the sounds have distorted across the open ground, making their origin difficult to find.

That reminds me of my time in the forest ... when ... the girl ran away ...

Another crack. One of the animals falls to the ground. It kicks a few times, tries to lift its head, another kick. It never stands back up.

"What's going on? Brin? Violet? What's happening?"

Brin curses through gritted teeth. "You've got to be kidding me! Today? Now?"

"What?"

Violet grabs my arm. "Let's get back to the car. It's for the best, trust me."

"No! Tell me what's happening! Were they ... gunshots?"

Brin stares off to the right, in the opposite direction than the unfortunate animal. "I can't see a transport of any kind. Perhaps it's just a couple of people under camouflage? Or in the back of a small truck?"

"What? Who's here?" I demand. Violet still has my arm but she isn't pulling any longer.

"I don't know who it is. I know it isn't safe, though. We have to leave, right now!" orders Brin. He is furious, yet not with me. It is because those who are firing at the animals have ruined something else for me, something that he has arranged.

"Can't you do anything?" My eyes open wide and fill with hope. "Can't you use your family name and power? Tell them to stop! Order them to stop!"

"It doesn't work like that, Elana," says Violet. Her style of apology is to speak her words at an almost inaudible level.

"No, it doesn't … but …"

"Brin … what are you thinking?" asks Violet. She has a cautious edge to her voice.

"If we're here to see the animals, they'll have to stop, they'll *have* to … or risk shooting us. I think Father's reputation will be useful in this case."

"Brin, it'll attract attention! We've got to be careful, remember?"

Another crack springs through the air. I don't look to see if another animal has fallen because I need to keep some memories pure, untouched, not associated with death.

Violet makes sure that she has my full attention and holds me in a stare. "I'm sorry that you saw this, I truly am, but it's just better that we leave. Forget this and we can concentrate on Mayor Hartner."

"Violet …," says Brin. He isn't angry any more. He sounds scared instead.

"What?"

"There are a couple of large trucks over there. I think they're …" Brin's face drops, "… carriers. We have to go, right now!"

"Carriers?" I ask. "What are carriers?"

"It's not important, Elana, honestly," lies Violet, although she isn't very good at it.

Carriers? Large trucks called carriers … what could? No … don't think it, Elana, don't! … But trucks called carriers … it means they are carrying … No! Don't think it! You're wrong! You have to be wrong this time!

Violet grips my arm tighter and moves me back to the car, pushing my body towards the back seats.

Brin hurries to get in and start the engine. "I'll drive fast and we'll be at the other house in a matter of minutes. It's just up the road. From there we will have a clear view of Mayor Hartner's residence and can start to research his daily routine. We have to remember the reason why we are here!"

I look out of the window to see the large trucks which have scared and caused Brin to panic so much. They are a dull green, moving along slowly on tyres bigger than me. A couple of guards walk to the back and pull open the doors. Then, they stand and point their guns inside. *What is in there?*

"Brin ... you have to let me see this ... I have to know ..."

"I don't want you to. I don't want you to have this as a memory," says Brin. He refuses to turn and face me as he speaks. The car doesn't move, as if he is stuck in a moment of indecision. He understands my request yet has to deny it at exactly the same time.

I watch out of the window as my earlier thoughts become a sick reality. The scene is created directly from one of my nightmares, ripped out of my dark thoughts for me to watch. It makes me retch yet I can't stop staring. I see people jumping down off of the carrier. Men and women, teenagers too ... all slaves, like me. They run off, desperate to survive and find somewhere safe to hide.

How can they do this? My hands push and slap on the window as more gunshots crack mercilessly through the hot summer air.

Chapter twelve

Brin rolls up his sleeves and snaps himself out of any confusion. He makes the engine roar like a caged beast and drives away from the scene as quickly as he can.

"Stop the car!" Tears are falling down my cheeks and my stomach has tightened. It's sending sharp pains corkscrewing through my whole body. I form tight fists and resist the urge to hunch forward in distress.

"What? No! I can't, Elana! I won't!"

"Brin, you have to! Please!" I scream as I grab at the door handle. I can't even grip it properly because my hands are shaking so much. *Come on! OPEN!*

"No!" shouts Violet. Her tone is so different than I am used to. She's angry, forceful and determined. "There is nothing we can do!"

"Please!" I beg.

Violet kneels on her seat and wriggles her body through to the back, so she can sit next to me. "He's right, Elana. We can't stop."

"How … how can they … hunt … people? HOW?"

Violet, with a strange mix of gentleness and authority, grabs my face so that I have no choice but to pay attention. Her eyes drill through my own. "I'm sorry to say it, but Brin is correct. We can't do anything." Her voice changes as she speaks: soft, calming and full of regret. "It's disgusting, Elana ... cruel ... sadistic ... They don't care."

I return the intense stare as I hold one of Violet's hands. "You two do. You two care. I know you both do."

Violet appreciates my words with a delicate smile which has no place in this dark moment. She wipes a tear off my cheek as it slowly falls over my skin. "Some people only hunt the animals, Elana. It was popular in the old world, long before the virus, a kind of sport. Then, one day ... I don't know when, or the name of first person to do it, somebody put a slave out there ... and pulled the trigger on their gun. They suddenly had a new game to play, a new sport to brag about with their friends. It's another way to prove to themselves, and everyone else who will listen, how powerful they are. To live when others don't is the ultimate power. It's a perverted thrill!"

I choke and raise my hand over my mouth, scared that I'll vomit at any moment inside the car. My stomach cramps are punching without remorse, only slightly soothed by Violet's actions.

"Just breathe, Elana. And look at me, don't look anywhere else." Violet moves my face as she grips my hand tighter. "We'll get them. I want you to know that, okay? I want you to know it and believe it as one piece of truth in your life which will never change. We will get them."

I watch Brin's hand as it turns the steering wheel in the driver's seat. *Listen to her ... listen to her. She is helping you ... Don't do it!*

I wriggle my hands free from Violet's, lunge for him and grab his elbow with as much tenacity as I can find.

DON'T ...

For strange reasons that can't be explained, I remember the military representative at my progression interview, wondering if he would be impressed with my current display of strength.

DO ... IT!

"What are you doing? Elana ... let go!" cries Brin as he tries to shake me off and keep control of the car.

The unexpected action causes Brin to lose his concentration and we veer off to the left. He pushes pedals below his feet - some unnecessarily - and the engine whirrs and screeches at a higher pitch.

"Let go! Elana!" Violet leans forward and wraps her arms around me in an attempt to break my grip.

I tug once more at Brin's elbow, aided by the anger inside. *I have to see this! I must see what these people do! I must ...*

"Elana! We're heading towards the trees!" warns Brin.

Only at this moment do I realise how much danger we are in - and all because of my rash behaviour. The speed of the car catches me off guard as I stare out of the window. A wide tree trunk stands many metres in front of us, yet, a second passes and it is just a few yards ahead.

"NO!"

Brin throws his elbow back and I lose my hold just in time. "HANG ON!"

What have I done? We're going to crash!

Brin spins the steering wheel left and right with rapid turns. His whole body moves in unison as the muscles in his arms flex to their limit. "Come on! COME ON!"

I feel a hand touch mine: Violet reaching out to me for safety. A cloud of guilt and shame descends over me, gripping my skin.

Brin regains almost total control, slams his foot down on the brake pedal and stops the car inches from a tree. "Hold on!"

The momentum sends us all flying forward with force. My body smacks the back of the front seat, Violet's shoulder hits the back of Brin's, and he hunches towards the steering wheel.

All three of us have our necks whipped backwards seconds later.

Brin! ... Violet! ... I'm sorry ... please don't be hurt ... please!

The sun shines in my eyes, flickering like tiny diamonds. I can't see very well, unable to know, for certain, what has happened to the others.

A low groan sounds.

Silence.

Another groan.

"Are you two okay? Violet? Elana? Answer me!" growls Brin.

A wave of relief pours over me. "Yes! Yes! I'm okay! Are ... are you?" My words are whispered, my voice stolen by shock.

"I ... I think so," says Brin. "... Violet?"

"I'm okay, I'm okay ... but my shoulder bloody hurts! And ... my glasses ... I can't find ... no, wait ... got them!"

A gunshot, followed by loud cheering, stops everyone from speaking another word.

"We're ... even closer?" I ask with a sense of defeat. "I ... I put us all in danger ... and all I've done is bring us nearer to the hunters!"

I cry while gritting my teeth. I move with care - my neck hurts because of the impact - to look out of the window.

"Violet, get yourself back in the front," says Brin. He sounds angry and has good reason to be.

I selfishly ignore everything going on in the car, choosing instead to stare at a distant blur of grey moving in the grass. *What is that? Is it one of the animals?*

I see it again, this time with a golden tint added, only for a second. It disappears out of view behind a tall tree and some grass.

Elana Mayne

"Let's take a minute to calm down, then we'll get to the house. Elana, we'll talk about this when we get there," demands Brin.

I'm not going to have a choice in the matter, yet I don't reply to him. I'm too focused on watching the grey and gold shape which has reappeared and moved upwards.

"Elana?"

"Erm ... yes, sorry. I'm sorry, both of you. I just ... I lost it ... I'm sorry ... this is ... it's so much ... too much to take in," I explain, however, as I speak, something changes. There is a new feeling inside my mind, a new thought. It is a noticeable shift in my attitude, a willingness to learn ... the first stage of acceptance.

If I am to stop this ... these people ... I need to understand them first ... but ... when did I decide to stop them? When did I decide that I would even try?

For a brief moment, the golden tint darts to the left and I see a blurred, distant face ...

No! No! It's one of them! It's one of the people ... the slaves ... being hunted! She's trying to climb the far fence!

"It's understandable, Elana," starts Violet. "I remember the first time that our father brought us to a pursuit."

"A pursuit?" I turn away from the window, looking at them both. Brin has a red mark on his left cheek, underneath his eye, where his face recently hit the steering wheel.

All my fault ...

"It's just the name given to ... this ... this sick sport!" replies Violet. Her eyes flick upwards - she's found a memory from her complicated past. I know it isn't a pleasant one as the now predictable lines of fought off tears are back in her eyes.

"I remember it too," adds Brin. "You cried for hours, and I didn't eat properly for over a day ... and then we both suffered from those terrible nightmares afterwards. I didn't stop thinking about it for a month, maybe even longer."

I need to start considering their feelings in all of this! I must try and see life from their point of view as well. They've witnessed far worse than I have, and had to deal with it all from such a young age. They couldn't complain ... just smile for their parents and pretend they enjoyed it!

"I can't imagine ... how you ... you dealt with that." I look back out of the window because more gunshots are cracking close by, somewhere beyond the line of trees.

"Look away, Elana, please. I'm okay now, I can drive to the house," says Brin. "At least when we get there, you won't have to see anything like this."

I touch Brin on the arm. "I don't think you'll understand this, or you Violet, but I need to get used to it. I need to force myself to watch. Exactly as you two have done in the past."

"Brin, look! They've noticed us," says Violet.

Everyone turns at the same time to see a Community Guard walking towards the car. Their automatic rifle is raised as a precaution.

"No! No! This is all my fault! I'm so sorry! I didn't want this to happen!" I say, regretting my careless actions. Even though I was completely out of control, I have to apologise once again for my strong emotions.

Brin places his finger on his lips and widens his eyes. He doesn't want the Community Guard to hear loud voices from inside the car.

"Elana, don't blame yourself. Never take the blame for being upset at what *they* do! Okay?" Brin grabs my hand in his own. I welcome the warmth of his skin as it sweeps over mine. "I'll stop this. I will."

"What are you going to do?" asks Violet.

"You know how Father always tells me that I need to toughen up?"

Violet nods but she is also keeping an eye on the

guard outside, still approaching the car with slow steps. "Yes. So what? He says stuff like that all the time, to me as well."

"Well, it's about time I listened, don't you think?" says Brin as he gets out of the car and slams the door shut. He walks straight towards the line of trees and confronts the guard.

"What is he going to do?" asks Violet as she pushes a button next to her. It lowers the window by an inch so that Brin's voice is clear.

"Guard, lower your weapon! You've been trained, yes? That means you understand basic protocol … you can see from the plates on the car that I'm no threat! I don't appreciate you creeping around with a gun pointed at my sister and me!"

I'm truly shocked to see Brin acting in such an aggressive manner. It looks so natural, though, not forced. *How much has Brin really learnt from his father, even if he doesn't realise it?*

"I apologise, Mr. Dencourt," says the guard. The quiver in his voice indicates fear and respect. "I know the car belongs to your family, sir. I only became concerned because of how long you've been parked here. I wondered if, perhaps, you had broken down?"

Brin keeps his commandeering stance: tightly clenched fists, unbreakable stare and his body standing tall and strong. "I have a new order for you. Get inside the zone and tell them it's over for today."

"Sir?" asks the guard.

"I don't care who it is. I'm here with my sister and we want to drive through to our property. This pursuit is finished! Do you understand me?"

"Yes, sir!" The guard runs off through the trees and I watch him open a gate, similar to the one I escaped through when leaving Brin's house.

How many times have I seen other people scared by

the Community Guards? How many times have I been terrified myself? Brin takes that fear away ...

I find the grey shape of the slave in the grass. She is waiting for a better moment to move and try to find a safe place to hide. *Hold on, just hold on and stay hidden ...*

A single gunshot bursts from inside the Wild Zone. The slave, probably driven by fear on hearing it, jumps at the fence again. Several more ring out seconds later, as does vile laughter and applause ...

No! No! Please ... no more ...

I follow the shape as it slowly drops to the ground.

The guard returns to the gate with a muscular man dressed in dark-green khaki clothes. Brin walks away to meet them both nearer the fence.

"Is this because of me, Violet? Is he acting like this because I grabbed him?"

Violet lowers the window by another inch and some much needed fresh air drifts through the car. "It's partly because of you, but not really to do with you trying to stop the car."

"I don't understand," I say as my eyes move away from the Wild Zone. I am full of sadness and fear, knowing the slave won't rise out of the grass ever again.

"He's getting annoyed because every single time he tries to talk to you, or take you out of this dark world, it's ruined by reality. Even we can't escape it, Elana, and there are plenty of occasions when that's exactly what we want to do. For us, it's strange. It's in our very blood. We are ... are trapped in our own lives."

I feel a warmth growing inside me. I have felt it before, when with Jackson. It radiates through my body and removes some of the pain and fear ... only this time, Brin and Violet are the cause.

"Talk to me, Violet, please? Keep me distracted. I can't ... I ... can't stop looking, even though I need to!" *I wake up. I wake up. I eat breakfast ... I brush my teeth ... I check the knife ...*

Violet closes the window. "We'll be away from here in minutes, Elana. Just look away. Look out of the other window … stare at my face … anything."

The sound of Brin's stomping footsteps catch my tortured attention. He opens the car door and sits back in the driver's seat. "I think that worked."

"What did you do?" I ask. *Don't look for the slave ... don't look! You need to accept what has happened ...*

Brin grabs the steering wheel, trying to calm himself down. I can hear him taking deep breaths and see raised veins on his neck. "It doesn't matter what I said. They're leaving, that's what's important. It's over."

"Thank you, Brin … I don't know of a better way to say it, but I want you to understand how much it means to me," I say as I reach forward and touch Brin's shoulder. He reciprocates, gently touching my hand back.

"One day … one day you'll see the world without this barbaric edge! This kind of …" Brin finishes the obscene sentence under his breath. Both Violet and I know it is only quiet out of politeness.

"Hood up, Elana, quick!" says Violet.

The Community Guard walks back to the driver's side of the car. "The zone is now clear, Mr. Dencourt," he explains with a wave of his hand.

"Excellent work." Brin closes the door and drives the car back towards the fence.

I have questions, yet I know that Brin is still full of adrenaline and anger, so I choose to speak to Violet instead. A gentle touch on the arm gains her attention. "Where have they gone?"

"The people hunting will start to travel home, I expect. Or they'll drive to another Wild Zone. The nearest is about an hour away, though, so they might decide it is a wasted day and leave it."

"And … erm … the people?"

Violet pauses as Brin slows the car so that it can manoeuvre through the gate. "Rounded back up and put in the carriers. They'll be transported back to wherever they are housed. They are safe today, but not forever, I'm afraid."

I don't want to ask, yet I can't stop the words. "What about … the body? The one I saw? That'll be taken away, right?"

"No. It'll be left … I'm so sorry."

I know tears are on their way yet again, and more nausea. *I want this day to be over! I can't take this! I thought I could handle it … but … but I have to at least try and be brave … I have to try!*

Brin notices my fragile state and decides to speak. "You want to save them all, don't you? You wish you could think of an idea, a solution? One that will solve every problem that you've seen or discovered so far?"

I gulp in some air. "There isn't one! I've thought about it … it never leaves my mind! It's been there since I met you, Brin … I fight it off, but it never goes away."

"It never leaves mine, Elana. I've thought about the same questions as you … and for a lot longer than you have. Violet as well."

Violet rests her hand on top of mine. "And I believe that the answer *is* out there. It hasn't been discovered yet, that's all. It's not only about finding the courage to act and defy their laws."

I can see a giraffe in the distance. I almost forgot such a beauty and magnificence lives and breathes so close to me.

"Wait!" I shout.

"What's wrong?" Brin is already driving at a very slow speed, so the car stops moving quickly. "Elana?"

I open the car door and jump out. My legs scramble forward for ten feet before I kneel down in the tall grass.

"Elana! What are you doing? It isn't safe! There are wild animals everywhere!"

I ignore Brin's warning with deliberate rudeness. I can see the grey and golden tint through the green blades of grass.

That's ... blonde hair ... long blonde hair ...

I've found ... *her* ... the slave shot down as she tried to climb the fence.

Be alive! Please, be alive!

A young woman with blonde hair and green eyes looks at me and and smiles. I'd guess her to be mid-twenties in age, yet it's difficult to be sure because of the dirt and sweat on her face. *She knows I am not a threat to her ... she trusts me? Does she know that I am like her?*

I lay a soft touch on the woman's hand. "Don't be afraid ... they've gone ... they won't shoot at you now," I say, noticing the dark stain spread across the shoulder of the woman's tunic.

There is so much blood. It has seeped through to the ground underneath her, coating the blades of grass.

I know enough about biology to realise this poor woman is bleeding out. *It's a miracle that you've stayed alive as long as this ... you have a strength that I need ... I know I'll need it very soon.*

"Try not to be afraid. Stay with me ... please ... don't ..." I stop myself from speaking of death. "What's your name?"

"It's ... Suzanne ... erm ... Suzanne ... I think. I don't know! I ... I can't remember who I am!" Her face contorts with confusion. "Why can't I remember anything properly?"

My chest tightens up. I close my eyes and inhale fully but it doesn't stop the crushing sensation around my lungs and across my back. "Suzanne, listen to me ... it'll be okay ... Suzanne ... close your eyes and rest ... please ..."

"It's cold out here, isn't it? Why is it so ... so ... cold?

The sun looks beautiful in the sky, don't you think? I don't see the sun … they don't let us see the sun …"

I feel Brin's strong grip around my upper arm as I reach for Suzanne.

I am suddenly back in the car.

Everything I look at has a blurred edge or a glow.

What's happening to me?

I'm reminded of my time in the Tower, yet there isn't any warmth flowing through me like I experienced back then. This offers me a different escape from the harshness of reality: a darkness … a loss of memory and emotional pain.

Give in. Give in and forget …

Violet speaks to me, yet I can't hear the words properly. They are muffled, dampened by a thumping noise from inside my own head and ears.

Put your head down on the seat and rest, Elana …

I don't know if those whispers are my own thoughts, or if Violet is still talking.

The world sinks beneath a dark-grey wave that floods over everything, pulling me along with it, dragging me under.

••

I drift through this new world - dark-grey and so cold - as if I'm floating or swimming on a layer of smooth silk. It wraps around me like a weightless cloak, brushing my skin like a winter breeze. Something so sublime shouldn't be feared, yet it forces dreams and nightmarish thoughts to unfold: Mayor Hartner laughing, my parents crying, Suzanne covered in blood as she stares blankly at the sun.

My body sinks inside the silk as a light appears … a street light. I float towards it, placing my bare feet on the ground that suddenly appears beneath me. I am in a familiar place: the train station platform near to my college. Although the street light still glows brightly, I sense it is actually during the day. *This is really strange ...* "Am I waiting for a train? Where am I going?"

"That is a very good question," says Blake. "Elana, it's probably the most important question you're going to ask yourself for a while." He appears next to my right, as if we have arranged to meet here, dressed in the tunic, trousers and plimsolls that I last saw him in. That I last saw him in *alive.*

"Do you have any ideas, Blake? Where can I go? You've helped me a lot so far."

Blake shrugs. "I have no idea what's going to happen next. I wish I could help."

"Is that why you brought me here as well?" asks Jackson as he appears on the left.

I grab him in a tight embrace. "I've missed you! Do you realise how much?"

Jackson smiles. "Probably the reason I've arrived. So, where are we going?"

"She doesn't know, I've already asked her," adds Blake. "You'd think she would have some idea, wouldn't you?"

"You don't know? But, you *must.* Why carry on if you haven't chosen where to go?"

"Sorry, Jackson. Sorry, Blake. I'm taking it one day at a time. There isn't another choice at the moment."

"I've got a question. Why is that guy digging in a big flowerpot?" asks Blake.

"What?" I say. "Which guy?"

"I've never seen him before, have you?" says Jackson as he turns around to investigate.

I swing my head, surprised to see Brin. He is on the edge of an oversized terracotta pot that has been placed at the bottom of the nearby steps, digging around in the dirt. The shovel sounds in a rhythmic beat as he turns the earth over and moves it about.

Jackson has an expression on his face that I can't

read. "Do you know him?"

"Yes, that's Brin. He's been really helpful. I doubt I'd have made it this far without him, if I'm honest."

"And me," says Violet. She appears on the information screen on the wall, sitting behind a desk. "But we aren't sure of what to do now, are we, Elana?"

"Not really."

"I don't trust him," snaps Jackson. "Did you hear that? I don't trust you!"

"Jackson! Stop that! Brin is my friend, accept it."

"Whatever. I have to go."

"Go? Go where?"

"I have to start my career. I wonder where I ended up?"

"You don't know?"

"I can't know, can I? This is your dream. If you don't know, then I don't. Anyway, see you around, Elana."

"I miss you!" I hug Jackson again.

"Good. I miss you as well." Jackson makes sure that he has my eyes in a familiar stare - one he knows I can't resist. "And, you already know this, but I'll say it anyway … I never believed it, Elana, not a word. I wonder if that changed my life too? I'd like to know where I am, right now. I bet I never made it to the library for extra study!"

Jackson walks to the train, laughing at his own joke. It arrived without anybody realising. Brin keeps digging. The sharp cutting sound of the shovel hitting dirt continues … dig and lift, dig and lift …

"Are you staying, Blake?" I spin around in a full circle. "Blake? Where is he?"

"I'm over here!"

I turn to see Brin and Blake standing together in the large pot, talking to each other. They smile as if they are close friends and have been their entire lives. "What are you doing, Brin?"

"Digging."

"Why?"

"I want to dig."

"Right."

"Yeah, so … that's why I'm digging. Is this complicated, Elana? It seems straightforward to me."

"It is," agrees Blake. "He wants to dig … so that's what he's doing. This isn't difficult to understand, Elana."

"Do you want to dig?" asks Brin. He holds out a shovel for me.

"Erm … no, but thank you for the offer."

Brin and Blake frown with disappointment before they carry on.

"Hurry up! The train is about to leave!" shouts Violet.

"Right, of course, the train. I have to catch the train? But … where will it take me?"

Violet cleans her glasses before she taps a few sheets of paper on the desk, arranging them neatly in her hands. "Elana! Come on, Elana!"

Chapter thirteen

"Elana! Elana! Try and open your eyes for me, please. It's Violet … don't be afraid … you passed out so we brought you to the house. You're safe now."

I slowly open and shut my eyes a couple of times. I can still hear the sound of a shovel hitting, and cutting through, the dirt. *Strange dream! I guess I'm not awake properly yet?*

"How long have I been …?" I stop talking and grimace in pain. "Oh, Violet, my … my head hurts! How long have I been … unconscious for?" I sit up and choose to focus on my right hand. I wriggle the fingers about until my head ceases its constant pounding.

Violet's face swirls as I focus. I'm greeted a few seconds later with a welcoming and beautiful smile. I notice her clothes are different from when we were in the car: black trousers, sandals and a red blouse.

"A few hours. You did wake up a couple of times but you were still light-headed and didn't say anything. Do you feel better now?" she asks while pouring me a cup of pink coloured juice. "Drink this, it tastes like strawberries, you'll love it."

I take a small sip first, then a large gulp. It tastes

sweet and quenches my thirst immediately. "Where's Brin?"

"He'll be back in a little while. He had a few things to do outside." Violet flicks her head at the bedroom window.

"Where are we? At the house?" I move my head from side to side. *Okay, I'm on yet another bed. Why do I always pass out and wake up on different beds?*

"Yes, we are at the house. Do you feel better?" Violet sits herself down close to me. "Your skin turned a frightening shade of white earlier, as if the colour had dropped right out of you. I'm glad to say you look a lot more human now."

I touch my face, noticing a sticky covering of sweat across my hot skin. I wipe it on the sleeve of my tunic and check out the room. It is, yet again, similar to the ones I've been in previously, at Brin and Violet's houses. The colour themes in use here are blue and cream, both in a few different tones.

"Is Brin still angry? It feels like I've done nothing but go against him today. First the car, then he had to stop the pursuit. And jumping out when I saw the slave …" I pause as my most recent memory returns. "What … what happened to Suzanne?"

Violet shifts herself along on the bed and lays her hand on top of mine, adding a squeeze of comfort as well. "She … erm … lost too much blood, Elana. There wasn't any chance of survival. It happened shortly after Brin put you back in the car. You didn't notice, because of what was happening, but there were a couple of hungry lions heading directly for you. We got you in the car and drove here."

I tighten my grip on Violet's hand. "Sorry, what? Did you just say lions? Are you serious?"

"I'm deadly serious, Elana! You jumped out of the car in a Wild Zone, remember? I know you had … other priorities … but it gave Brin and me a shock, I can tell you that much."

My head spins a couple of times, lasting for about

five seconds. I quickly down more juice and try to rid my mind of images relating to savage lions.

"At least the other people out there are safe for today, like you said. I can't imagine how scared they must have been."

But Suzanne, if that was her true name, still died. How much more death will I see? How many more will I see die before I find some sort of ... of normality?

Violet nods and smiles. "It's a tiny positive in a world of negatives, Elana, but it matters. It matters to *them*. You'll understand that, I know you will."

I do and smile back. "It wasn't until earlier, in the car, that I understood you both ... if that makes sense? Your lives and how you cope."

"No, I'm not sure it does, Elana." Violet's lips purse as she thinks for a second. "It's probably best if we all try to forget what happened in the car. It was horrible for all of us."

I continue because I wish for Violet to know my thoughts. "What I mean is, you two have had to live, and survive, with this ... cruelness ... for a lot longer than I have. And you are surrounded by others who agree with it as well. I can't imagine how lonely that would make you feel. Every other person flaunts it and doesn't care."

Violet doesn't reply. The corner of her mouth twitches, as if she is trying to smile, but it never fully appears.

"What time is it?" I ask, needing a way to change the topic and flow of the conversation. "When can we begin to watch Mayor Hartner? Are we doing it from the house, or somewhere else?"

"Slow down, Elana! Take a breath!"

"Sorry. I'm too eager, I suppose." I listen to the advice and act on Violet's words. I relax my body, breathe deeply and remind myself that the end is not actually in sight. Our actions now are just another part of the larger story, and they need to be carried out correctly.

"Right, let's start at the beginning. It's one o'clock in the afternoon. As soon as Brin returns, we can look through the database, check the mayor's schedule and the maps of his land. I suppose we'll know where we have to be, once all that is completed. If you look out of the window, you can see one of the buildings on his land and a corner of his house. I haven't noticed anything yet, but I've been more worried about you."

"Thank you. I keep saying it, but I mean it. Where would I be without you and Brin?"

"Oh, probably by a tree somewhere, eating insects, or causing trouble," replies Brin as he joins the conversation unexpectedly. He walks in the bedroom with a towel around his hands, rubbing them clean. He has changed his shirt to a dark-blue, long sleeved top. Once finished with his hands, he rubs his sweat covered face as well.

"How do you manage to be so quiet with those heavy boots on?" asks Violet.

"It's easy to hide my footsteps when I've got you two chatting constantly with each other!" Brin laughs at his own joke. I don't join him and neither does Violet. "You're looking a lot better."

"I must have needed the rest," I reply. "I'm … erm … I've caused a lot of trouble today, Brin. I want you to know how sorry I am."

Brin doesn't smile straight away. He wants me to know my actions were erratic and could have resulted in us all getting hurt. His silence and eyes show me this fact all too well. "I've already got the oven on downstairs. I'll cook, we'll all eat, and then we can start out by walking along the fence boundary. You'll have to put your hood up, in case of patrols, but I don't see any other complications."

"Great!"

Brin looks at me. "Elana, do you actually know why you sound so enthusiastic?"

"Huh?"

"Elana, you're excited that we have arrived and are about to begin ... but ... what is your actual plan here? I want you to think about that, and I mean *really* think about it. This could still end up leading us all nowhere. We could find nothing of use here. It's important that you prepare yourself for that."

"I try not to, Brin. I know that's not what either of you want to hear. I can't stop myself, though."

My eyes flash to the pocket in my trousers ... and the knife. *Maybe I do have a plan? Maybe I know what will happen when I see Hartner ... but I can't admit it to myself, or you two?*

Nobody has anything else to say. The bedroom falls silent.

••

After eating another of Brin's delicious soup creations, lots of buttered rolls, a salad platter the size of a tyre on the car, and grapes for dessert, the three of us return upstairs.

Brin opens the laptop as he sits on the end of my bed. This room has now been nominated as the 'girls room'. Violet will sleep in here with me while we are at this house, with Brin across the hall. He moved the bed in from the other room for Violet to use and brought up a mattress from his car - one that needed to be pumped full of air.

Brin taps at a few keys after the laptop loads up. "Have you ever used one of these before, Elana?"

"Yes, at school and college. Students were only permitted one hour of computer time per day, though, because of the limited resources. I was allowed more because I had to study videos of experiments, or case studies, that were important to my science curriculum."

199

"Another blanket over the eyes of the residents, courtesy of Central Government," adds Brin.

"A lie? How so?"

"Technology is more advanced than you are told, Elana. The world was a connected place when the virus hit, and the first new government salvaged and maintained that function. Back then, practically every computer in the world had the capability to connect to another … and the system to allow that still exists today. I'll explain more, as I need to, but you'll be surprised at what we have at our disposal."

"I can't wait," I say. This piece of information interests me a great deal.

Brin types on the keyboard again and moves the cursor around on the screen. "The only thing I can't do is access any remote data. It will be logged and our location noted. For the moment, that is something I want to avoid."

"But … don't people know that you and Violet are here already?"

"Yes," starts Violet, "but if we start searching through sensitive information, it will raise questions. Brin has enough on the computer to help us, though."

"Here we are," says Brin.

I move so I can see the screen. "This database has a list of all active government officials, and every member of the population as well. We can find a lot of Hartner's details and the public schedule. It will also tell us the number of Community Guards at his disposal, and maybe even security measures on his land. All of that could lead us towards the next step."

I look at the image of Mayor Hartner displayed in front of me. I see his photograph immediately as a clever mask, part of a false identity. It portrays him as a caring man, which I know to be untrue. The soft eyes and genuine smile conceal much darker traits that I've seen first hand. *Blake* …

"What does it all mean, Brin? Most of it looks like

code, or abbreviations."

"It would take me a long time to explain all that, so don't worry for now." Brin points to the screen. "This one, though, *is* important."

I take a closer look and read the information on the screen. "Hartner, Charles. Eleven years in mayoral office. *AL3*. What's AL3?"

Violet answers. "Authorisation level three. It indicates how much of the truth Mayor Hartner is permitted to know."

Permitted to know? I let the explanation sink in. "He doesn't know everything?"

"No. Few actually do," replies Violet. "Even those in power keep secrets from each other."

Another question jumps forward. "What level do you have? And you, Brin?"

Brin turns to face me. "It's different for us, because of our father and family history. We don't have a classification, as such, but it would be level two. There are files that even we aren't permitted to read and certain knowledge isn't entrusted to us. I'm not sure if I ever want to see them, or learn anything new, to be honest."

Your father owns the country and you don't know everything?

"Why not?"

Brin taps at his chin. "I know a lot already, as does Violet, but I can't begin to imagine how terrible the secrets would need to be to shock us now, after everything we've had to grow up with."

"What doesn't Mayor Hartner know about? Does he realise this?" I'm slowly forming an idea, or the spark of one at least. "Is it an advantage to us, somehow?"

"He's fully aware of the system," answers Brin. "I'm afraid that isn't a viable way to hurt him. Everyone already in power understands that hard work, loyalty, being someone they can trust with secrets … it helps you to climb the ladder, so to speak."

"You sound like an information message, Brin." I pause before continuing in a fake tone of voice that makes me sound eloquent. "Aspire to serve your Government, to be a person of virtue, of understanding, of loyalty. You could be rewarded as well."

All three of us laugh together as Brin clicks at his keyboard a few more times. A detailed three-dimensional map appears. "Okay, pay attention, you two. This is important."

"Yes, sir!" jokes Violet. She salutes Brin while trying to stifle a laugh.

"Very funny," says Brin as he begins to point at the screen. "The fence outside … that's it. This section is where it joins with our land so we have a large area to work in."

"I think it's making sense. I think." I lean in closer to the screen, trying to understand the diagrams and graphics.

"Look out of the window, Elana. This building here," Brin points to a grey cube on the laptop's screen, "is that blue and white building that you can see on Hartner's land."

I watch and listen, connecting the maps with my current surroundings. I need this information. I need it to be fresh in my mind, unable to measure or comprehend it's true importance to me at this moment. Every detail, even the most insignificant, must be learnt and mastered. A guard walking around a corner, or how long it will take me to sprint to safety. *Everything* has a deciding factor with regards to our success.

"Shall we go and look? It does seem a little bit strange to be staring at the laptop when everything is right outside the door, don't you agree?" suggests Violet. The planning and preparation is obviously not keeping her attention very well.

I voice my concern. "It isn't dark yet, though."

Brin places his hand on my shoulder and smiles with reassurance. "Put the hood up. Violet and I will be with you every step of the way. You're are in *our* territory now, remember."

Violet walks to the bedroom door. "If we meet any guards at the fence, just …"

"Stay quiet and obey orders," I interrupt. "Yeah, I remember that part."

••

Because I fell unconscious in the back of Brin's car when we arrived here, this is the first chance for me to become accustomed to the new house.
It dawns on me, as I walk on the grass outside, that I wasn't able to explore Brin's home, or Violet's either. This is an entirely new experience and kind of freedom, different from the orchard visit. The fact I can leave the house at any time, albeit with a hood pulled over my head, unlocks the subconscious shackles and chains always weighing my mind down.

The house itself is larger than the two I've seen before, with flowering vines growing up the walls, creeping and stretching along the bricks. Inside, the lounge and kitchen are joined together, running from the front of the building to the back. Two thick archways, constructed so that the bricks are still visible, are placed for support and aesthetic appeal. They allow a rustic atmosphere to flow, as does the wooden flooring. Terracotta paint, highlighted with areas of cream, completes this setting, as does the furniture: two beige sofas, pine shelving and a unit for the large screen, plus a few potted plants. Their green leaves bring a striking colour and contrast to the living space, blending with the view through the windows.

Outside of the back door, an area is concreted over

with dark-red slabs, surrounded by smaller flowers and plants in tubs or pots. A dinner table and some chairs, placed centrally, draw me in to the peaceful area.

In front of the house, the grass covers a large section of land until meeting with a line of trees. *How big is this place? The trees are at least five-hundred feet away ...*

I turn myself in a slow circle. To the right, the Wild Zone, to the left, more grass, flowers, thick bushes and shrubs. Above the continuing tree line, something cuts across the sky in the distance. *Is that one of the train tracks? Does it connect with my community ... my home?*

"Elana," says Brin. "Did ... erm ... Violet tell you about Suzanne?"

"Yes. I know that she ... died." I try to pinpoint the area in the Wild Zone where I spoke to her, but my memory won't allow for details. "I hope her mind was clear of confusion before she passed ... even just for a second or two."

"Anything else?" asks Brin.

"Erm ... no, not that I remember. Did I forget something, Violet?"

"No, Elana, you didn't. I never told her, Brin. She opened her eyes just before you came up to the bedroom. I didn't have a chance to explain properly." Violet walks away so that she can study Mayor Hartner's land.

"What are you two talking about?" *Am I going to hate what he has to say?*

Brin stops walking. He turns to look at a large bush and brushes his fingers along the deep-red petals on the radiant flowers. "I gave her a proper burial. I didn't just leave her out there in the Wild Zone."

I swing my head around to gaze once more upon the area that caused all of us so much personal and physical agony. I can't see any of the animals. "Oh."

"After I got you back in the car, I drove through the

grass to get the lions to retreat. Once I knew it was safe, I collected her body."

I move my arm slowly out to the side, letting one of my fingertips touch the back of Brin's hand. "Thank you," I whisper.

"If you ever want to talk about it, just let me know, or Violet. We can help." Brin looks at me with regretful eyes. "It … it stays with you, trust me on that. You'll never forget Suzanne."

"Or Blake."

"Or Hannah …" Brin controls the sadness he is hit with on mentioning her name. "So many people. At least we know their names, and we *will* remember them."

"Brin, Elana … come here, quick!" says Violet. She beckons with her hand, gesturing with what can only be seen as excitement.

"What is it?" I ask.

Violet indicates with a move of her head. "If we stay here, it won't arouse suspicion. We're far enough away, yet we can still see the main residence, well, part of it at least. Look at that building, though. I just saw Mayor Hartner go inside. He was carrying a bottle of something … might have been whiskey from the colour."

I notice that Mayor Hartner's house is much larger than the others I've been in since opening my eyes at Brin's, after he rescued me for the first time. It isn't possible to see all of it from this viewpoint - only part of the back and one side of the building - yet the size is obvious just from that. I count ten windows on the ground floor and eight on the first.

You live well, Hartner. How many have suffered at your hands to provide you with such luxury? How many secrets do you keep so that you can sit on a balcony in the sun?

"You have the eyes of a hawk, Violet! Are you absolutely sure?" asks Brin. He peers towards the building, hoping and wishing to find something of vital significance, although he knows life isn't usually that accommodating, or steered by luck.

Violet cleans her glasses before replacing them."I'm sure. Is it some sort of hangar, or large garage? Why go in there to get drunk?"

"Maybe he wants some privacy?" I suggest.

"No, that doesn't add up. If he wants privacy, he simply tells everyone to get lost and give him some. They aren't going to say no, are they?" states Brin.

"Maybe he's checking on something? A car? His personal collection of alcohol?" The sarcasm creeps in at the end of my sentence and I don't try to stop it.

"It's a starting point, and one that we didn't have five minutes ago. We stay here and wait for him to come out … *hopefully* come out," says Violet.

Brin sits on the grass, as does Violet. She kicks off her sandals and sinks her toes in the grass.

"What do I do? Am I allowed to do that too?" I ask. "I doubt it's the typical behaviour of a … someone like me."

Violet pats the grass next to her. "You sit here, Elana. Brin, you move in front of us. To be honest, I don't care who sees you, but it's better to be safe than sorry."

I join Violet with rushed excitement. I take off my plimsolls and slide my feet along the low cut, soft grass, amazed at how much it adds to my new sense of freedom.

Such a beautiful place to live. I feel safe here … or do I just feel safe with Brin and Violet? I wonder where I'll be tomorrow, or a week from now?

As the thought of safety crosses my mind, my eyes focus on the thick bars of the fence that separate the Wild Zone from the areas of private land. A warm breeze blows my hair and I watch the tall grass inside Mayor Hartner's land shimmer gently.

I focus my attention over Brin's shoulder, wondering

how I hadn't noticed the difference in security since leaving the house. *The fence between Brin's and the mayor's is nothing compared to the other one! It's just thin, woven, wire! I could probably ... probably pull it up? I could get to the mayor ... face him?*

I cut the ideas and my vengeful imagination off before they both race away from me. Dangerous thoughts are being created ... frightening thoughts.

You will have to face him, Elana ... you can't expect this to end any other way. What will you do when that happens? What form will your anger take? That knife you carry is so important now. You always feel for it in your pocket. The familiar handle and blade. Why do you do that?

I close my eyes and exhale, trying to forget about my weapon. "I'm guessing that Hartner trusts you two?"

"Huh?"

"The fence. You forget that I've seen a few of these now ... and this is not as strong or as well constructed as the others. I guess living next to Dencourt land provides its own security, right?"

Brin laughs, awkwardly. "You learn fast."

A couple of Community Guards appear from one of the doors on Mayor Hartner's house, followed by a line of about a dozen men. Some look the same age as Brin, others much older.

"What is going on over there?" I watch the men being marched to the building. They are dressed in grey tunics and trousers, and the mixture is confusing to me as well. There isn't an obvious pattern to see: young, old, thin, tall and short. There is even a man at the back of the line, slightly separated from the others, with a severe limp.

He looks familiar. How can that be? I don't know anyone with a limp.

"We'll have to wait and see," suggests Violet. "After all, that is what we are here to do."

I know that I have to be included in the reconnaissance effort, and that I'm a vital part of it, yet the thumping headache has returned, punching behind my eyes. "Do you two mind if I go back to the house for some water?"

"No, of course not. Do you want me to come with you? Or Violet, if you'd prefer?" offers Brin.

"It's fine. Is it ... erm ... safe?"

"Yes, completely," replies Brin. "We'll stay here and see if anything else happens."

I walk off and breathe in the evening air of summer. It is brimming with the powerful scents of flowers, grass and trees. The varying aromas remind me of the different steps of my journey since Blake died.

I stop halfway to the house, beside another rose bush with deep-red petals. The ground around it has recently been disturbed, and I can clearly see boot prints stomped in the surface.

Why has this been dug up ? ... Oh, Suzanne ...?

I turn around to see Brin looking directly at me, his face solemn and peaceful. He nods once.

"We will have our revenge, Suzanne," I whisper as I stand for a couple of seconds, giving her a peaceful moment of my time.

Once I return to the kitchen, I notice something immediately. *The computer is still on ...*

I stare at it on the kitchen table as my glass fills with water. *Perhaps there is something on the map that we missed earlier? It might show me what is in that building?*

I'm unsure how to open the software which Brin used upstairs. I revert to my own computer knowledge and start with the main directory. It lists the folders so I click on *database* and a browser window opens.

"I need to get Hartner's file open, then click from there to the map of his land ... I think? I'm sure that's how Brin did it?" I ask myself.

I stare at the screen for a second, trying to recall all his previous actions, but I wasn't watching his exact movements when we were in my bedroom. "There must be a search feature? Erm …"

I see a blank field in the top right corner of the browser and type in Hartner. I click 'find' and am soon rewarded with a list of all the family: Charles, Elizabeth - spouse. Jonathan - son. Beth - daughter. Other family members are also listed underneath a sub-header link. *Extended relations.*

Elana, forget the map … you know what you really want to do …

The thought appears from nowhere and suddenly a list of nearly half a dozen names have appeared inside my mind, all circling about, each one trying to prove it is the most important to me.

Father … Mother! I type in Mayne and hesitantly click. The list appears and I can't look away. Nicholas, Anne, Elana(C/PE/D). *C? PE? D? I need to find out what those letters mean!*

I shoot a look out of the window to see that Brin and Violet are still sitting on the grass, talking to each other as they watch the building on Mayor Hartner's land. I move the cursor to the *Nicholas* link … *Father …*

A second later, an image of his face stares back at me. It causes instant tears and I reach forward to touch the screen. *Where are you now? I hope you and Mother are safe … don't let the worry and fear control you both … I'll find my way back to you …*

I do exactly the same for my mother's image. Again, it proves to be an emotional choice. *Can I find them on here? I must be able to see which Community Zone they were relocated to?*

"Are you okay?" asks Violet as she enters the kitchen. "I thought I'd check on you. Well, Brin was going to come back but he suggested that I do, in case you needed my amazing feminine powers again. He makes me laugh. So intelligent, yet so clueless at the same time."

I shut the laptop and jump to my feet. It knocks the chair over and I back away from the table with a few quick steps. There are now too many loud questions, and thoughts, buzzing inside my head.

"What's the matter with you?" asks Violet. "It's only me. What are you so anxious about?"

I watch as her eyes jump from the laptop to the fallen chair. The expression of sadness on her face shows that she has easily worked out the answer. "What did you do? Let me guess, your parents?"

Talk to her. Violet is your friend! She's been that since the moment you met her ... or she has tried to be a better one ... trust her ...

I sit down, sipping the last of my water. "I saw the laptop still open ... I ... I thought we might have missed something, about that building. As soon as I sat down, though ... I ... don't know ... I just thought about them, and everyone else who lives in my mind all the time!"

Violet refills my glass and pours herself one as well. She joins me at the table, choosing to sit close. "So, what did you see?"

"I didn't discover anything, not about my parents or friends. I saw myself ... I'm C ... PE ... D, whatever that means? Then I clicked on my parents ... once I saw their faces, though ... I couldn't go any further ... and that's when you came back in."

Violet sighs and momentarily avoids eye contact. She grabs my hand with the care and warmth that is required. "Conditioned. Public exile. Erm ..." Violet pauses to sip her water. "Deceased."

"What?"

"Your codes. That's what they mean. There isn't any

point in making you wait for an explanation, is there? You should know how the system views you … and that's how."

My life … it's been reduced to nothing more than codes in a computer file. This world … the true world … will I ever understand it? Will I ever see it through the eyes of those behind it? The powerful … such as Brin and Violet's father?

I take a quick drink. "I'm okay, Violet, honestly. I shouldn't have done it, should I? It was a stupid thing to do! I knew it would only upset me!"

"Elana, listen to me." Violet moves my face, as she had to do in the car near the Wild Zone. "As soon as you decide that you're ready to search for them again … your parents, your friends … you tell me, straight away. Do you understand? I will drop everything at that very moment and sit with you. This isn't something I want you to do alone, so you won't be."

"Thank you, Violet." A tear falls down my cheek.

••

After five minutes, Violet and I return outside carrying hot drinks. I used the time indoors wisely to dry my bloodshot eyes and calm myself down. Violet and I decided we shouldn't mention searching on the laptop to Brin right now. A better time to discuss it will arise soon enough.

I hand him a cup of tea as he picks at blades of grass, always with his eyes on the mysterious building, waiting for something to happen.

"Thanks. You two were in there for ages. What were you talking about?"

"Mind your own business. Girl talk," says Violet. She winks and smiles at me.

"I'm fine, Brin," I say as I sit back down on the grass next to him. "I think everything that has happened today is

211

catching up with me, that's all. Once I've had some more sleep, I'll be back to my normal self … whatever that is these days."

Brin laughs. "Hartner and the men have been in there for quite a while. Did Violet tell you my idea?"

"No. What are we going to do?"

Brin turns to face Violet and me. "Not we, just me on my own. I think an impromptu visit might be a good idea. It'll either stop Hartner, or I will be invited to join him. Either could be useful to us."

He waits for the replies, concentrating his eyes more on mine, trying to sense what I might be thinking.

"Isn't that dangerous?" I ask. "In there? With … him?" My imagination has always portrayed Hartner as an evil man, I don't want Brin being hurt inside my mind as well.

Brin shrugs. "Dangerous? Why would it be dangerous?"

"Brin," Violet starts, "he might not be a threat to us, but to Elana, he is the epitome of evil, try to remember that."

"Sorry, I don't think that way … like you do. To me, though, it's a good idea. You two can stay here and keep your eyes open. The only consequence is that Hartner will know, for certain, that we are staying at the house. It could impede us at a later date … and you might have to be much more inconspicuous, Elana."

Violet purses her lips as is customary when she wants to decide on a situation. "Okay. It gives us a pair of eyes inside, so we can't waste that opportunity."

"Agreed," I say.

"Be careful, Brin." Violet touches her brother's arm. "We already know he's a monster in a suit."

"He's no different than everyone else we've ever met, Violet. We invite those people to our houses all the time, sit with them as if they are our friends, or eat dinner with them. Besides, I'm a monster in disguise too … you saw me with that guard near the car. I scared myself!"

Brin walks off laughing at his own words. He has managed to absorb any anger from today and channel it in a positive manner.

"How long will it take?" I ask, sounding nervous.

"For Brin to get there?"

I nod as I pull my hood forward a little further, always fearful that a Community Guard will patrol nearby and see my face. I know that Violet will always protect me, but the fears never let go.

"Five minutes, probably less."

"Hartner's that close?"

Violet moves to the other side of me, so she is in the best position to watch the building, and points behind us. "We can't see it all, because of the trees, but the fence bends around in that direction. There is an entrance to Hartner's property on the other side."

I'm five minutes away from my enemy ... the one I have decided is responsible for everything that has happened to me. Only five minutes away.

"I really hope this works. We only need ... I don't know ... one tiny detail, one piece of information ... something to scare him for a change. I've never wanted anything so badly in all my life!"

"Take it easy, Elana. Anger can drive a person. You won't succeed if it ends up controlling you. My father told me that. For once, I actually listened to him."

"You're right, Violet, I know you are. It's like I'm fighting myself with every thought and decision most of the time. One part of me wants to jump that fence, run and find him ... then ..." I shake my head. "Another part tells me to play the long game ... be patient, make it work."

We sit for a couple of minutes, drinking in silence, before Violet stands up. "Elana, look!"

"What?" I ask, jumping to my feet as well. *I hope*

nothing has happened to Brin?

"It looks as if my clever brother's idea … don't tell him I said that … has been successful. He's out of the main house and being taken to the building," explains Violet as she cleans her glasses.

I watch two Community Guards walking with Brin in the distance. He looks safe and even turns around to speak with one of the guards. "No sign of Hartner, though. Will he have been told that Brin is there?"

"Definitely," says Violet. "Although, as you already know, our family name means a lot. Excuse the obvious expression, but it really can open doors for us. Hartner will be thrilled to have a Dencourt visit him."

Brin reaches the building and walks inside. He doesn't look over his shoulder in our direction.

"What shall we do? Stay here and wait?" I ask. "Do you think he'll be in there for a long time?"

Violet finishes off her drink. "It's impossible to know, I'm afraid."

What can you see, Brin? What are you and Hartner talking about at this very moment?

"Come on, Elana. I'm going back to the house to make another drink. To be honest, I might go to sleep as well. We left my house hours ago and I haven't rested at all yet. You must be tired as well? Today has been … challenging, to say the least. I know you rested after, you know, the Wild Zone, but we don't know when Brin will be back. It could be in one hour, or we might not see him again until the middle of the night."

I am tired, really tired, but I don't want to leave, though. I want to be here … to see Brin …

"Do we have to go inside?"

Violet smiles. "Missing my brother already?"

I blush. "No! It's … erm … just in case he comes back, that's all."

Violet puts her hands on her hips and a knowing smile forms on her lips.

"Well, maybe a little bit."

Violet laughs. "We'll go to the kitchen, have another drink, and then check back afterwards. If we don't see him, we'll call it a night. Yes?"

I nod as my eyes focus on the building once more. *Be careful, Brin ... please! Be careful!*

Chapter fourteen

I open my eyes and smile at the beauty of the moonlight as it beams in through the bedroom window. The silver rays cast striking patterns and lines across the walls and floor.

I'm sure I heard a noise? Is that why I woke up?

I look across at the other bed to see that Violet is fast asleep. *Is Brin back? Maybe I should get up and have a look?*

Despite waiting for him - I'm still telling myself he isn't in any danger - Brin didn't return from visiting Hartner. Violet and I went to the bedroom an hour-and-a-half after sunset.

We talked for another hour or so about the true world, which made me angry. Then, boyfriends, which made me feel awkward. The subject changed once again to Brin's ex-girlfriends. That made me feel *extremely* awkward. Violet also spoke about the countries which she has visited, mostly with her family.

I wonder if Brin and Violet will ever take me to another country?

I listen carefully, trying to pick out any sounds from inside the house, yet nature and exotic life inside the Wild Zone are all I can hear.

Violet rolls over in her sleep as I reach underneath the

mattress of my bed and grab the hilt of the knife. It's been with me ever since leaving Brin's house, and I don't plan on giving it up at any time soon. The bottles of medication are also close by at all times. *Are they all part of my daily life now? When will I be able to sleep without a weapon close to me? I want feel safe enough to put the knife away, once and for all ...*

I tip-toe out of the bedroom and cross the hall first. I see Brin isn't in the bed he pumped full of air earlier this evening, so I move quietly downstairs with my hand gripped firmly on the weapon. *Did we leave the light on in the lounge?*

I walk to the doorway and peer in. *Brin!*

He is asleep on one of the beige sofas, still in the same clothes and shoes. I don't know why, or how, yet one of the flowerpots has been knocked over, spilling dirt on the kitchen floor.

What's happened here? Why didn't you walk up the stairs? Were you worried we'd both wake up? I think, placing the knife back in my pocket.

As I ask myself questions, I study Brin's eyes. It is obvious to me that he's been crying, or trying not to. The skin underneath his eyelids looks red and tender.

"Brin? Are you okay, Brin?" *What's wrong with him?*

Brin coughs then rolls over, planting his face in one of the pillows. He mumbles a couple of words, nothing coherent, and an aroma lingers in the room: savoury and strong.

Has he been drinking alcohol? Is that what I can smell? Is that why he fell asleep here?

I know from Central Government warning messages, as well as previous scientific lectures, that alcohol has a variety of effects on the human body. *If he did drink, it was probably out of politeness, I suppose? He couldn't have pretended like he did with Saskia. But what did he see that*

217

upset him so much? Was he so shocked that he had to drink ... to try and forget it?

I pace around in the lounge for a couple of minutes before pouring myself a glass of water. I also search in the kitchen to find a dustpan and brush in one of the cupboards.

As I clean up the mess from the flowerpot, my mind tries to piece together what might have happened.
I want to wake Violet but decide against it, knowing that there is only one thought in my head, one decision that has *already* been made: *I'm going inside! I need to see what is in that building for myself!*

••

I reach the bordering fence and stop by a large tree trunk. It forces me to remember the forest and both of my escape attempts. *I need to get up high, or ... low ...*

A thought from earlier yesterday evening returns with a loud voice. *I can get through underneath the fence!*

I rush back across the grass to find Suzanne's grave and look around by the rose bush.

There it is!

I grab the shovel Brin used to dig and tell myself it can work, that it *has* to work. *I only need a small space.*

If I can create enough of a gap between the fence and the ground, I'll be able to squeeze through to the other side. The long grass will help a lot, hopefully concealing patches of disturbed earth from any of the patrolling guards.

I have to be quiet ... no sound ...

I place the tip of the shovel in the ground and push on it with all my strength. It sinks in the dry ground easier than I thought it would and a large chunk of grass covered dirt lifts away. *Keep going! This won't take long!*

After a couple of nervous minutes, I kneel down with my face planted on the grass. I slide the shovel under the wire and pull it back, lifting it by about a foot. I am trying to decide if there is enough room for my body to push through, and I'm also hesitant about continuing. Seeing Brin so upset caused me to react with such anger and irrational motivation. I know this may be nothing more than rash impulses, yet I don't want to stop. I can't.

No, don't change your mind. Go! Now!

I sit down on the ground and carefully move through the gap feet first, then, I drag myself forward on my back, pulling with my heels and pushing with my hands.

All the effort with the shovel worked better than I expected and, after less than a minute, my eyes are level with the fence. *Just a few feet more ... don't stop now!*

My hands grab at the tall blades of grass, using them to anchor me and pull on, as my heels dig in a few more times until my head clears the fence line.

I've done it. I am here. I've crossed a mental and physical barrier. I've moved from a place of safety to a place of ultimate danger, separated only by a thin fence, only a few centimetres thick. Two worlds exist, so different, situated directly next to each other.

Get to the building! I set off in steady bursts. My body crouches and crawls in an attempt to avoid moving the grass around me too much. Guards may see it and become suspicious.

I look around the large side of the building for any kind of opening: a window, a door or a loose panel, but there isn't anything. It also runs further back than I previously anticipated. From my position on the other side of the fence last night, the true depth wasn't visible. It's got to be a couple of hundred feet, minimum.

"No guards," I whisper.

I walk back to the front of the building and peek around the corner. I'm surprised because there aren't any patrols outside either. I sneak towards the front entrance in the centre, seeing that it is actually nothing more than a hinged panel with no locks.

If the men are still here, why don't they run? Why don't they try to escape? Maybe they are so changed, so conditioned, the temptation to be free never enters their broken minds?

I push on the panel and it swings inwards by a couple of feet. I squeeze through the tiny gap before I've even had the time to take a couple of sharp breaths, surprised by my own courage and determination.

It is very dark inside and the moonlight doesn't enter. There is a dull glow ahead of me, running along the walls and high ceiling, but it's still difficult to make out any structures.

What do you do in here, Hartner? What purpose does this place hold for you?

I find a wall and press my back up against it, moving sideways, step by step. I want to see everything in here and try to remember the exact details as well. Getting trapped is an instant death sentence, I'm sure of that. Knowing how to escape - escape at speed and in darkness - will prove to be invaluable information.

What are all those bars for? I stand at the beginning of an open area, the main part of the building. Despite the lack of lighting, metal bars are visible, running along both sides, cut in identical sections. *Stairs as well ... and a mezzanine floor ... so, whatever they are, the mysterious Mayor Hartner has them stacked on top of each other?*

The dull glow I saw is produced by strip lights on the ceiling and walls, although on a very low setting. I wish I could adjust their brightness and see everything around me more clearly.

There's a constant noise in here ... but ... what is it? It's coming from all around ... like ... people breathing?

I move forward by a couple of cautious steps. The floor changes underfoot from a hard surface to a dusty, and very fine, sand or dirt. *This stuff is all over the place. I can't work this building out ... it makes no sense ...*

A long shadow covers the ground in front of me. I can see the silhouette of a tall platform near the far end of the building and decide to investigate. If I can identify what it is, I may be able to ascertain its true purpose. I notice footprints and dark stains below me while walking. *Is that ... dried blood? What did you see in here, Brin?*

As I get closer, I see that the platform is actually a raised seating area, made from thick metal, with stairs on both sides. It's like a mechanical throne: Hartner's seat of grotesque power.

And this is where Hartner sits? He watches from above? I don't get it ... he must have watched the men earlier ... but ... but what were they all doing in here?

I hear a noise near the entrance and freeze. *It's the door! Move!*

I spin around, searching for a place to hide. My terrified eyes realise the metal beams of the platform are welded together in a lattice design. *Quick! You have no other choice!*

I twist through the diamond shaped gaps in the metal, squashing my body in the back corner. The panels under the stairs cover me in shadows, hiding me from sight completely, offering safety. I'd call it the perfect place if it didn't also remind me of the sickening time underneath Blake's home.

The lights grow brighter and, although my cloak of shadows grows deeper, my thoughts steer towards the negative. *Did someone see me sneaking about outside? Maybe one of the patrols noticed the gap in the fence?*

I grab the knife from out of my pocket. I don't let my mind consider that it will be useless against automatic weapons. *Who is here? Is it a guard?*

A few more excruciating seconds pass before my questions are answered. *It's ... it's him!*

Mayor Hartner stands near the entrance. He too looks at the blood stains on the ground, but not with the disgust that I had. He scuffs them away with one of his expensive shoes, sweeping them from existence with ease.

A couple of Community Guards join him and they speak with each other, yet I can't hear the words. Mayor Hartner points to the bars and only then, when the expressionless faces appear between them, do I understand their purpose ... their design. *They are cages. This building ... it's used as a prison.*

The people look out but make no sound. They don't cry for help or beg for release, and I wonder just how conditioned they are. *Do they know what awaits them? Have they been brainwashed to accept all of this?*

Mayor Hartner walks towards the platform and I hold my breath, hoping he can't see me.

The metal clunks above my head as he climbs the stairs to one of the raised seats. The Community Guards make their way to the prison cells and let a dozen or so girls out. Their ages differ as far as I can tell, although it is difficult to be certain. To me, some don't look healthy at all. They are thin and fatigued, slouched over and walking as if they have to force their own legs to move.

And what happens next? Is this how it played out last night, for Brin?

"You two ... and you," says Mayor Hartner from above. The Community Guards take three girls forward, closer to the platform.

I can see their glinting eyes as they look up at him. They don't seem scared, they don't seem to know what to do at all, except await their next orders.

"You are a Community Guard ... I shall call you ... Emma."

A blonde girl nods. "My name is Emma. Yes, sir."
What? They must have had all their memories taken

in the Tower! Suzanne had a lot of trouble remembering her name as well ...

I take the bottle of lilac liquid out of my pocket. *Anaesthetic suggestion ... psychological conditioning ... one in the same?*

Mayor Hartner points to the next girl in the line: short brown hair, tall and thin. "You are a fifty-fifty. Answer to the name ... Carla."

"My name is Carla. Yes, sir."

"Finally, you are friends with both of these people. In this exercise, you'll be referred to as Lily."

"My name is Lily. Yes, sir," says a girl of average build and height, with black hair.

"The guard will attempt to apprehend the fifty-fifty, which is the lawful course of action. Lily, you must decide what to do, and which person you will help. Do you all understand me?" asks Mayor Hartner.

"Yes," say three voices in unison.

It's some sort of physical exercise? I don't understand. I can't see any sport here, any kind of game ... unless Hartner enjoys watching people fight? Nothing would surprise me any more!

"Guard ... Emma, you over there. Carla, you on the other side. And you, Lily, you stay close to me, until your decision is made. Then, when you've chosen which side to assist, you will act."

One of the guards walks up the stairs to join Mayor Hartner. I can't hear the conversation properly, only picking out certain words: *protocol, stimulant, experiments.*

I suddenly see the building as a different entity altogether, the people inside too. I don't want to watch another second yet my eyes refuse to look anywhere else. They are fixed on the imminent experiment, the hypothetical situation that Mayor Hartner has created. I know, though, that these three girls will believe it, feel it as unquestionable reality. They are about to fight.

"There are no guns in your possession, yet you do have a standard protection baton each," instructs Mayor Hartner. "Remember the specific roles that I have assigned to each of you. Do not hesitate. Do not show remorse."

No! I put my hand over my mouth, so fearful that I will make a noise and reveal my location to Mayor Hartner and the Community Guards.

I've seen a protection baton used before and it is a violent and formidable weapon. A weighted bar of steel with a rubber covered grip that fits over the knuckles of its owner.

Brin ... wake up ... wake up! Realise what a mistake I have made. Come and find me like you did before! Come and stop this ... take me away from it!

"Begin!" shouts Mayor Hartner.

The blonde girl, Emma, in the role of a guard, lifts her baton off of the ground and holds it up. "Stop! Put your hands out to the side!" She stands in an offensive stance, facing her 'adversary', the brown haired Carla - the 'fifty-fifty'.

I remember those words so well. The exact same were yelled at the beginning of everything which has happened to me. My innocent visit to the college library replays as a daydream, allowing questions and possible answers to emerge. *Is Hartner training future guards? Will that be the outcome of this experiment? The strongest are trained further?*

"No! I'm not doing anything you say!" shouts Carla. She moves quickly to the middle of the sand covered floor and stands her ground.

"Stop! I will use force if necessary!"

Carla lunges first with her baton and Emma jumps out of the way, striking down swiftly with a counter attack to the wrist. There is a cry of pain as Carla rolls away and regains her footing.

Emma surges forward, raising the baton above her head in preparation to swing downwards. Carla predicts this move and holds hers up, blocking it. The sound of screeching metal rings out and echoes through the building, stabbing at my ears. The two girls fight and push with all their strength, desperate to overcome each other.

Where did they learn to do that? Could other information be placed inside their minds, apart from obedience? My thoughts confuse me. Even though it is terrifying, I suddenly wish to return to the Tower with the hope of discovering secrets. That place manages to haunt me, every minute of every day.

Carla kicks Emma in the thigh, sending her leg backwards, knocking her off balance. She takes her chance and swipes the baton downwards. It strikes Emma on the side of the face and she falls to her knees.

I am fifty feet away yet I can still see the red line on Emma's cheek and jaw. *Brin ... please ...*

Emma jumps up and catches Carla with an unexpected blow to her ribs. It's followed with a punch to the shoulder, strengthened by the steel knuckle-grip.

I shut my eyes. I close them so tightly it makes the muscles in my face hurt. This fight ... *experiment* ... is heading in a brutal direction and I do not care to see its conclusion, yet, despite the nausea, the need to scream, the sheer horror of witnessing Mayor Hartner's secrets, my eyes force themselves open again.

"Have you made a decision yet, Lily?" asks Mayor Hartner.

"No, sir."

Two against one! Is that the game here, or does Hartner carry all this out with a twisted and scientific purpose in mind? I remember he mentioned controlling behaviour and conditioning when he spoke to Blake. Is this how they do it? They test chemicals on these people?

225

Elana Mayne

Emma runs towards Carla with a couple of long strides. In a swift move, she drops and slides her body along the floor. The momentum knocks Carla over, then, they both swing their batons behind them and another loud crash of metal fills my ears.

Lily chooses this moment to join the fight. She picks up the baton in front of her, walks a few steps, then speeds up.

What are you going to do? What have you decided?

Lily crunches her baton on the back of Emma's neck. Her eyes glaze over for a second, then, as if the bones in her legs have crumbled to dust, she drops to the ground. Carla takes a few deep breaths and then stands up.

"Is that it? Is it over now?" says Mayor Hartner. "You chose to help the fifty-fifty? You chose friendship over following the law?"

I'm so afraid of the tone in Hartner's voice. It reminds me too much of how he spoke to Blake, right before the gunshots rang out. Right before he killed him … killed my friend … an innocent sixteen year old boy who dared to answer back and confront the powerful lies.

"No, sir," answers Lily. She swings again with aggression and strength, catching Carla in the stomach. As she doubles over in pain and shock, Lily takes her legs out with two snapping blows, right behind the knees.

I hear Mayor Hartner talking above me. "Interesting," he says. The word carries an edge to it … almost an admiration. "Tell me, Lily, if I told you to kill them both, what would you do?"

NO! DON'T DO IT! I hold one hand on my stomach, the other over my mouth.

"I would kill them both, sir."

A silence follows. It is the longest ten seconds of my whole life.

"Do not kill them. The fifty-fifty is still able to

retaliate, though. You haven't finished yet, have you?"

Lily clenches her fingers through the knuckle-grip on her baton and throws a punch across Carla's chin. It knocks her unconscious and a pool of fresh blood soon stains the ground.

"It's over, sir."

I let my eyes close. Instead of forcing it, I concentrate on nothing else than relaxing my body. I think of the soup that Brin prepared for me when we first met, how gently he spoke to me through the bathroom door when apologising, his smile that seems to lighten even the worst of situations.

"Guard, did they all meet the requirements?" asks Mayor Hartner.

"Yes, sir."

"Are you sure? Even Emma?"

"Yes, sir," repeats the guard. "All parameters have been reached."

"Interesting. I thought we would need to dispose of her. I'll run it again later with her as a subject again. Make sure ten are injected. I need to complete a multiple adversary simulation."

I hear Hartner speak but ignore his cruel words. I've never regretted my actions as much as I do at this exact moment in time.

He told you, Elana ... curiosity killed the cat ... you shouldn't have come here ... you should have stayed with Brin and Violet.

"Lily, return to your cell," orders Hartner.

"Yes, sir."

My eyes follow Lily as I wonder how long I will have to hide here for. This building has now become the most dangerous place that can exist for me. I am in Hartner's domain, his sickening world, all alone.

I think of my new life, the different life that exists on the other side of the thin wire fence. *I have no choice but to wait here.*

The Community Guards collect up the batons and place them inside a locker at the side of the building. I notice that it isn't secured afterwards with a key.

Hartner is very confident in his set up here, maybe too confident? He relies entirely on the obedience of the slaves and their cages ... he has to. The security measures would be much more strict otherwise. I walked in through the front door! Did Brin realise this as well?

Carla and Emma are dragged away, both still unconscious, to the side of the building. I'm relieved to see one of the Community Guards taking the time to check both their pulses.

Have others died here? Brin had to watch this too ... he had to sit with Hartner and pretend to enjoy this! Now I understand why he had been crying ... he must have held it all in until he got back to the house!

Footsteps bang on the panels again and Mayor Hartner strolls off through the building. He has completed another of his experiments, causing pain and suffering to others. In his eyes, the eyes of the creature that he has become, it is simply another part of his work for Central Government, nothing else.

Chapter fifteen

I find strength of character, willpower, *and* a level of patience inside me that I didn't realise was possible. Fear, disgust, and regret all combine until I want nothing more than to run out of this building. This fight zone, prison, laboratory … it has many titles and uses, all abhorrent to me.

The Community Guards won't stay in here all day, will they? I need to get back to the house … to Brin and Violet! This place is crushing me and I don't know how much more I can take!

Twenty minutes slowly tick along as I repeat the calming words I've used so many times before: *I wake up … I eat breakfast … I brush my teeth …*

I watch as the two guards complete paperwork - a report of the experiment - that they have attached to clipboards. *So, is that sent to the Science Department now? Hartner works for them, or does everyone in power have to do this?*

To my immeasurable relief, Emma and Carla finally regain consciousness. They don't even notice that they are covered in blood and painted with fresh bruises. They stand up slowly, awaiting the next words of direction. The guards order them back to their cells and they are as compliant and obedient as expected. They ignore any pain, show no hesitation and ask no questions as they shuffle across the floor.

The guards are leaving!

They walk back to the front of the building and I clearly hear the door's hinges creak as well. The lights dim again moments later and I know my chance to leave has finally arrived. *I'll go back exactly the same way ... out of the door ... stay low, stay hidden in the grass ... under the fence and back to Brin.*

A couple of minutes are added - I need my confidence to grow - and then I start to climb out through the metal beams of the platform. I squeeze my body between the gaps and run to the edge of the building, taking a different route than before, finding the thickest of shadows.

It is impossible, yet I try to avoid the eyes of the people inside the cages as I move. They look at me, through me, hold me with stares that make my heart ache with pity and sorrow. *I wish I could open your cells. Do you all know that? Do you have any idea what I'm thinking?*

I stop when I see Carla in her cell. *Oh, Carla ... look what they've done to you!*

Blood stains the skin on her face and hands, her tunic as well. Dark bruises scatter themselves across her legs.

"Carla?" I say and wait as this poor girl slowly turns her head.

"Yes. I am called Carla."

I can't do this! I can't stay here and look at you ... at how they're treating you!

I let the tears flow down my cheeks and don't even try to stop them. I want Carla to see me cry. I want Carla to see someone cry *for her.* "I'm ... I'm sorry, Carla ... I ... I can't help you!"

"You are sorry," repeats Carla in a low tone. "You can't help me."

I quicken my steps and ignore the others in their cells as my heart shatters inside my chest. I can feel their eyes penetrating and crawling over every inch of my skin.

You're here, Elana ... you're at the door ... you don't have to see the suffering any longer ...

Next comes the most feared and dangerous part of my return - venturing back outside. I pull the door so that a thin gap appears, just as I had done on entering.

I give myself thirty seconds to mentally prepare, and listen for any guards nearby, then shoot out at speed, reaching the grass and some cover. Sunrise is approaching and already Mayor Hartner's land is much brighter. The extra cover of darkness I had on my way here won't last for much longer.

I don't have any time!

I reach the fence within a couple of minutes, using the shovel on the other side of the wire as my guide and compass point to safety. *Under the fence ... quick! Slide back under ...*

I pull again at the dirt with my heels and fingers ... *Please! Let me do this! Let me do this!*

One more second, my eyes are level with the fence again ... another second ... I can see the sky above ... I sit up and push my legs, throwing my body away from the fence line.

I've done it! I've made it! Calm down ... it's over ... YOU - ARE - SAFE!

I pant out a long breath as my legs buckle underneath me, shaking at the same speed as my heart beat. I've made it back. I am close to Brin and Violet once again ... I'm untouchable, away from Hartner's grip of power.

"Elana? Why are you up and out here so early?"

I grab the shovel and throw my body up with a burst of energy. My legs are still weak but I manage to stand.

"Hey, take it easy! It's only me," says Brin. He holds his hands up in feigned surrender and smiles. "You're on edge. What's wrong with you?"

"Nothing … nothing. I … you … you made me jump, that's all." I drop the shovel next to me.

Brin rubs his eyes and his forehead. "I needed some fresh air."

"Are you okay?" I ask. "I hate to say it, Brin, but you look … ill … I mean *really* ill."

"Yeah, thanks. It's a headache, that's all."

"Right. Nothing to do with the alcohol?" I sound more sarcastic and condescending than I mean to, knowing Brin's head hurts for other reasons. "Take some painkillers, you'll feel better."

Brin's eyes begin to quiz me, then, they move to the shovel and a few clumps of the disturbed dirt near my feet. "You didn't?" He asks, noticing that the fence wire has been pulled out of shape. "Did you really think about doing it?"

"Doing what?"

"Come on, Elana! The shovel … the fence … and you have dirt all over your hands. You were thinking about going under the fence, or something like that? Right?"

I don't answer. Brin has pieced the situation together correctly, yet he's missed out the crucial part where I actually carried through with my stupid decision.

I don't want to lie to Brin … but … I think I'll let him believe what he is saying … for now.

Brin walks to the twisted part of the fence and pushes it down with one of his boots. "I can't believe it even crossed your mind!" He does the same with the lumps of dirt. "Do you know how dangerous that could have been? And what exactly would you have done when you got there? Walked up to Hartner and … what? Told him off for being nasty?"

I gaze at the ground with regret, although I'm only half genuine with these actions. *He really doesn't know! Let him moan and get worried for a bit, then he'll calm down … but he doesn't know I went through with it!*

"I'm … I'm sorry, Brin. I wasn't thinking straight. I had a nightmare … it made me so angry that I decided to come out here to clear my head. I noticed that you were on the sofa … I … erm … you looked upset, and I could smell the alcohol. I wanted to see what had made you that way and as soon as I saw how basic the fence was, and the shovel … I don't know … I … wouldn't have gone … I wouldn't have."

Brin shakes his head with severe disappointment and concern. "You shouldn't worry me like that, Elana. Please, don't do it again?"

"I've been … been sitting out here for a while, like a complete idiot! I would have come back to the house soon … you know that."

I feel uncomfortable with this untrue version of events, yet I decide that it will protect Brin from his own levels of stress and panic.

Brin pushes with his boots once again, until he is completely satisfied the fence and ground resemble their previous states. He stares across to Hartner's land as well, checking for any guards on patrol.

"Come back inside, Elana. I'll make you a hot drink and then I can tell you more about what happened last night. I was so tired when I came in."

"Water will help. I learnt that in college. It's great for … you know … the after effects of alcohol."

"It's called a hangover. But I don't have one. This is a headache, nothing else."

"Whatever. I'll make us some tea. You can sit and rest," I suggest as I touch his wrist. "I'm sorry that I scared you but you scared me too. It hurt me to see you like that. It's the only reason I thought about going over there."

••

In the kitchen, Brin sits at the table with one hand

shielding his eyes from the light. They are still red, although this time it is due to lack of sleep and the alcohol, not tears.

"So, what happened? Did you discover anything useful?" I ask as I wash my hands free from any mud. Then, I start to make two cups of tea.

My eyes stare out of the window as I watch the tall grasses move with the morning breeze. My memories keep swimming back to the building, back to Carla.

"You must have been over there for hours. I don't know what time Violet and I eventually went to bed, but it was dark outside," I say and grab a carton of milk from the fridge.

"I lost track of the time as well. It was worth it, though, all of it. He's alone over there, I found that much out. His wife and children are in Japan … but …"

"What, Brin?"

"I wish I hadn't, if I'm honest …"

I finish making the drinks and sit down at the table. "Drink this, Brin. You should really get some more sleep as well."

"We were right about him … Hartner … so right about him! He's a monster! A psychopathic beast!" Brin spits the words through gritted teeth and they are coated in a growing rage. His hands form fists and his muscles tense.

I become understandably shocked at this sudden change in his attitude. "Hey, calm down, Brin. What's the matter? What happened in that building?"

Brin turns away through shame, or male bravado, I can't decide which. "I … I … shouldn't have gone over there. I wouldn't have seen .. I wouldn't know any of this if I'd just stayed here!"

"What? You have to talk to me, Brin!" My concern escalates. I think about waking up Violet. "Drink some of your tea. We can talk about it, or not. I'm here to help you, remember that."

Brin's shoulders lower as he slumps down in the chair, so very tired and confused. Whatever he witnessed, it has torn at his soul. "Thank you." He smiles and laughs a little.

"Did I say something funny?" I ask, confused. I can't see any humour here.

"No, well, yes. Isn't this scene usually reversed? I save you and then calm you down?"

I smile too. "Ahh, I see your point."

Brin sips more of his tea. "Experiments, Elana. But not the kind you would have studied at school or college."

"Experiments?" *Act surprised ... remember, he doesn't know that you went through the fence ...*

"It seems that Mayor Hartner is very well connected to the Science Department. I missed it earlier when I was looking at his details on the laptop. He started there, in his career, and has worked his way up. But, he has never lost contact with them."

"I'm not sure that I understand, Brin." I notice that his skin has turned pale. "You look awful. I think you should go back to sleep. We can talk later once you have rested."

"Thanks for your honesty."

I blush at his words. "Sorry, but you know what I mean!"

Brin laughs.

"Not funny!"

Brin finishes his cup of tea with large swigs. His face drops within an instant. "I saw ..."

He must have seen the fights, like I did ... it's sickened him as well ...

Brin lowers his head and covers his face with his hands. "It was savage, Elana. Hartner ordered the men we saw to fight. And one to ... to break ... break his opponent's neck."

Remember, act surprised ... Wait ... what?! I did not

expect to hear the final part of Brin's sentence.

"Someone … died?"

Brin forces himself to nod.

Hartner asked Lily if she would kill the other two … Emma and Carla … but … he actually made one of the men do it? He ordered another death and Brin watched it?

"He justifies it all underneath a warped blanket of research. He's testing chemicals on the people in the buildings, sent from the Science Department."

"And it makes them fight?" I ask, despite already knowing the answer. I wonder if it is possible to keep my secret for much longer.

"It makes them controllable." Brin stares out of the kitchen window, letting the sunrise hit his face and the warmth calm him down. "The men we saw walking from the house last night were drug free. They were taken to the building and had to fight others always kept inside. Test subjects who have been injected with varying doses."

I stand up, needing to move, to do something. "I need another drink … we both do."

I remember meeting Brin for the first time, and how, as he said a couple of minutes ago, things are now reversed. A thought sparks in my mind and I reach for the pocket on my trousers. *No, you can't, Elana, you can't! But, it will help him. I want to help him! I want to take his pain away. I … I care for him. I … care for him? Yes, I do …*

"Elana, I know I've been somewhat … hesitant … I may have come across as overly cautious, especially when you have spoken of revenge. After last night, I am with you, completely, with all my heart and soul."

I smile as I put one drop of the lilac liquid in Brin's tea and stir it thoroughly. "Thank you, Brin. I never thought that about you, though, not once. It's taken me a while to realise it, and accept it as well, but I've always known that you are helping me, protecting me all the time." I return to the kitchen table. "Here, drink some more. You've had a terrible shock."

"Where's Violet?"

"Asleep upstairs. Do you want me to go and get her?" I offer. I'm not sure how to know if the liquid anaesthetic has worked.

"No, leave ... leave her there. I'll talk to her ... in ... erm ..." Brin loses his train of thought and stares at his cup of tea, watching the steam rise in tiny trails of spiralling vapour.

"Later? Once you've had some more sleep?"

"Erm, yes, later. That's what I wanted to say." Brin rubs his eyes and runs his hands down his face. "Wow! I am so tired! It's just hit me. Boom! ... I feel ..."

That's it! He's much calmer now, it must be working.

I reach forward and grab Brin's wrist. "It's okay, Brin. You rest again. I'll help you to the sofa, so you can sleep some more. I want you to relax. We'll talk later, I promise."

"Thank you, Elana. Very clever ... you're very clever ..."

We stand at the same time and I help Brin walk through to the lounge.

Very clever? Does he know that I've drugged him?

Within seconds Brin has fallen asleep again. I sit opposite on the second sofa, watching him, protecting him for once, until my own eyes drift shut.

••

"Elana! Elana!"

Violet?

"I've made you some tea. Brin is in the kitchen, cooking."

I open my eyes. My neck feels stiff due to the uncomfortable position my body has been in for too long. "Brin's awake? How is he? What time is it?"

237

"I'm fine!" calls Brin from the kitchen. "It's nearly lunch. Get up!" he adds, laughing.

"Come and eat, Elana," starts Violet. "Brin has made scrambled eggs, toast, fried tomatoes and mushrooms. Delicious!"

"That sounds amazing. You're such a great cook, Brin!" I call out.

"Yeah, I know!" he calls back with pride and a dash of inflated ego.

Violet stands over me, beaming a smile across her sunlit face, wearing the night clothes which she slept in: a large t-shirt and knee length shorts, both in light-blue.

I swing my feet off of the sofa and allow myself a few moments to wake up. *No dreams? No Hartner nightmares?*

I can see the sun flooding through the room and it feels so warm, so nurturing. The doors from the kitchen that lead outside are open, letting a breeze drift in, carrying the scent of grass, flowers and trees with it.

"So, do you two want to tell me what happened during the night?" asks Violet as I walk through and sit at the kitchen table.

Brin shoves a large piece of toast in his mouth as I begin to fill my plate. *I'm so hungry!*

"Anyone?" pushes Violet. She gives Brin and me equal time to answer, and identical questioning gazes.

Brin swallows his mouthful of food and drinks a large swig of tea. "We had a chat by the fence, Elana made me some tea, we talked some more ... she drugged me, you know, the usual." His tone is nonchalant, as if the events were part of a normal day for him.

"What?" asks Violet with surprise. She turns to Brin. "She drugged you?"

Don't be upset, Violet ... I had to do it! Please, I don't want you to be angry with me!

I very nearly choke on a mushroom. I quickly regain my breath and sip a little tea. "You … erm … know I did that?"

"It was for my own good, right, Elana?" Brin doesn't act bothered at all by what happened during the night. He fills his plate with more mushrooms and scrambled eggs. "It's fine, Elana," he adds as he begins to devour more food.

"Well … erm …" I mumble my attempt to answer. My face turns red and I can't think of how to explain my actions. At the time, I'd acted out of necessity. "Brin was in a state … and … erm … I thought about how he had calmed me down … erm … after we first met … and …"

Violet puts her hand on my shoulder. "Hey, relax! Take a deep breath before you pass out."

"Elana," says Brin, "Violet and I have done the same over the years. We've had no choice."

"What?" I ask, puzzled by his relaxed truth. *Why would they resort to taking the liquid anaesthetic?*

"If we needed to, yes." Brin grabs another slice of toast. His behaviour is surprising to me because I honestly thought he would react in a different way. He should be angry and disappointed by my actions.

"Think about it, Elana. There have been *many* occasions when we have needed to," adds Violet. "After seeing something that has upset us both, like the pursuits for example, or we've been told one of the truths about the world. Does that make any sense?"

I think on her words for a second. "It does, actually. I … erm … I couldn't think of anything else to do. I just wanted to give you a chance to rest, Brin."

"After my father … erm …" Violet stops talking mid-sentence and drinks some tea. She pulls her feet up on the chair too. "After … what happened to Brin, we moved our beds around in the house so that we shared a room. One end was full of my stuff, and Brin had the other. Half each. We wanted it that way … we decided that we wanted …"

"Needed," says Brin, interrupting.

Violet nods. "Yes, *needed*, to be together. Neither of us could sleep at night, not straight away, so our personal physician prescribed it. Back then, in the months that followed Hannah's death, Brin would wake up after horrid nightmares, or I'd start crying without reason."

Brin's face is blank as he recalls this troubled time in his life. Then, as if he relishes the personal triumph over the past, he smiles, wanting to bring the conversation away from its upsetting path.

"Aww, you two, always helping me out."

He stands up and quickly plants a kiss on my cheek, then skips across so that he can do the same to Violet as well. He bursts out laughing at his show of affection.

My face matches the colour of the tomatoes on the plate in front of me. I sit with the cup of tea close to my lips, hoping it will cover all the blatant signs of embarrassment.

"Urgh! Boys!" Violet giggles and then takes a short pause to clean her glasses. "Now that we are all awake, it's the perfect time to continue with our plans. Brin has already told me about the … erm … what he saw in that building, Elana. It's horrible, sickening! We know people are used like this, to test new serums and other chemicals, but to order a person to …"

Violet stops talking. She doesn't want to mention death, none of us do, yet it seems to be everywhere we go, following us. It is always snarling behind our heels, ready to attack like a pack of wolves.

"It's terrible. He's defiling scientific research with such … I don't even want to call them experiments. I can't imagine how many people have …" I stop mid-sentence and turn my head, instinctively searching for the building beyond the fence. I find it but close my eyes immediately. It is too painful to look at. "… All so that they're able to control people more efficiently! Produce better slaves!"

"We have another chance to get inside," says Brin as he takes his empty plate to the sink.

"What?" asks Violet. "I think I should come with you next time, if that's possible?"

"We do? When? How?" I add. *Why does this excite me so much? Why do I want it? Have I decided something - what I will do to Hartner - without realising it?*

"This evening. Mayor Hartner has invited us over for dinner, Violet. I politely accepted," he says and returns to the table.

"Dinner?" asks Violet.

Brin leans back in his chair and grabs his tea. "It was an obvious move, Violet, if you think about it. He isn't going to waste a chance to impress and please a Dencourt, is he? He'll want us to mention his generous hospitality the next time we see Father."

"That's true. It *is* a great opportunity. One we shouldn't miss." Violet's eyes contemplate the situation.

"Although, career progression didn't seem evident from our conversations last night. He's content at the moment. He's reached a level that is comfortable for him, that fits his personality. It allows him to do everything that he wants," continues Brin.

Like experiment on humans! I take a calming deep breath. "At least you two will be safe over there. I'll wait here in the house until you return, as usual."

"No, Elana, you won't."

"No? Why not?"

"Because you're coming with us."

"Oh, I see." My heart jumps for a split second. *I'm going inside Hartner's house? I'm going to be so close to him ... but it won't be the same as when I had to hide at Blake's ... or the Tower and last night. I'll be standing near him! Will I be able to control my anger for much longer?*

••

I sit in the kitchen watching Brin move the knot on his tie about.

"I do not like wearing these bloody things!" he moans with frustrated pulls and twists.

I hide my smile and the laughter trying to escape.

Brin sighs and mumbles a few extra words under his breath. The rest of his clothes - a grey suit, blue shirt and polished black shoes - are not causing him any problems.

I eventually have to laugh, I can't stop myself. "At least you can dress up smart for the dinner at Hartner's. I get to wear my tunic and hide underneath the hood!"

"Your very *clean* tunic," mutters Brin.

"Clean?"

Brin pulls at the collar on his shirt and adjusts the tie some more. "The one you had on earlier was filthy. Almost as if you had been rolling about in dirt. Strange, don't you agree?"

He does know! Has he worked out that I went under the fence?

I look around the kitchen, trying to act innocent. "I … must have rubbed my hands all over it. It was dark, I didn't really pay much attention to be honest."

"Yes, that must be it," adds Brin with a mild cynicism attached to his voice.

Violet joins us in the kitchen and her dress makes me instantly jealous. It is a shimmering burgundy colour, running over one shoulder and under the other, with small diamonds sparkling across the hems. It flows to just below her knees, where more glittering stones have been set in the intricate black lace work. Her black shoes are low heeled with straps that wrap around and up her ankles.

"You look so … so beautiful!"

I catch Violet's skin as the sunlight streaming in through the window coats her. Every part of her glows with a golden tint, from her toes to the deep red colour on her eyelids. She has styled her hair so that it drapes down one side of her face, held up on the other with a diamond studded clip.

"Oh, thank you! I can never hear that enough!" Violet puts a finger to her eye as she shuffles forward and kisses me on the cheek. "Stop, though! I'll cry and my make-up will run."

I get up from my chair, take Brin's hands away from the tie and push them down. "Leave it alone, you're making it worse. If you need to, undo your top button and cover it with the knot. Like this."

Brin blushes as I, unintentionally, run my fingers along the skin on his neck.

"There, done. You look ... erm ..." I lower my voice due to embarrassment. "You look very handsome, Brin."

"Thanks."

Violet coughs to break the awkward silence. "So ... are we ready? Elana, are you sure that you can do this?"

I hope so. I shouldn't make promises that I have no intention of keeping ...

"Elana?" repeats Violet.

"I'm not, actually." I turn away from them both. "It might be safer if I stay here. There's no fear of complications if I'm not around to cause any."

Brin moves next to me but avoids direct eye contact, knowing it will embarrass me. "If that's what you want, I won't argue. I know you can do it, though. I know, somewhere inside, you *have* to do this."

"It's a victory," adds Violet. "Your chance to face Hartner. Your chance to walk alongside him, in his own house, knowing that you're here, alive. You're not codes in the computer, like he believes."

"You're right, both of you" I say, accepting their words as if they are my own guiding thoughts. "I can. I won't mess it up for you both … but …"

"What?" asks Brin.

"I'm worried about you and everything that happened last night. You keep asking after me, but how will you cope? You witnessed horrible acts of violence in that building. And now you're going straight back."

"I can't react, Elana, it's that simple. Once we are inside Hartner's house, Violet and I will change. We'll become different people, especially to you. Our actions and behaviour, every word we speak, it's all an act. It's how we've coped over the years. Our chance to hide the truth from them."

I remain silent, unsure if I can endure their false transformations. Brin and Violet are my world at this moment. If they change, I fear the consequences.

Brin rests his hand on my shoulder. "Don't take any of what we say at face value. We're on a different path over there, living a totally different life. I need to wear my mask, as does Violet. I don't know how it will proceed, not exactly, but we'll probably be taken to a lounge before the meal. Just sit yourself away from Hartner and keep the hood up. He won't question anything … he will … oh, it doesn't matter."

He adjusts the cuff links on his shirt as a deliberate ploy to try and diffuse or end the conversation.

"What, Brin?"

Violet decides to answer instead, sensing that her brother has grown uncomfortable. "Mayor Hartner won't acknowledge you … at all. He sees you as inferior to him, and you … erm … you belong to us. He has no place talking to you because of that. Because you are … our property."

I turn away again. Violet's words are painful for me to hear, causing me to view my place in this world with such blunt, truthful eyes. "I see."

The aroma of Brin's aftershave gains my attention as he moves closer to me: sweet and fresh, with a citrus edge. I'm reminded of cutting oranges with my mother.

"Elana … if …"

"If what?"

"Listen, if you need to get out … if it is too much for you, signal to me. I'll be playing the dinner guest role, I know, but I'll always be checking on you as well. This isn't going to be easy, as we discussed earlier. You've only seen glimpses of Hartner's evil, now you're going to be consumed by it."

I make sure I have Brin's eyes firmly held by my own. "Thank you, Brin. We can't miss a chance like this, though, we can't. We're so close, I can feel it."

Another silence falls over the room, again broken by Violet. "Right! Come on, you two, we need to get moving. Brin, you escort me. Elana, you walk to the left of Brin."

••

We make our way out of the house in silence and walk across the grass, leaving through one of the entrances around the land boundary.

I am soon confronted with large gates, standing tall and menacing in front of me. They are created in iron, hammered and twisted to form the insignia for Central Government. *More of Mayor Hartner's exuberant style!*

"Here we go," mumbles Brin as a Community Guard approaches from inside Hartner's land.

"Good evening, Mr. Dencourt, Miss Dencourt. Please follow me and I will take you inside."

I keep my head down, watching Brin's polished shoes move forward. I mirror my own steps with his as we walk up the brick pathway.

"Mind the steps, Violet," says Brin. "You don't want

to trip."

I know that his words are for me as well, not just his sister. I flick a glance forward and climb the deep-set steps.

This is ... amazing! It's ... like a palace!

On leaving the Tower, I had a need to stop and stare in awe. That feeling, that urge, has returned to me now.

It's twice the size that I imagined, maybe more ...

Yesterday evening, I remember how I counted ten windows, yet that figure was only a small part of the true proportions. The rest of Hartner's secret home spans further across the land, with a second floor extension added at the far end.

"Brin! Excellent to see you again! And Violet, what a beauty you are! The last time I saw you must have been ... Paris?"

Violet smiles in a coy manner. "Oh, Charles, thank you. Yes, your memory serves you well. Paris, three years ago, for my mother's birthday."

Mayor Hartner!

He stands in between the main doors with his arms open, as if greeting old friends or family members. He too has dressed in smart clothes for the occasion: a light-grey suit, white shirt, and a blue tie.

Every muscle in my body reacts to his presence, tightening. My mind sees Blake at the window of his home, in exactly the same state. *Can I do this? Can I honestly say that I won't react? Should I signal to Brin now, before it's too late?*

I am scared, angry and vengeful. I am afraid of my own thoughts and the actions they may produce.

"Come in, both of you! It's a pleasure to have you as guests in my home," says Hartner. He smiles the twisted smile that I am so familiar with from the nightmares.

Both of you? I don't even exist ... Violet told me as much. I wonder how much longer that will last? How much longer will I be unknown to you, Hartner?

The large doors close behind us all and two Community Guards take up their positions. I stand still, unable to move, realising how dangerous the situation really is. I am in terrible danger, yet so are Brin and Violet simply because of their connection to me.

Don't let the fear in! I wake up ... I brush my teeth ... I reach for my knife ... I feel safe with the knife ... Mayor Hartner is in danger too ... he should be fearful of me!

I stare at the tiles on the floor in a daze, created by an unseen mist of anger that surrounds me. I welcome it and fear it equally. A fleeting thought - running forward and attacking Hartner - it is locked away before it has a chance to grow and spread. I know that three people fighting against an army of guards isn't even an option worth considering. It isn't an option at all.

This is not the time ... this is not the time! You've travelled this far, and you're still alive. You have to wait. You have to hold all of your anger inside ... until the perfect moment ...

Chapter sixteen

The main foyer is a large circular space, attached to the front of the main house as an extension. Four hallways run off of it - two on each side - with dark-red paint decorating their walls. Sunlight pours in through the panels of glass in the ceiling, landing on a soft and plush carpet which covers the floor completely in grey and white tones.

I wait until Hartner isn't looking in my direction before I stare upwards through the glass. The outside of the house rises above me like an ancient monolith. It is a magnificent visual spectacle, one designed specifically to impress all those who walk underneath it when they enter. A grand staircase runs centrally towards a stained glass window, splitting off to the left and right, curving back up and around to join with the upstairs landing.

This is ... amazing! I don't want to admit it, yet I'm enjoying the splendour of my surroundings. I quickly remind myself of how Hartner acquired such luxury. *I wonder if all the houses ... all those that are hidden and kept a secret, are like this?*

"You have a beautiful home, Charles," says Violet. She spins herself around in a slow circle to admire the interior. I can't tell if she is genuine or not with her compliments and behaviour.

"Yes, I agree. This is stunning. I wish I'd had a chance to look around properly yesterday," adds Brin.

"Thank you, both of you, thank you," says Hartner, delighted by their complimentary words. "It has taken me a long time to get it exactly as I want it. My wife and daughter work wonders with the décor and furnishings ... not my area of expertise, I'll admit to that." He smiles and laughs. "And many years of hard work as well, as you can understand."

"The rewards outweigh the sacrifices." Brin smiles at Hartner after he speaks.

What is that? Some sort of motto for the people in control? Do they say that to each other at parties while they drink too much and discuss slaves dying?

"I've renovated over the years as well. Believe it or not, a long time ago, this used to be a private school." Hartner indicates towards the landing above him with excited gestures. "Upstairs has been converted for recreation and business needs. The broadcast room is up there, the gymnasium, my personal office, and the apartments for the children."

Broadcast room? He can transmit to the Community Zone screens from here? I let the idea swirl around inside my head, imagining my face on those screens. My face, more determined and stronger than any person has ever seen it, shouting the truth for all to see and hear.

"How long are your family in Japan for, Charles?" asks Violet. "Recreation or business?"

"A bit of both, my dear ... and they return in a fortnight."

Brin brushes by me and I feel his arm touch against mine. "You don't mind the solitude? I only ask because I've met many people who own large houses, such as yourself, yet they feel rather alone due to the size."

Hartner smiles. "Not at all, Brin, not at all! I have my

work, of course, which keeps me busy, and my various appointments in the Community Zone as well. I've never really given it much thought."

Did Brin and Violet ask those questions for my benefit? Are they gathering information from Hartner?

"We must have a quick tour before dinner. Even if it's just down here. I'll admit it, Charles, I love this house!"

Violet has changed in front of my eyes. She has become an excitable young woman, full of energy, throwing enthusiasm around. Brin warned me earlier of such actions, yet it is still strange to see them, and how easily she can alter her personality.

"Of course. We're due in the dining hall in twenty minutes. The staff have prepared an excellent dinner for us all," says Hartner.

"I can't wait," smiles Brin.

Hartner walks off to the left, taking the first hallway. I can't quite believe how wide it is - easily ten feet, minimum. There are black leather sofas, bookcases made of dark wood, and tall plants in large pots along the wall. They all face the bay windows which overlook the front of his land.

"This is one of my favourite places in the entire house. I often have a whiskey here in the evening."

"Oh, don't mention that word. No more whiskey, Charles. My head still hurts from last night!" laughs Brin. "I was in such a bad state this morning ... well, I think it was still the morning!" He pats Hartner on the shoulder in a friendly manner.

Hartner joins in with a sickening smile painted across his face once again. To him, this is a triumph in regards to his social standing. I can easily imagine how he will brag about it in the future, at *every* given opportunity.

"We did have rather a lot to drink, didn't we? I had to finish up some work first thing this morning, after you left. It didn't take long so I managed to get a few more hours of sleep

… and I've had plenty of coffee today too!" He laughs at his own words. "You just can't keep these people waiting, though. The Science Department are known for their strictness and impatience."

I was there, Hartner! I saw you finishing your work! I was there, with you, when you decided to let those girls live!

We all turn right at the end of the hallway, and, when Hartner isn't looking in my direction, I examine and study everything: the approximate number of steps from the foyer, how the windows are locked, if any guards are patrolling. I stay behind everybody else by a few yards to give myself the opportunity to raise my eyes away from the floor. *You don't want to acknowledge me, Hartner? I'll use your arrogance for my own needs!*

Brin stops by large wooden doors to his left. Hartner sees this and continues with his explanations, eager to impress. "Here we have the library. It runs all the way to the back of the house and takes up this whole side … thousands of books … I've collected many rare titles. The other side of the house contains the swimming pool, jacuzzi, sauna …"

"If I get a chance, I'll most certainly visit the library," remarks Brin.

He plays the part so well. I wonder how many times he's had to do this before? Maybe with his parents? Act like the obedient and understanding son?

Violet gains Hartner's attention with a touch on his arm. "We don't have a swimming pool next door. I have been meaning to install one for quite a while now. If you hear splashing in the middle of the night, Charles, you'll know that I've sneaked over!"

They turn right again, all laughing along with Violet. Even I manage a smile underneath the hood of the tunic because Violet's new persona is quite comical at times.

Hartner isn't suspicious, that much is obvious.

I map out the route in my head as we enter another

wide hallway - more red paint, less furniture. I see a couple of doors, paintings of family members, or enlarged photographs of Hartner with other people who wear suits and have an air of importance around them. *This runs parallel to the first hallway ... we'll be back in the foyer when we reach the end.*

"The dining room, communal study, and lounge are all at the centre of the building. When we eat, we will have a view across the fields towards the tree line. It is glorious at any time of the year." Hartner's smile boasts about his wealth and lavish property for all to see.

Brin nudges by me again, feigning interest in one of the paintings on the wall. "You live very close to your zone, Charles. The mine field is only beyond the trees. Does that work well for you? I've seen others who live further away, by request. They want to distance themselves from the illusion."

What? The mine field? It's close? The dangerous thoughts return and my hand slides down towards my pocket. I tap at the bottle of liquid anaesthetic and my knife, unsure how my furious mind is planning to use them. *I can't attack him here! No! No, the guards will find me ...*

"It works very well for me, Brin, yes. I don't have to travel far when duty demands that I am in the community. All of my official appearances can be carried out promptly as well, which keeps the reputation solid. They adore me in there, respect me completely."

"Yes, I see what you mean. Very interesting advice. I think I'll try for a position soon. I have to start my career somewhere, don't I? Perhaps Mayor Brin Dencourt will be a good first step?"

"Wise choice," says Hartner. "I'm sure that will make your parents proud. *Especially* your father."

I cringe under my hood as Hartner takes Brin's arm in a firm grip. The smile on his face is so repulsive to me.

"Any help, any questions, you contact me, Brin. I'll do everything that I can to assist you."

Is he lying? Does Brin really want to control a zone? I don't know what his real ambitions are ...

As I expected, we soon return to the foyer. I believe I have memorised the layout of a part of Hartner's house and tell myself it is both useful and required information.

I could be running through these hallways soon. Will I have armed guards chasing me once I decide on Hartner's fate?

"Shall we take a quick drink before we eat? The dining room is back this way," says Hartner as he points to the right.

"Excellent idea, Charles," says Violet. "I've heard stories about your wine cellar. They can't all be true, can they?"

Hartner revels in the attention that he is receiving. He takes Violet by the arm and begins escorting her back through the hallway. "My dear, *all* the stories are true! And there's still more to tell you! I have collected some of the finest wines this world can offer."

Brin walks behind his sister and Hartner, letting them chat to each other. He turns his head for a split second and smiles at me.

Still keeping me safe ... as he promised to.

••

The dining room runs for one-hundred feet in length, lavishly decorated with silvery velvet and silk material. It is draped across the tall window frames, along the walls, and down wooden beams that support the high ceiling. It is the most magical sight that I have ever witnessed in my life.

Remember, all this ... this house ... all that Hartner owns ... it is tainted ...

The table itself is easily thirty feet long, made of an expensive dark-red wood. Bowls of fruit, bread rolls, and assorted drinks run along it, plus vast arrangements of flowers as well. Three places are set near to one end and I have to restrain myself from becoming lost in the opulence. The wine glasses sparkle as if cut from diamonds, the cutlery could be pure gold, the tablecloth looks to be woven with strands of silver thread.

Slaves! I see a group of people dressed in grey: five male, five female. Their ages range from mid teens to early twenties. They all stand in a line, heads down, awaiting instruction. They are voiceless pawns on a chess table, awaiting the next move from their master.

Ever since I escaped the Tower, beauty has been ruined by the truth many times. This is yet another.

"Greet my guests!" calls Hartner, followed by two claps of his hands.

Now the powerful mayor shows himself. The man who controls others!

"You!" calls Brin.

Is he talking to me? He must have a reason ...

"Yes, sir," I say with politeness and respect in my voice. *Did I learn to behave like this in the Tower? I didn't need to force the words.*

"Wait just outside, by the doors. Return only if we summon you." Brin manages to flash a smile at me because Hartner is too preoccupied. He's watching his own slaves take care of Violet, wanting everything to be perfect for his important guests.

"Yes, sir." I turn and walk away. *He doesn't want me in here? Is he afraid I'll do something, or has he given me a chance to search the house?*

As I take up my new place by the dining room doors, I see that Brin and Violet are being shown to their seats by two young men. They both have wine poured out for them before the slaves retreat backwards by a few steps, staying close in case they are required for service again.

I know that Hartner will take the other seat, at the end of the table. *If I stay here, by the door, I can still see Violet and Brin ... but Hartner won't see me! Oh, Brin, you are clever ... I'll probably never tell you that to your face, but you really are!*

"I think a toast is in order, don't you both agree?" says Hartner as he moves to his own seat, satisfied that his slaves haven't ruined the occasion. He raises his glass. "To friends, to company, to the life we all live. May it continue in the manner that we are all accustomed to."

Brin sips his wine, as does Violet. Hartner is still revelling in the fact that he has members of the Dencourt family at his table.

I hear a door open to the left and look down the hall. A line of slaves walk out in single file. They are carrying plates and trays of food to the table, soon setting it down for Brin and Violet to admire. *I don't even recognise some of that food! And there's far too much for them all to eat!*

I remember the food rations that were delivered to my home every week, when I lived with my parents. Unpacking the boxes with my mother was a required household chore, yet also an enjoyable time. The elation we used to feel on seeing fresh fruit, or different coloured vegetables, seems trivial to me now. Hartner has prepared vast amounts of meat and fish, and one of the slaves places a large pot full of soup on the table.

"This looks marvellous, Charles. You're going to ruin my figure with all this delicious food!" jokes Violet.

Hartner snaps his fingers and the slaves walk away, back towards the door. I watch them file out to the hallway and walk back through the other door. *The kitchen? I need to search this house ... I need to ... it must be why Brin put me out here?*

"You. Come here!" orders Hartner. A young woman stops, puts down a bottle of wine and walks over to him.

"Yes, sir?" she asks.

"Go to the kitchen and fetch my whiskey. Brin, I won't force you, but have a glass if you want to!" He laughs, loudly.

The other slaves walk from their line at the side of the dining room to begin their serving duties.

Follow her ...

The young woman ignores me as she walks through the doors on her way to fetch the bottle of alcohol. She is in her early twenties, with light-brown hair and green eyes.

I catch Brin sneaking a look towards me as she disappears behind the kitchen door. I hear more laughter from Hartner, Brin and Violet.

I haven't seen a single guard since we arrived here, only those by the front door. Where are they all? Perhaps Hartner feels safe in here, with them all patrolling outside for him?

My hand reaches for my pocket and I tap the liquid anaesthetic bottle once again. *Hartner must enjoy drinking whiskey ... he will drink the whiskey ... Mayor Hartner will drink the whiskey!*

After a few steps along the hallway, I realise that my fingers have proceeded without my permission and grabbed the small bottle. They are rolling it and picking at the lid. *Hartner will drink the whiskey!*

The idea swirls about, screaming loudly inside my mind, as I step inside the kitchen. More slaves are present here, performing various duties: cooking, cleaning, and preparing the food. Not a single one of them speaks.

The young woman walks through to a small side room and I follow, unaware that I have entered a daze. My thoughts and movements are slow and disjointed. Every action is clouded by the vengeance that wants to claw its way through my skull and take control.

The window, Elana! Look out of the window! It's the

line of trees ... the trees that are close to ... the mine field! It would only take ten minutes to walk there ... or less ... not far away ... my home ...

I stop moving and lift the hood on my tunic, yet none of the kitchen slaves pay any attention to me or my behaviour. The thoughts suddenly snap together to form one piece of clarity ... one moment of decisiveness. I feel as if the last few minutes have been a daydream, with my body moving about automatically.

I join the young woman in the room. Cupboards run around the edges and bottles of alcohol are lined up on shelves.

"You. Stop!" I order, staring at the slave's glorious green eyes.

"Yes?" she says, softly. I see something in her expression ... it looks like physical pain.

Stay strong! I think, wanting to immediately apologise for my tone. "Give me that bottle of whiskey!"

The young woman holds it out in front of her without any resistance. It is as if she isn't looking at me at all, more through me. She is unable to see the person, just my attitude and the voice of control. *That expression reminds me so much of Carla.*

I swipe it out of her hand with unnecessary force. "Stay still. You can take this back to Mayor Hartner in a moment."

I unscrew the lid and set the whiskey on the floor. *Do it!* I grab the bottle from my pocket and hold it in my hand for a moment. *It will break his mind ... he'll be mine to control as soon as he drinks another glass! And then ... and then ... I'm sending him back to where all this began ... I'll order him to walk through the mine field!*

I empty all the lilac liquid - three-quarters of the original amount - straight down the neck of the whiskey bottle. I hadn't seen it with Brin's tea, or the soup, yet it dissolves within seconds and leaves no trace colour behind. My shaking hands screw the top back on as I stand up and take a deep breath. My revenge has finally been set in motion. It is impossible for me to pinpoint the time when I decided it, but it seems that I *am* the type of person who can carry out such actions on other people … *people like Hartner*.

I remember my own reflection in the mirror at Brin's and how the Elana staring back at me was almost unrecognisable. She … *I* … had been changed by others, moulded to fit their needs.

"Here, take it. Take it back to Mayor Hartner." I hold out the whiskey bottle. *You do realise that it might kill him?* I shake my head to ignore my own thoughts.

"NO!" booms a male voice from behind me. "Put that bottle down and take this one instead."

A guard? Defend yourself! I spin around and pull the knife out of my pocket at the same time, ready to strike back with the only weapon I have in my possession. I grip the handle with all my strength and thrust out my arm.

NO! That's not … not possible! It … it can't be! I know you … I know who you are!

"Elana?" asks the man. "Elana Mayne?" He steps back away from my knife, shocked, and his eyes open wide.

What … are you … you doing here? You're … you're Blake's father! You can't … can't be here. You're … dead!

Chapter seventeen

"Elana? Elana Mayne? I know you, don't I? Nicholas and Anne are your parents?"

John Wright … *Blake's father* … the man I believe to be dead, walks forward one step. His eyes switch between the knife and my stunned, horrified expression. "We used to live near each other in the estate housing. You remember that, don't you?"

I nod as the female slave leaves the room, carrying a new bottle of whiskey.

This … this can't be real! How can this be real? My hand refuses to let go of the weapon. I slowly look him up and down, fearful that panic and adrenaline have caused me to hallucinate. *Maybe I touched some of the liquid anaesthetic?*

My eyes focus on the intricate stitching of his dark-blue tunic, the tiny droplets of sweat on his forehead, the grey hairs that poke through the natural black on his head and in his stubble. *Can I imagine such details? If I am creating all this in my mind … would they look so vivid?*

"But … but why are you here, Elana? Why would they ever take you?" asks John. He is visibly upset, angry, and confused to see me.

What do I say to him? I don't know WHAT TO SAY!
My eyes fill with tears of shock and sadness.

"Put the knife down, Elana. I won't hurt you." John reaches out his hand but doesn't move any further forward. "Have you remembered? Have your memories returned, Elana? I've seen it happen with others, like yourself. The fear must be … be terrible."

I stare at John's leg. It's easy to see how it makes his body lean slightly to one side. I know now why the man with the limp seemed so familiar to me yesterday evening. *I don't understand! John, I don't understand how you can be alive!*

"Give me the knife, Elana. Please? I can try and help you."

My hand shakes as a growing tightness wraps across my back and chest, pounding at my lungs. I have tears running down my cheeks as I gulp in mouthfuls of air.

I … don't …

My fingers loosen … they let go … a whole part of me gives in and lets go of the pain and torment.

… understand …

The knife falls to the floor and I rush forward, embracing John with such force that he stumbles backwards.

"Oh, Elana! What have they done to you?"

Why did Hartner bring him here after the announcement about his death? I can't work it out! I can't see the truth here … I can't see it!

"Elana, you have to talk to me. I need you to take a deep breath and calm yourself down. I want to know how you got caught up in all this. What could you have done that warranted exile?"

He wouldn't know that I witnessed Blake's death … Blake's murder … he doesn't realise how his own story weaves along the same path as mine …

"Elana?" John grips my arms, gently pushing me backwards. He has a few tears in his eyes as well. "What did you do?"

I hold my breath and try to lower my heart's furious rate. It's so fast I can't even distinguish single beats any longer. The words are there, they want to come out, they want to be spoken and heard, but it won't happen. I feel as if an invisible hand is in the room with both of us, wrapping itself around my throat, squeezing tight.

"Let's start with something easy ... something we can work with," says John with a soft and understanding tone. "What do you remember? What is your last memory?" He opens a cupboard on the wall to the right of him and takes out a bottle of water.

Does he know about the Tower? Has he learnt the truth about the world since the explosion, as I have?

I open my mouth but nothing comes out. *What's the matter with me? TALK TO HIM! TALK TO HIM!*

John gives me the bottle of water and I swig down a few rushed mouthfuls. It is cold on my throat and refreshes me instantly.

"It will make you feel better, Elana, trust me. Take your time. Mayor Hartner is busy with a formal dinner, so we won't be disturbed."

I hand the bottle back as my legs bend without complete control. I fall awkwardly to the right and end up slumped sideways on the floor.

Stay in control ... focus on something ...

I'm worried that my voice will never return. My mind is about to disappear inside the shock that is creeping through my body like piercing shards of ice. My skin pulses yet feels numb at the same time. *Come on, keep it together! I wake up ... I go to college ... I study ...*

"I ... I ... saw ..."

John's eyes sparkle with joy. He is so relieved to hear me finally speak, worried I had been changed and broken beyond repair. He smiles and carefully sits himself down on the floor next to me.

"It's working. Keep going, Elana! Tell me, what did you see?"

I don't think of Blake, I think of Brin and Violet instead, sitting at the dinner table not far away. They are with my enemy ... our enemy. John and I both have reasons to see Hartner punished. *Snap out of it! Get up! GET UP!*

My hands push on the floor and I manage to stand up, however, it is a dangerous test of will and strength, both of which have left my body. It takes a lot of effort and my lungs beg for air once again. "I ... I need ... to get ... get back to the dining room. Brin ... he's ... he's waiting."

"Brin ... Dencourt?" asks John. "You're here with the dinner guests? They are the ones you serve now?"

"No! No, it isn't like that." My voice returns to me and I wonder if the need to defend Brin and Violet is the main reason. "They're not like the others ... not like Hartner! I wouldn't be alive today if it wasn't for them." I wipe my tears away on the sleeve of my tunic. "They ... saved me ... I trust them ..."

John's face changes on hearing the word. "Trust? It means nothing to anybody! The world is ... it's ..."

"I know what it's like! I've seen a lot ever since I escaped," I say, interrupting. An element of calm returns to me, yet it only lasts for a second.

"Escaped?"

I nod.

"That's why I'm here," mumbles John. "The main reason that Mayor Hartner keeps me here now."

"What do you mean?" I ask. The urge to feel my knife in my hand again fills me. I dart my eyes around the room, searching for another.

"I have to prove to him that I can be trusted." John stands up and stares across the room, caught in a memory. It lasts for a couple of seconds so I guess it is a powerful one, focused on his family.

"When did they take you, Elana? I don't remember hearing about it, so it must have been after the explosion at the steel plant?"

I do not reply. All I can think about is getting out of this room, getting to Brin and Violet. *I don't want to be here! I don't want to talk about it ... about Blake ...*

"Mayor Hartner told me he had to invent a cover story for the media to use. There had to be a plausible explanation for my absence after the explosion. As far as everyone else believes, I am in Europe because I need extensive physiotherapy on my leg. Do you remember any of that? Did your parents talk to you about it?"

What? That's ... that's not what everyone else believes! That's not what we were told!

I recall the moment when John's death had been announced. I was sitting on the Town Hall steps, scared, confused and ready to run. *NO! NO! Another lie?*

My body shakes and I have to consciously force my legs and hands to stop trembling. A crushing fear emerges for reasons that I can't explain. It is as if I am walking through a thick nightmare, hindered by a clinging fog. My mind knows danger, fear, and terror are close by, yet it cannot identify the source. *Why am I so afraid of John's words, his very attitude? What is it about all this that frightens me? It feels ... as if ... something is missing ...*

Fortunately, John doesn't notice my behaviour and continues. "Try to remember for me, Elana, please? I never had a chance to see my family before Mayor Hartner brought me here! I just want to know that they are all safe and well ... my wife, Blake, the girls ... I miss them all so much!"

Oh ... no ...

I realised why fear has taken me in its frozen embrace. The nightmare reveals its purpose, its meaning, its cruel conclusion. The missing piece to John's behaviour punches me in the stomach and my world dissolves. The primal need to survive and run returns. He is not talking or acting like a father who has recently lost a son. He still holds a hope inside that this ordeal will end one day. He honestly believes the life he knew before still exists for him.

Blake? He ... he doesn't know? What twisted game is Hartner playing here? Oh, how can I tell him the truth? How can I be the one to let him know what happened?

I move for the door as my stomach and muscles tense without mercy or remorse. I must escape again, unwilling and unable to tell John the truth. I've evaded many Community Guards with weapons since leaving the Tower, however, this fear is so much worse. I hold the key to John's personal prison ... *our* prison, and I fear what will happen once I open the door.

"I ... need ... need to get back. I'm ... I'm sorry ... I don't know anything!"

"What's the matter, Elana?" John's tone of voice and body language tell me all too clearly he senses something is wrong, *very* wrong. He knows I'm avoiding him and his questions. He moves in front of the door, raises his shoulders, widens his stance and blocks my exit.

"Please! Let me out!" I beg. "Please!"

"Elana! Talk to me!" John's voice is balancing on a line between anxiety and understanding. He wants to know my thoughts, wants to hear my words, yet fears them as well.

"NO! Get out of the way! Please!" I grab John and try to push his body but it is pointless. He is tall, muscular, and he doesn't move an inch despite my best efforts.

"Elana ... please? If you know something, you have to tell me! There are too many lies in the world, you know that now, just as I do ... please?"

What can I say? Should I lie to him? Should I keep the truth from John? NO! Never question yourself! He needs to know what happened! If you nurture these lies, you are as cruel as Hartner!

I step back, only noticing then how much I'm crying. "You … you're …"

"I'm what?" pushes John. His mind is running at a million miles per hour, creating thought after thought, waiting for my answer.

I wipe my eyes and try to take a deep breath. My lungs tighten and I choke. My attempt to regain control of my emotions fails and I sink to my knees. "Both you and Blake … you're … both dead! That's why they exiled me, because I saw the guards and Hartner …" *SAY IT! TELL HIM!* "… kill Blake!" I cry out.

John's normally kind eyes vanish behind an empty void, as if replaced by a dark, foreboding sky. His face drops and sets in an expressionless state, as if it will never move again, and the muscles on his neck bulge and twitch.

What have I done?

John bends down and picks up the knife. He looks at the reflection of his own eyes in the blade, seeing a passion and anger staring back.

John? What are you doing?

"I … I'm so … so sorry, John!" I say through gasped breaths. I've seen this before. I've seen a different person looking out of the mirror.

"Get out of here, Elana." John stares at the knife again, his face contorting with inner torture and decisions that need to be made. I can see them dancing behind his eyes.

Are his thoughts like mine? Has he chosen an enemy?

He eventually turns the weapon, holding it by the blade. "Take it. Be safe."

I grab the knife handle and feel a rush of security. John walks out of the room, back to the kitchen.

"John! John! What are you going to do? Where are you … you going?"

"All of you, out!" shouts John. He opens a door and

the slaves in the kitchen do not question his words. They file out to the land surrounding Hartner's house. "And you!" he adds, turning his gaze on me. He is a different person with fires burning across the darkness in his eyes. There are no more decisions. His purpose is now clear.

"I … I can't! I have to stay here … with Brin and Violet!"

John clenches his huge fists as he changes again in front of me … the final transformation brought on by utter grief now complete. He is a single minded beast with only rage and violence screaming inside his body and mind. The sacred bond between father and son has been violated and cut, ripped apart, mutilated.

What are you going to do? I need to warn Brin! I need to get back to the dining room!

John grabs cloths from out of the kitchen cupboards, cutlery and cardboard boxes as well. He stomps around the kitchen turning all the electric hobs, ovens, and micro-cookers on to their highest settings. All the food that has been prepared for the dinner ends up thrown to the floor with violent swipes of fury. Glasses and bottles are also smashed. His strength terrifies me. It's bordering on unnatural, beyond human.

Is he … going to burn everything? What do I do? I can't stop him!

John shoves tins of food and cutlery inside the micro-cookers, throws the cloths inside the ovens, and places boxes on top of the hobs. Smoke begins to drift from all the appliances and fill the kitchen. He grabs a bottle of liquid and pours it over some more cloths.

NO!

John cries out for the first time since I told him the truth about Blake, venting some of his pain, screaming with sorrow as he throws the liquid and cloths towards the ovens. A wave of roaring flame flies across the kitchen seconds later.

I dive to the floor to protect myself and hold my breath. I pull my body along the tiled floor, heading for the door the slaves used.

John leaves the kitchen through the ever thickening dark-grey smoke, heading back to the hallway. Back to Hartner.

I have to get to Brin! I can use the doors at the back of the dining room!

I imagine myself inside the house and search my recent memories, quickly gaining a sense of direction. "It has to be this way!"

I pull the hood of the tunic up, put the knife inside my pocket, and force my legs to walk instead of run.

The others! The slaves from the kitchen stand around me with no idea of the danger. "Get away from here! Walk away from the house, all of you! Move towards the fence." I cry in a commanding voice.

I hear a woman scream. It's coming from somewhere to my right. *Violet?*

I walk to the next corner of the house and poke my head around, seeing open doors running along the wall only twenty feet away. *That's the dining room!*

"Answer me, Hartner! Why did you kill my son?" John's voice bellows out of the house.

No! He's already in there!

I reach the doors and my eyes find Brin and Violet on their feet, standing away from the main table. *They're safe! Calm down, they're safe!*

I look to my left to see John with one of his strong hands around Hartner's throat. Plates, food, and smashed glass are scattered on the floor near to Hartner's seat at the table.

He's going to ... kill him!

"My son, Hartner! My son!" John spits his words

with a venom and purpose. He pushes Hartner back to the table and grabs an unopened bottle of wine. "You will *never* hurt anyone ... ever again! Nobody can have your power. Do you hear me?"

Don't watch, Elana! Don't watch more suffering ... more pain ... Hartner is about to die! Do you want to see it? Do you need to?

John lifts the bottle but stops as soon as he sees me by the doors. His lips twitch, as if I have the power to force a smile from deep inside his furious mind. His cold, determined eyes change back to normal, for less than a second, and he mouths only two words to me: *Thank you.*

"Elana!" shouts Violet from across the room. She beckons with her hand. "Over here!"

No ... I need to see this ...

John lets go of Hartner's neck and punches him in the face as he lifts the bottle. "For Blake," he says in a calm tone, as if peace has been found, right at the end, right before he takes revenge. Before he becomes the type of person who can.

Brin rushes around the table and grabs me. I push his body out of the way and keep my eyes fixed on the dinner table, staring at the merciless attack. Staring as my enemy is finally defeated.

John brings the bottle down with all his strength, cracking it on the side of Hartner's head. Violet rushes to me as well and puts an arm around my shoulder.

John swings the bottle with a backhand, hitting Hartner again, then another swift forehand. I can see blood dripping off of the bottle and running down John's hand. Hartner's face is covered in it as well.

This is my fault. I may not have used my knife on Hartner, but my words ... my truthful words ... John became my weapon.

John roars again as his hand raises for the final time.

He swings with every emotion inside his mind.

"STOP!" shouts a voice.

I watch as Community Guards run through the doors to the dining room, at least ten of them, all with their guns raised. Brin and Elana make sure they are shielding me.

Multiple shots ring out through the room and John's body writhes and jolts as he is hit with bullets. Spurts of blood cut through the front of his tunic. He looks like a puppet, dangling in mid-air, waiting for the strings to be pulled by his master.

I can see it, John. I can see your smile. You are free now, at peace.

His body falls to the ground a second later.

"Mr. Dencourt, are you hurt? Miss Dencourt?" calls a guard.

"We're okay! We're fine! Secure this room, the house … and get my sister and the girl out of here!" orders Brin. He manages to meet my eyes with a relieved stare before the guards surround me. They grab me by the arms and march with unwavering speed out of Hartner's house.

Chapter eighteen

I know that I am outside, safely away from Hartner and the horrendous scene at his house. The sun warms my face, the grass brushes against my plimsolls and ankles, although a blanket of darkness clouds around all of my senses.

I stop moving for a few seconds because the group of Community Guards make me do so. I hear metal creaking, a breeze rustling through leaves, birdsong.

A hand touches mine. *Violet? Is that you?*

I start walking again but my bloodshot eyes aren't paying attention to anything. I see blurs of dark and light, changing constantly, yet no details. I allow the strength of the hands gripping my arms to pull me along, to lead me to safety.

The warmth on my face disappears soon afterwards and the ground turns solid.

"Guards, return to Mayor Hartner's … to my brother. Get the staff inside the house for now. I'll be fine here."

"Yes, Miss Dencourt."

Where am I? I can't … can't feel anything. Where's Brin? Violet? Did I really see Mayor Hartner die? John as well?

Something, or someone, touches my hand again. It

sends a shock of sensation running across my skin, like a jolt of electricity. *I'm sitting down ... when did I sit down?*

"Elana? Come on, Elana ... it's me, it's Violet. Look at me ... look at my eyes ... try and concentrate on my voice."

Violet? Is she with me, watching over me, talking to me?

I replay Hartner's death in my mind and at my own pace. I see details that were initially missed during the chaos. They are memories, ones I have planted like seeds, ready to sprout at a different time. I can stare at John's unrecognisable face, twisting with pain and anguish. I can watch the tears on his cheeks fall as the sun reflects off of them. I can look at Hartner's eyes, so full of fear as blood spatters on the food and dining table ...

"He's ... he's dead? Hartner is ... gone?" I ask as the world returns around me in a swirling mixture of colours. The terracotta paint on the walls, the beige sofas, and the green leaves of the plants.

The first thing I see with focused eyes is Violet's face, pale with worry, covered in tears and stained make-up.

Violet lunges forward and squeezes impossibly tight. "Don't do that to me, Elana! Don't ever do that!"

"I'm ... sorry, Violet. I ..." I take a deep breath and exhale slowly because a stab of nausea cuts through me. "I don't remember getting here, back to the house, though ... what happened?"

Violet lets go. She strokes her hand down my face with one hand and wipes her own tears away with the other. New streaks of mascara and golden eye shadow line her face afterwards. "The guards brought us here, and they move fast when you tell them to. I knew something was wrong with you. It was your eyes ... they ... changed."

"Changed?" I ask.

"They were open, but you were just staring, nothing

else. It was as if all the life inside you had … disappeared. Don't ever do that to me again!" she repeats with some added fear and anger.

"I'm sorry, Violet. It's strange, though. The same thing happened to me a while ago, when I ran towards the perimeter mines around my Community Zone. I didn't realise what I had done until it was too late."

I reciprocate the caring gesture and take Violet in another embrace. "What about you? How do you feel?"

Violet sighs. "I'll be fine. We're safe now … but …"

"What?" I move backwards. I want to see Violet's eyes.

"For a moment there, back in Hartner's dining room, I wondered what would happen! That man … I've never seen anybody so … so …"

"So angry?" *Did that anger free me? Did John's rage put an end to my own torment?*

"No, it wasn't anger. It was so much more than that. He'd focused every ounce of pain, loathing, hatred … all that he could find inside or create, and directed it at Hartner. It frightened me so much." Violet clenches her hands to try and stop them from trembling.

I am about to speak when an aroma drifts close by and catches my attention: sweet and fresh with a hint of citrus. *I recognise that … is it the flowers from outside, maybe? I can't remember …*

"Brin!" cries Violet. Her eyes raise to a point above and behind me. The sight of her brother banishes an unspoken and crippling worry from inside.

I spin my head around just as Brin's hands reach out for Violet's and mine. He holds us both with the perfect grip - caring yet forceful, protective yet commanding.

"Hartner is dead. Do you understand? You realise what just happened?" asks Brin. His eyes are pieces of shining glass, hypnotising me so I can't move.

"Yes, I understand. I know he's dead … it's … it's over." I don't feel any relief after the words are spoken and it scares me. I'm telling myself, expecting myself, to feel different. I want the experience of … freedom … freedom from the power which has held me for so long.

"And the man … he mentioned the name Blake?" asks Brin. "Your friend?"

"Yes. That was his father, the one I told you about before. I don't know why, but Hartner took him after the explosion. He's been working over there ever since, believing he would be returned home."

"But … his death was announced to the community, right?" checks Brin. "There wasn't any chance of him leaving. Not ever."

I nod and keep my head low with sadness. "It was all a … sick joke!"

"I can't believe any of this!" screams Violet. "No wonder that poor man attacked Hartner."

"Listen to me, both of you, carefully. There are things I need to do, and I need to do them right away," says Brin as he lets go of our hands, crosses his arms and starts his thoughts dancing for a moment.

Violet and I can't take our eyes away from his. We see him as the answer to all our problems. He will make a calculated decision and soothe all the pain away.

"I'll be with you both as soon as I can. Violet, take Elana to the kitchen. I need to use the screen for an urgent communication."

Communication? I suppose Brin has to try and sort this mess out now? How will he explain it?

Violet holds out her hand. "Do me a favour?" she asks.

"Of course," I say. "Anything."

"Stay with me? I don't want to be alone."

I stand up with a confused smile. I'm still having

273

trouble understanding how I can ever provide any help or support to Brin and Violet. Despite their upbringing, despite everything they have seen, the event at Hartner's house has still shocked them both. Knowing the truth about the world hasn't prepared them for all they will experience with their own eyes. There are still fears they have to confront.

"Who do you need to contact?" asks Violet. "I'm not as knowledgeable as you are when it comes to political protocol. What are we supposed to do in a situation like this?"

Brin turns the screen on and stands directly in front of it, clenching his jaw. A small square in the corner displays his face a few seconds later, indicating the built in video camera is ready to record and transmit. "I'm not following the rules today, Violet."

Violet lowers her eyebrows, questioning Brin's comment. "What does that mean?"

I find a smile inside me, caused by Brin checking his appearance on the screen. He runs a finger across his eyebrows and makes sure that his hair looks smart.

"I'm calling our father. Stay in the kitchen and keep quiet." His eyes flick to me. "Especially you. Not a sound."

"Father? Why?" asks Violet. Her hand squeezes mine a little tighter at the mention of him.

They have a fear of their own father. It must be terrible to live with that feeling inside you. I think of my own parents and a warmth pulses through me.

"I'll explain soon." Brin touches the screen and a menu appears. He scrolls through with swipes of his finger, finding the communication link. A numerical keypad appears and he taps in a set of numbers.

Violet steers me to a chair at the kitchen table. It is a deliberate manoeuvre that ensures the camera can't catch a glimpse of me in the house. She puts a finger on her lips, to warn me once again that complete silence is important, as she kicks off her heeled shoes. "Bloody things are hurting my feet!"

I listen carefully while Violet walks away and starts to make hot drinks for all of us. *What will their father say? How will he react to Hartner's death ... Hartner's murder at the hands of a slave?*

"Brin? This is unexpected," says a powerful male voice.

Marcus Dencourt!

"Hello, Father. How is your visit to the United States?" asks Brin.

I want to see this! I want to watch this conversation! I force myself to stay seated, despite the urge to move.

"Here you go, drink this," whispers Violet. Her eyes keep flicking towards Brin but she doesn't seem eager to enter the lounge. "I wish I knew what he was doing."

"Work is work, Brin," replies Marcus. "Now, why have you contacted me?"

His voice is transmitting through the speakers on the side of the screen, yet it feels as if he has taken control of the room with a demanding presence.

"I'm currently at our property near to the Essex Community Safe Zone," explains Brin. "I'm afraid there has been an incident ... with Charles Hartner, the mayor."

"Hartner? What's that awful drunk gone and done this time?" jokes Marcus.

"It's serious, Father." Brin pauses, readying himself for the announcement. His jaw clenches a few more times. "He's dead."

The entire room falls silent. I try to imagine Marcus' facial expression.

"How did it happen?"

"Murdered, Father. I haven't pulled up every file yet, so I can't give you all the details, but one of his staff attacked him while Violet and I were having dinner."

"You were there?" asks Marcus. "You're both safe?"

He sounds ... worried, like any father would. Perhaps I can't judge him on their stories alone? Perhaps I'll have to see him in person to make my own mind up?

"We're both safe, Father. Shocked, but safe," answers Brin.

"Thank goodness!"

Violet smiles and looks at me with emotional eyes. "He has his moments," she whispers.

Brin continues his explanation, trying to stop his teeth grinding. "From what I've read in the files, though, it does seem that Mayor Hartner had his own agenda here. In my opinion, Father, it looks like a power game. One that has, unfortunately, horribly backfired."

Again a silence falls. Violet sips her tea, as do I.

"Send me a full report as soon as you can. And when I say soon, I mean an hour ago, do you understand me, Brin? Don't waste a second here."

"I understand."

"What a mess! I'll have to contact Central Government and rearrange new leadership as well. His family, do you know where they are?"

"In Japan, Father. They aren't due to return for a fortnight."

"I'll speak to them right away. No point dragging out or delaying these matters."

"Erm ... Father ... I ... erm ..." Brin speaks in pauses and his voice has quietened.

He sounds nervous, but why?

Violet moves her head slightly, so that she can see Brin. Something obviously worries her because her face and eyes change to show a growing anxiety.

"Spit it out, Brin! Hesitation means you're not sure about something. Be sure, be certain, or don't bother! I've told you that a million times before!" The words are so sharp, so direct.

I can't see Marcus ... he isn't even in the same country ... but he terrifies me!

"I'm sorry, Father." Brin pauses for breath and finds his courage. "Don't contact Central Government. I'll take the position."

"What?" asks Marcus. "What did you say?"

Brin wants to ... be the mayor?

I touch Violet's arm and receive a shrug of the shoulders and a shake of her head in reply.

"I'm serious, Father. Let me take leadership of Hartner's zone. I'm here, Violet is with me should I need her advice, and I assure you that the transition will run smoothly."

Marcus does not reply. I imagine him on the screen, staring at Brin to see if he will back down or change his mind.

"I can do it, Father, I can. You can count on me."

I look at Violet again. Her face has a shocked expression across it which won't falter. *So, this is a surprise to both of us?*

"I can't believe this!" whispers Violet. "Why?"

My eyes open wider as I display my own surprise. "I can't either."

"Listen to me, Brin."

"Yes, Father."

"Don't mess this up! DO NOT MESS THIS UP! I'll be back in a month and I will drive straight there to check on your progress. Understand?"

He spoke with Hartner about this before the dinner. Perhaps it was all true?

"I understand."

"Send the files over. I'll contact Hartner's family."

"Thank you, Father."

"Make me proud, Brin."

"I will."

Another silence covers everything and everyone.

Marcus has managed to remove any sound from the room ... the entire house.

"He's gone. You two can stop hiding now," says Brin. He walks through to the kitchen area and pours out a tea. "That was so much fun. Remind me to do it again sometime. Like, never." His sarcasm hits a peak.

"What was all that about?" asks Violet. She is on the verge of shouting at her brother.

"What?"

"Mayor? Since when have you wanted to do anything like that?"

I decide to stay quiet, not wanting to involve myself in a family argument. *He never mentioned it to me. Maybe this has been part of his plan all along? I've had my secrets, has Brin had them too?*

Brin sits down and glances at Violet. "I've never wanted to do anything like this, you know that. But, it's done now. We have a community to run, and we have a place to hide you, Elana."

"Me?"

"Oh, I get it now!" interrupts Violet. "The long game." Her face brightens. "Elana, do not play my brother at chess ... ever! He's beaten you before the first pawn has been moved, trust me on that!"

What? I don't get it ... I don't understand!

"Can one of you explain this to me, please? I'm lost! I have no idea what you two are talking about!"

Brin smiles and some of my frustration and fear melts away. "Running from one house to the next is no way to live. Now, you'll have a place to call, well, home. I can hide you in Hartner's house much more easily, and there are others there as well ... slaves ... you can blend in, walk about as you please. The Community Guards will never bother you. It isn't perfect, but ... it's a new beginning. Call it whatever you wish. The next part of your life. Understand?"

My body shudders. It isn't caused by the thought of my new life, it is because he sounds too much like his father. "I do … I think."

Violet and Brin both smile.

My new life … my new sense of … of freedom? Protected by Brin and Violet …

A tear, created through a mixture of joy and fear, falls gently down my cheek.

Chapter nineteen

I stare out of the passenger seat window of Brin's car, admiring the trees and wild flowers as they all bathe in the summer sun.

It's over, Hartner is dead ... but ... I still don't feel as I hoped I would. Do I need to try and change my own thoughts? Do I need to change the way I see my life? Or has Hartner's grip been replaced by that of another ... the system itself?

"Not far to go," says Brin. He is now, officially, Mayor Dencourt, yet he isn't wearing a suit. Today, out of the Community Zone, he decided that his familiar clothes were a better choice: black boots, trousers, and a navy-blue top.

"Are you okay, Elana?" asks Violet, sitting in the back of the car. She's wearing a light-blue dress and sandals. "We can stop and turn back if you want to?"

"I'm fine, honestly. This is ... it's something I have to do. I can't explain why," I say. I don't look at Brin or Violet, wanting to avoid their eyes.

It has been two days since Hartner's death. I've spent all of my time at the Dencourt house while Hartner's possessions are removed from the larger property. An entire life, the belongings of an entire family, all loaded inside of trucks and taken away.

I wonder how Hartner's wife and children are? I knew him as a monster, but ... how did they see him? Did they know and accept the truth of the world?

"Elana, can you check the map, please? I know it's here somewhere, but we can't get too close because of the mines," says Brin.

Violet hands the laptop through from the back seat. I open it and check the screen, seeing a small blue pyramid - Brin's car - on a three-dimensional map. Graphics of dark green surround it: the large area of grass and trees we are currently driving through.

"The perimeter mines are five-hundred yards ahead. Hang on, let me zoom in on the zone," I say and tap a key. "I want to get this as close as possible."

"I'll get the binoculars ready. You'll need them," says Violet.

I see the compass move on the laptop's screen, indicating that we are heading in a north-easterly direction. Brin slows the car down to a speed of only a few miles per hour. My finger starts to trace a line on the screen from the Town Hall building to the blue triangle.

Is this it? Are we here?

"Ready?" asks Brin as he stops the car. He touches my hand and smiles. "You might have trouble explaining this to yourself, but I can see why it is important to you. After Hannah died, I used to sit alone in the dining room for hours."

"You're both coming with me, right?" I ask.

"Of course we are," says Violet.

"Try and stop me. I'm the mayor now, remember? I'm important and I demand respect. And don't forget I'm important!"

I burst out laughing, as does Violet. Brin frowns at our behaviour.

We all step out of the car and walk a little closer to

the minefield. It is marked with metre high steel posts, placed one-hundred feet apart.

I stop before the others and spin around in a full circle. My eyes follow a line in the distance: one of the raised train tracks, heading in the opposite direction, ensuring none of the houses are seen. Then, the one thing I came here to see, directly ahead. The one thing that I need to see.

Home ...

"We can't get any closer, Elana," says Violet. "This is our limit, unless we all want to get blown to pieces by the minefield. Which I don't."

I look across the flat ground, trying to pinpoint where the grass stops and the dirt and gravel begin.

Home ... this is where I ran ... across the gravel over there. The guards took me, drugged me. It all started right here.

I hold out my hand and Violet gives me a pair of binoculars. "Thank you," I say and put them up to my eyes.

Due to the digital zoom and enhancements, I'm able to see for a substantial distance. "I think there are a couple of guards ... yes, they're patrolling." I readjust the zoom to its highest setting. "... and there's the street ... the street I ran down ..."

"The street that I have cleared of any residents today, so that we aren't seen," adds Brin. "I must be *really* important. Did I already mention that?"

Stop it, Brin!" moans Violet as she smacks his arm.

The streets that I have walked along all my life. The streets that carry all my memories ... my parents ... my friends ... Jackson! I haven't thought of you as much as I should have. Where are you now?

Violet puts her arm around me. "It's in the past. Always tell yourself that."

"I try, I really do ... but ..."

"Yes, Elana?" asks Violet.

"What do I do now?"

Brin joins in the conversation. "You know the answer to that, Elana. You're going to be living with us. The larger house will be furnished within days, and I've studied the architectural plans, so has Violet. There are rooms that we can conceal, or mark as private. You will be safe."

"And after that?"

"After?"

"Brin, you have given me freedom, but what about everything else? My parents? I can't just forget them! And what do I do now that I have seen the truth? Do I accept it and walk around your house and land, satisfied with my new life? I don't mean to sound rude or ungrateful, but ... oh, am I making any sense at all?"

Brin nods. "Of course you're making sense, Elana. It's just ... I don't have any of the answers, that's the problem. Violet, any other suggestions?"

"No, sorry ... I don't know what to say. I promised you that I'd sit with you, though, when you are ready to find out where your mother and father were relocated to. That offer still stands."

Brin's eyebrows lower. "When did you two talk about that?"

"Mind your own business," says Violet with a smile. "Elana and myself are *always* chatting to each other ... mostly about you, actually."

Brin blushes and decides not to carry on with his questions.

I look through the binoculars again. "Don't worry, I won't do anything stupid. It's going ... going to take some time for me to adjust, though. I have too many unanswered questions and they won't stop."

Brin puts his hand on my shoulder. "Questions?"

"Well, for example, the woman who slipped that note inside my tunic could be walking around in the zone right now. Others like her could be all over the world. Wouldn't you like to find out who she is? I know I would!"

Brin smiles in agreement. "Holding the mayoral seat will help a lot. If I do start to investigate residents, it won't raise questions."

"We all need time to adjust, Elana," says Violet, "and, fortunately, we now have that luxury ahead of us."

"We'll do it together," adds Brin. "Now that we aren't running or hiding, you can try to find some of the answers to these questions."

I lower the binoculars. I've returned to one of the places that holds a strong significance for me. It grants a feeling of inner calm, although I can't explain why. "Thank you, both of you."

We all return to the car. *For now, I must live the life I have been given. It isn't all that I want, it never will be ... but I must try. Hartner's death didn't take away all the pain. I don't know what can do that for me, not yet.*

"Double cheeseburgers for dinner tonight, Elana, as promised," says Brin. He starts the car and drives slowly back in the direction of the trees.

I smile, yet it is forced, only half genuine. "I can't wait!" I say without complete conviction or enthusiasm.

I will find my way back to you ... I will find my way back ... I promise ...

THE END

My long journey to sincerity

Elana Mayne

Another message from the author.

Hi. I hope you enjoyed Elana's journey :) There will be more books, you'll (hopefully) be pleased to hear. Now I have altered this title, so it is being told from Elana's point of view, I can open up her world and expand on the characters. I believe a story such as this should focus on all the emotions, feelings, and actions. The reader needs to be there, as they happen.
The original book: The Long Journey to Sincerity; 9781906529529, will stay in publication.

I have included a preview of a new title - Female: 918, on the following pages. It is one of my current works in progress, so I am aiming for a release date in the latter part of 2016.

Thanks for reading :)

Female: 918

Exist. Survive. Live.

Jason Ellis

Female: 918

By
Jason Ellis.

Exist.
Survive.
Live.

Female: 918

Published by;
Jason Ellis/ JTT Publishing.

Front cover by Sharon Stone. Copyright © 2016 Sharon
Stone.
https://www.facebook.com/SharonStoneArtpage

ISBN 13: 978-1-906529-91-8

JTT Publishing books may be ordered through all internet
booksellers, or through your local book retailer.

Printed in the United Kingdom.

<u>Prologue</u>

Complete darkness surrounds my body. This is a place where light is forbidden, even unwilling and scared, to enter.

Every attempt I make at movement feels constricted, like I am swimming, or trying to, through thick, black oil. Every breath I draw in has a flavour. The air is laced with a corrosive mix of heat and fear ... an intimate fear, one I can instantly recognise.

Am I alone here? I think. I wait for an answer from my own mind.

I can feel another. I can sense another soul swimming with me. They are different. Yes, they can move through the oil with ease. Their soul is somehow connected to this place, as if the same heart beats for them both.

Who are you? Where are you? For whatever reason, I don't have an audible voice here. My words have been stolen by the darkness, swallowed back up as quickly as they are produced.

The odour of salt and sweat swims side by side with the oil. If I let it in, if I let it pour down to my lungs, I know it will scrape at them from the inside and invade my body.

"Take aim!" A female voice, acidic and dominant, slices through the murky depths. The thick oil is split by the words, as if they are a sharp sword.

That voice ... no ... you can't be here with me, that is impossible! You can't hurt me ... I am not afraid ...

"... And ..." A deliberate pause follows. It *always*

follows. The feeling of power and the exhilaration it offers has to be extended and savoured. The moment between life and death is one of ultimate and infinite possibilities: a millisecond in time, a lifetime of memory, a wide universe or a grain of sand - they all exist there, waiting for their chance to stand at the forefront, waiting to be chosen as the final thought.

This place is changing. Somehow, I am now able to see through the pungent gloom that clings to my skin. In front of me there are … *NO!*

How am I able see them? I do not understand this place! I wish for the darkness again because I am confronted with a line of grey and terrified faces. A mixture of eleven people in total: male and female, teenagers through to the elderly. They all close their eyes as blindfolds - grey rags ripped up in strips - float through the air and wrap over them.

"… FIRE!"

••

"NO!" I cry as I sit up in my bed, woken with hateful precision by the nightmare. *I can still taste it! I can taste the oil … the salt and the sweat!*

My stomach and lower back muscles clench with sharp pulses, as if I have been punched while asleep. I lift my maroon nightshirt a few inches, with care, and massage across the painful areas.

The early morning sunrise layers through the horizontal slats on the window-blinds and I can see my bedroom glowing. I feel and experience the calm familiarity of my life around me: my clothes are on the floor, as are my black boots, and the furniture is where it has always been. *Do you see that blue top? That pair of jeans? You wore those yesterday … you took them off last night … when you were safe. You are still safe. You are.*

I'm slowly brought back to the present moment, out

2

of that place, that darkness, away from that ultimate and intoxicating power.

"Just a dream. Just a stupid dream, nothing else," I say in a quiet voice, glad that my words have returned with me from the nightmare.

My eyes, dark-brown, focus on my arm as I watch a bead of sweat trickle down the golden skin for a few seconds. It is the result, the end product, of an exotic mixture of harvested DNA. Apparently, so I have been told over the years, it creates my alluring, Asian elegance.

As I sit, I lose myself completely to the refracted and reflected spectrum inside the miniature drop of liquid. It is so full of colour, so bright. I need it, this timeless contrast. I need the light to defeat the darkness.

Loud footsteps thump along the hallway outside of my bedroom. "Aunt Rain!" Daisy Coast, my seventeen year old adopted niece, cries out as she flings open the bedroom door. Her blue nightshirt runs a few inches lower on the left shoulder and her blonde hair has obviously been on a pillow very recently - probably less than a minute ago - hence its unkempt style.

Daisy's hazel eyes widen with love and concern as she runs across the room. "Are you okay? I heard you scream! What happened?" She jumps up on the bed and takes my hands in her own.

I force a smile and open my eyes fully. "I'm fine, Daisy ... I just need a second to get my head together, that's all," I answer.

"I hate it when you have these dreams."

"Me too." I nod as I free one of my hands from Daisy's tight grip. I run my fingers through my own hair; long, straight and deep black, like a night sky void of any stars.

"It's been a few months since the last one, at least," Daisy reminds me, attempting to bring a positive to the moment. "They're still less frequent, aren't they? It isn't like years ago, when we were younger."

I decline to answer as I sit back on the bed and bring my knees up closer to my chest. Daisy follows, resting on my shoulder.

"I'm sorry that I woke you up, Daisy. What time is it anyway?" I ask.

Daisy turns her head to the right. The projected readout - a flickering and translucent turquoise light - from my mobile communicator hovers in the space above the bedside cabinet. "Ten minutes to six. It's not far off the alarm … so stop worrying. I've told you a million times before that I don't like it when you apologise. You never need to apologise to me, Aunt Rain."

We sit in complete silence for a few minutes, allowing the day to begin. The lack of words do not bring forth a problem, though, for we have a bond, we are two pieces of a whole. Years of peace, trust and calm silences have passed between us already.

The alarm - with a gentle crescendo - plays birdsong. "Right, six o'clock. Time to get up and check the perimeter," I say.

Daisy nods and sits up first. "I'll go and get dressed," she says as her legs spin around off of the edge of the bed.

As I move, a noise, one so quiet that I question my own sense of hearing, hums from my left forearm. I look down and rub at the skin.

"Is something wrong?" asks Daisy as she swipes her hand over a sensor on the wall. The blinds rise up, stacking themselves neatly at the top of the window with automated movement.

The room floods with more sunlight and growing warmth, pouring in like a waterfall. I move my eyes around for the second time, still taunted by the nightmare. My furniture, inanimate, sparse and boring, helps to ground the troubling thoughts. A wardrobe along the left wall, a dresser opposite the bed, two bedside cabinets and the burgundy carpet that feels soft under my feet - I can use these everyday objects as anchors. I can mentally grab them and hold on, or pull myself back to reality.

"Aunt Rain? Is something the matter?" repeats Daisy. Her voice wavers ever so slightly with the growing concern.

I shake my head. "Sometimes it hurts … my arm … even after all these years. Don't worry yourself. Go and get dressed … and …"

"Yes?"

I turn myself around so that my eyes lock with Daisy's. "Stay with me this morning. We'll walk the fence together," I say, unashamed by the words. I don't want to split up when carrying out the security checks, as we normally do. I want her by my side. I want her there in case the black oil returns for another attempt to smother me.

Daisy nods. "Of course." She leaves my bedroom as a smile tries with bravery to form on her lips.

I run my forefinger along my left arm, from the wrist to the elbow. It feels like bone under the skin, even though it is actually a prosthetic creation of metal and wires. I stop at a specific point and push with a little more force. There is a slight dent under my finger, a line of about an inch-and-a-half. *You can't hurt me any more. Never again,* I think and the darkness clouds across my eyes for another second.

••

Outside our home, both Daisy and I admire the early August morning. Again, we are silent. We don't always need words to communicate with each other.

It doesn't matter to either of us that, in truth, the house isn't anything more elaborate than a two-storey brick cube in the middle of a field. The building and land have always been our very own part of the world since shortly after Daisy's birth - a few thousand square feet to live in, at peace, in safety.

The ground slopes with a slight gradient towards the front fence, then, at a much steeper angle, it drops towards the Thames Estuary. This allows us both to view the beach, the sea and the half-mile wide road and train network that leads out across the water. Somewhere in the distance stands a vast floating city, one of the entrance points to this area, known as Aegis.

"Aunt Rain, are you ready?" asks Daisy. She stands outside the front door of our house with a handgun holstered to the waist of her black trousers. She is also wearing brown boots and a maroon sweater that looks to be tight-fitting.

"Almost," I say and check my right boot. A knife sits inside a leather sheath attached to the side. "Yeah, I'm ready. We'll start by the lake and work our way around. Anticlockwise today. Never get set in a routine, Daisy, always remember that. You never kn ..."

Daisy jumps in and finishes the sentence for me. "Know if you are being watched. Routines give them a chance to learn, or discover, a weakness."

I swing an automatic rifle over my shoulder, roll up the sleeves of my beige top and check the back pocket of my jeans, feeling the mobile communicator inside. "Good girl. Shame you don't listen to me with that kind of enthusiasm when I ask you to clean up your bedroom," I say with a dry tone.

Daisy rolls her eyes and smiles as she starts to walk across the short grass towards the perimeter fence. Even though she can't see my face, she knows it carries exactly the same expression.

Daisy and I arrive by the lake a few minutes later. It is an imperfect circle with an approximate diameter of three-hundred feet. I do swim here, just ... not very often. It's too painful ... emotionally painful.

Although we are there for more important reasons, we both stand for a few moments, mesmerised by the tiny flecks of morning sunlight catching the surface of the water.

They dance from place to place and glide across the ripples.

Daisy walks away and checks the fence. "Green lights here, Aunt Rain."

"Same here." I nod my head after doing the same.

The border of our property is completely surrounded with electrified movement detectors - poles of steel alloy that stand eight feet high. They are all fitted with an array of sensors running from ground level.

I wait for Daisy to walk the ten or so strides between the poles and join me. "I'm sure I just saw a few fish by the surface. I should really get down here more often," I say.

Daisy takes my hand in a gentle grip. "I'd love that," she says. "It's one of my favourite places to sit and read, draw … listen to music. I'm meeting with Sky and Jay down here later this morning."

My memory sparks, in a positive manner, as Daisy mentions the names of her friends. I travel back in time for a moment and see their parents standing beside me. "You're lucky, as I was at your age, to have such close friends," I say as some of the events from my past flow through me. "Sky has learnt a lot from her mother … so courageous and intelligent." The past continues through my mind. It stops at Jay's father, *River,* and an unexpected kiss. I roll my eyes and smile widely. "Keep your eye on Jay. He's a handsome young man … and *too much* like his father at that age!"

Daisy laughs. "I've heard these stories before … and you always stop at the good parts!" she says, willing me on to add more details.

Despite the jovial conversation, my serious attitude returns without warning. It's always with me, I can never escape from it. "I know it's an amazing place, Daisy. It's … difficult, that's all. You see beauty, I see something … something very different."

Another memory sparks which does not cause a smile. Instead, it causes my heart to thump hard in my chest and my stomach to tighten. "And … you know why," I say as

7

my eyes scan across the water.

Daisy looks across the small lake, as I do, back towards the house. I can read her face. I know she is trying to imagine the scenes that I have described to her over the years. How can she, though? How can she imagine them? Bombs exploding all around me, bodies scattered on the floor ... blood and screams everywhere. At least twenty died in the crater that would become this lake. I remember that morning. It's burnt inside my eyes for the rest of my life. An impulsive memorial, built and reinforced by hundreds of hands in a matter of hours. I have every right to see a different side to it because my tears flow in this lake, my sorrow swims unseen through the water.

"Let's keep moving." I walk off, sober in thought, heading up the slope to the back of the property.

Almost ten minutes later, we reach the second corner and check the sensors. Each step forward, each reassurance of safety eases my fears. I know they aren't warranted after so many years, I do. I can't escape my past, though, and I know that. It has moulded my present self and become a part of me ... a part of my personality, my inner self.

"Are you going in this morning?" asks Daisy.

My shoulders are low, my muscles tense up and I take slower steps near this part of the field. I don't need to answer my niece's question with words. My body language speaks instead and only years of practise and control manage to stop me from screaming out a reply.

A section of the grass here has been clearly marked with a line of stones, just three or four high - the most basic of walls. It doesn't fit with the whole scene, though, and looks out of place, even out of time. Rustic and hand-crafted skills sit next to the present day technology of the motion sensors. I want it to stand out. I want it to be different.

"Maybe later." I mumble my answer.

Two rusted platforms - large discs that moved and spun around at one point in my past - mark the entrance.

Time has covered them in grass and sprinkled tiny wild flowers all over, like natural guardians, rising to protect those lain for years behind them.

I flick a glance at the larger stones inside, some with flowers near to them; bellflower, fuchsia, dahlia. A wild and random blend of colours and aromas. There are words - some unusual - scratched and painted on the stones; Ocean, Leaf, Blossom … Loudmouth, Gappy, Tick-Tock. I remember every letter. Some are by my hand, some by others.

I pause as my eyes force another look. I have no choice but to submit and give myself permission to smile, despite the mental pain. I can't deny or smother the memories.

Daisy is watching me as I stand by the cemetery. I can feel her eyes on me, wishing me to feel anything except sadness. She will wait until this moment has passed, with silence and respect. It is now a routine for her, as this is for me, one that she has learnt during her upbringing. I'm proud of her, I hope she knows that. So very proud.

I brush my hand through the grass on one of the rusted platforms and the edges of my lips twitch. I can hear them crying out from the past. I can hear the gun turrets that lived here. They screamed in such a unique way, such a stuttered and violent voice as the bullets flew out. My eyes are hazy, glistening with the promise of a tear. *You lost. I planted many of these flowers … I carried the stones … as did my friends. I told you there could be a different world, a different way of life! I see these flowers grow throughout the year … smothering the skeletons of these weapons with their … their power to live and survive! These … these machines of death. They will never harm again …*

Wait! What's that? I hear a noise. I hear a soft noise that shouldn't be near me. With a sudden skill, one that I have mastered through necessity, my feet and hips move and shift to a firm stance. I lock my body in position. I am a stone statue. I am immovable. *Listen. Ignore all that should be here. Focus only on that which does not belong.*

The automatic rifle arcs off of my shoulder, like a part of my body, my wing preparing for flight. I hear it cut the air and the strap rubs over my shoulder. It feels perfect … as it should. My hands raise and the rifle lands in my tight grasp.

My eyes dance left and right. I point the barrel just beyond the perimeter fence and peer through the scope. *Listen* … I push my finger on the trigger in preparation to fire as my nostrils flare and I control my heart rate and breathing.

Out of the corner of my eye, I can see that Daisy has raised her own weapon. Another reason that I am so proud of her. I know what it feels like to be protected by friends, by those you love and trust, and I know the responsibility of being the protector, too. It weighs on your shoulders like a boulder that you *want* to carry, that you are honoured to carry.

Daisy has never questioned my advice or training through the years. She mimics my posture, as she has been trained to do, and aims at the exact same location.

"It's okay, Daisy. It's a deer, that's all. Let's finish up and head back home," I say and allow my muscles to relax. I keep the rifle in my hands for a few more seconds - not unusual in situations like this. I'll fully relax when my senses calm themselves.

"I don't see it, Aunt Rain. Are you sure?" asks Daisy. The grass beyond the perimeter - the back of the property that belongs to Sky and her family - grows much taller, making it difficult for her to see anything.

"It's there, trust me." I walk away from the cemetery as I speak.

"Where?" Daisy holsters her gun just as the head of a deer bobs up from the grass. She smiles and continues her morning duties.

••

I decide to sit outside the house with a hot drink after my breakfast and an envigorating shower. I will sip my tea, watch birds fly by and listen to their amazing sounds. They soothe me - one of the reasons that I wake up to birdsong from my alarm. For many years, too many, I sometimes woke to other sounds: screams, gunfire ... explosions.

There is a patch of the field now covered in flowers, right outside the house. Daisy and I designed it, cultivated the soil and planted the various seeds. It provides the ideal location for such a morning as this. The amazing colours: green, red, purple, and yellow - in varying tones - bring the area to life somehow, they give it a voice and a presence.

"I'll stay with you today, Aunt Rain, if you want me to?" offers Daisy as she walks out of the house carrying a canvas bag and a sketchbook. She has changed her clothes after the morning security checks and now wears a long and flowing yellow dress. Her hair is neat and tied back with a white ribbon. The warmth of the day, although early still at eight-thirty in the morning, demands that she also be barefoot.

I decline with a shake of my head. "Don't be silly, Daisy. I'm fine. If you want to go anywhere else, though, let me know first, that's all I ask. Don't go out of sight for too long."

Daisy places the sketchbook in her bag as she walks closer. "I won't, I promise."

She's still unsure about leaving me after the nightmare. I don't blame her in all honesty.

A ladybird lands on my arm and I watch it walk slowly across my skin - the smooth and the scarred. I own healed lines that run alone, or intersect with others, almost forming their own brutal alphabet. I know the language that my scars speak. I learnt to speak it years ago, as did many others.

"Go on, Daisy. Meet with your friends and have some fun. It's warm and beautiful out here. I promise I'll join you later … I promise."

Daisy kisses me before walking away in the direction of the lake.

"It's been beautiful out here for a long time." I add more words as the ladybird flies away towards one of the flowers. I smile. I have many reasons to.

Part I

Exist

Chapter one

As sunrise creeps ever closer, the sky creates its own natural and evolving masterpiece. It paints with sweeping strokes and floods colours across the limitless canvas. Blue, purple and pink stand alone in horizontal drifts, daring to mix with each other, wanting to bring more radiance to the morning, yet waiting patiently for the correct and perfect moment. White clouds - tinted with coral and amber - float at an imperceptible rate, oblivious to their importance in the ceaseless work of art.

A thin sea mist surrounds the anchored city of Europa-Four - one of the thousands around the world - a colossal structure, twenty miles in diameter, housed underneath transparent domes. It swirls on contact and crawls up the steel, glass and thermoplastic in slow drifts, shimmering like a veiled wall of satin.
Waves from the surrounding North Sea lap in a soft rhythm, almost three-hundred feet below the surface. Their gentle ripples are lost, though, overpowered by the usual hum of

mechanical and industrial components.

Such an exquisite scene demands attention and many oblige, particularly the enslaved. Those with broken souls and desolation forcing their hearts to beat, their supply of hope already run dry. They lose themselves, incapable of resistance, needing to feel free and alive as the imminent sunrise plays with their senses.

Three blasts of a klaxon sound, filling the air, covering every inch of the city. Any notion of freedom shatters, as if a bullet - a physical manifestation of suffering and control itself - has been shot through a sheet of glass. The beauty dies at this exact moment, ruined in mere seconds by the sirens, by their significance. *Executions.*

Fear, nausea, shock and disgust flood through Europa-Four, with dominance and greed directing the waves, steering them so that every person is drenched by their force.

A scream shoots through the air - one of the caged and condemned. It only lasts for a couple of seconds yet manages to tell a much larger story to all those it reaches: one of a terrified woman ... a woman pleading for forgiveness, for mercy. She knows of the fate which awaits her - she knows, without any doubt, that her life will end soon.

Selected panels of the dome darken in rectangular areas as hundreds of concave screens are created in the sky. They are positioned around the perimeter of Europa-Four, measuring four-hundred square feet, to ensure that every person has a view of the upcoming punishments.

The televised brutality will also be broadcast directly to every other screen available in the domain. All eyes need to view it, soak it in, fear it - and fear it completely. Executions will never serve their ultimate purpose if they are not seen and experienced. To witness others being shot - a peer, one that you know, one that shares your despair - the bullets are a powerful and widely employed deterrent, on a global scale.

••

There are seventeen inked dots on the inside of my left forearm - to indicate my age - plus the identifier, *F-918*. That is my name, the only one I have ever been known by. Both the physical alterations are placed there permanently with a chemical procedure. It always stings for a few hours afterwards, the skin raises and it even bleeds sometimes. The procedure began for me at a young age, though, becoming just another part of my life, an aspect I've endured and adapted to.

In truth, I have no choice but to accept. Like millions of others in the world, I have been created through IVF - in vitro fertilisation - then incubated and grown in an amniotic chamber. I am a biological product. I am here solely to serve and toil for others. I do not have any rights, I do not have a name or a voice that can be heard in the world, except my own thoughts, my own internal monologue.
I use mine to drift through Europa-Four, like an invisible entity, unknown to all ... free from my physical life. I can stand in the wheat fields of Octant one, sit by the edge of the glinting water used for vast aquaculture hatcheries inside Octant three, or walk amongst fruit bushes and trees in the Octant two orchards, even climb and sit in the branches. My daydreams have evolved to become a method of escape, of finding peace and of subconscious survival.

I always wear a short-sleeve shirt, trousers and canvas shoes, all in deep burgundy. My body looks naturally thin, bordering on undernourished, and I'm five-four in height. As is standard for females, my black hair has been deliberately cut to only a couple of inches in length. In my imagination, I can change all of that. I can be taller, stronger, or wear different clothes. I choose how I wish to live.

My brown eyes are locked on the smaller screen attached to the wall as I stand in one of the kitchens that cater for senior military and security personnel, situated in Octant four. *I don't want to see more people die ... why do they force us?*

     The screen is still black as it awaits the live transmission feed. I usually take this opportunity to look at myself in the reflection, to study my face, to see if they have changed me at all, made me age ahead of time. I know of others in their thirties and forties with skin like cracked leather on the soldiers boots, such is the price of their toil and stress.

Fortunately, I possess a natural beauty which, in my own eyes, still radiates and glows, despite my malnutrition and forced appearance. From the basic geographical education provided in my younger years, I can see that my DNA is of East Asian origin, although I have never been to that part of the world.

     There are two security guards standing by the only door to the kitchen, holding automatic rifles. I can see them behind me in the reflection. They always wear black military uniforms, bullet-resistant vests and helmets. Their unyielding and stern eyes watch the screen with the same intensity as mine do, although they have no reason to fear what is about to happen.

     "Listen up!" shouts the kitchen manager, Darius Marnett. "As soon as the killings are done, you get back to work!" He always speaks with animated hand gestures and lets his muscular body and six-four height pulse superiority throughout the room. He is one of the many people I am scared of.

     There are two slaves on early duty this morning. I am here with a younger boy. He is taller than me, five-eight, with blue eyes and blond hair that has been recently shaved to the regulation length of two millimetres. His arms are thin, like mine, like so many others. We both nod with a tense obedience towards Darius.

     Are you angry today? Please, don't be angry ...

     "I want this floor mopped, the dishes washed ... breakfast for the officers mess is in one hour!"

Darius doesn't need to shout his orders, he carries a menacing appearance with him at all times: cropped brown hair, pumping veins on his neck and face, wide brown eyes that shoot a permanent, terrifying, gaze and a square jawline that could have been chiselled from a slab of rock.

The screen on the wall fades in from black to show the central quad. Ten wooden posts are lined up along a brick wall, ready for their fatal duty, ready to hold their prey in position as the bullets fly through the air.

I don't want to watch this ...

The quad is located at the entrance to the administration complex - the entirety of Octant six and seven - which houses all the lavish and extravagant homes on Europa-Four. They belong to the privileged, the rich and powerful, plus, of course, those in control. A quarter of the domain handed over to unimaginable luxury.

A woman in her late-forties, Warden Celestia Horrell - the most important person to reside in Europa-Four - walks across the quad, looking with a cruel admiration at the posts, almost as if she relishes their purpose, their ultimate role in her career and life. She is the person I am most scared of.

Warden Horrell adjusts her military blazer and runs her hands down any tiny creases in her trousers, both in dark-grey. She glares once more at the posts, kicks one with her black boots to test its firm standing, then climbs a few steps on the side of a raised platform. The assembly of surrounding video cameras zoom in on that location, magnifying her, filling all the screens with her tyrannical presence.

Warden Horrell's face always looks unnatural, as if carved out of grey stone, then covered in wrinkled and ashen skin. Deep eyes - that always appeared totally black - stare without mercy, without any spark of emotion. Her wide nose points down and her lips are just a thin, unmoving line. The streaked grey and black hair on her head has been styled with a tight plait this morning. It runs a little lower than her shoulders, like the coiled tail of a scorpion, poised to strike a dose of fatal venom.

"Discipline is key!" she says with a clenched fist. "Without it, there is chaos. Without discipline, we have nothing!"

An uncharacteristic pause follows as Warden Horrell looks around the quad, and further at the outer dome, with tight eyes. She has addressed the half-a-million strong population many times before without the need to reflect, or contemplate her words. "Let this be a reminder to you all that I will not tolerate chaos here!"

The cameras pan and zoom out, adding the row of security guards near the platform to the screen. They salute Warden Horrell and she reciprocates. "Bring them in!" she says in a cold and even tone.

In drilled unison, the guards march away to the holding cell area on the opposite side of the quad. It is an unnecessary display of the regime and all its might ... prove you have authority when there is no real need. We are more powerful than you can imagine, fear us.

We do fear you ...

The boy working in the kitchen winces at the screen and his eyes narrow. His head turns with a controlled speed so that he can look around the kitchen.

Yes, it is disgusting. It is cruel. I feel the same way, I think on seeing his eyes. Perhaps I should drift away? I could climb a tree in the orchard until the executions are over.

"What?" asks Darius as he wipes two huge hands across his white overalls. "You got something to say to me, boy?"

The boy turns away and chooses to remain silent.

Don't ... don't ignore him! Answer him! I make sure that my attention is on the screen and nowhere else. I'm scared. I have seen what happens to people who annoy Darius. *I can't escape inside my mind, not now ...*

"What?" Darius' voice rises as he speaks the angered word once again. "Hey! Why did you look at me?"

18

Again, no answer comes. Darius grits his teeth and a vein swells and pulses in his neck. "Don't ignore me!"

The boy turns around again with slow and hesitant movements and I get to see his identifier for the first time that morning. He has M-532 and sixteen dots inked on his left forearm. "Yes … sir?" he whispers.

Darius doesn't even bother to speak again. He stomps forward with two long strides and punches the boy in the face with a monstrous fist.
The boy's head snaps back with a sickening crack as he screams in pain and crashes to the floor with blood across his mouth.

Darius stands over the boy. His nostrils flare and it is obvious that he is deciding whether or not to let another punch fly. "You, girl, over here!" he orders.

Me? Please, don't hurt me …

I obey without hesitation and move across the room, forcing myself not to look at the injured boy on the floor. "Yes, sir?" I say.

Darius grabs my arm so that he can see the inked number. "918 … You're due for fertilization harvesting after the breakfast shift, correct?" he asks.

"I am, sir, yes." I nod and keep my eyes firmly on Darius. I do not want to enrage him more and fear that a slap or a fist might come my way. I've been hit for a lot less in the past.

Darius nods towards the floor. "Leave now and take him to the hospital with you. Explain to any security that he was punished for insubordination." Darius pauses and only then his fist opens, albeit begrudgingly. "Just … get him out of my kitchen!"

I allow my eyes to find the boy … M-532 … his neck and hands are covered in blood. There are darker patches on his burgundy shirt as well. He is frozen with terror and pain, still on the floor with a hand pressed against his split lip.

"If they need to contact me for an official report, they

can." Darius turns back to look at the boy. "Know your place!"

I kneel down and know that Darius can't see my face. I smile as I look at the boy's eyes, saying so much to him without the need for spoken words. *It's over ... he's calmed down ...*

We stand up together and walk towards the security guards by the door. The boy pinches and presses at his lip with blood stained fingers.

"I have to take him to the hospital and report myself in for fertilisation harvesting. Mr Marnett has ordered it," I say to the guards.

Darius, on hearing his surname, turns around and nods his agreement to the security guards. He returns to the screen and the imminent 'killings' straight after. His misaligned judgement has made him care more for the executions than the fact that he has just attacked M-532, a boy half his age and physical size.

One of the guards opens the thick steel door and waves his rifle to usher us both outside.

••

A couple of minutes later, once a safe distance away from the kitchen and security mess hall, the boy and I stop walking. We stand next to one of the many train lines that connects Europa-Four with other anchored cities or countries: thousands of miles of iron and steel are spread across sea and land, like strands on a spider web, linking the globe together. The sun, still rising, lights up half the city while it covers the rest in deep shadows. Tall buildings glow as if made of pure light, just as others strike dark and angry vertical lines. Steel and iron alloys shimmer and hide in obscurity at exactly the same time, unable to exist together in the same space.

The large screens on the dome show Warden Horrell pacing up and down the quad. She checks the chains securing those due to be executed to their posts - another futile exercise with no other purpose than to breed fear. I have worked in the steel mills of Octant four. I know that a slave has trouble finding the strength to even lift a heavy chain, let alone break through its metal links.

"What were you thinking? Do you not know about Darius' temper!" I ask. I can't decide if I am upset, furious or concerned for M-532. I can feel my heart beating faster than normal and my eyes are constantly scanning for nearby guards. The whole situation has filled me with a tingling sensation, one that is distressing, one that is too difficult for me to ignore.

The boy lowers his hand and cringes. His lip on the left side is swollen and disfigured - it looks as if he has something in his mouth causing the skin to bulge out. A deep split almost an inch long runs through it, still pumping out blood. "I haven't been here very long. I won't forget, though, trust me. I'll probably have a scar as a constant reminder."

"Where did you transfer from?" I ask as I grab the boy's arm. We start walking again, towards the hospital complex on the outer edge of Octant five. I don't want either of us to be questioned by security guards as to why we are talking with each other on the pathways.

"I spent a little over twelve years in the United Territories. After that, I've moved around quite a few times."

The boy holds his lip again, for a few seconds, and takes some deep breaths in an attempt to ease the stinging sensation. "I've worked in the South and North Atlantic cities and the Equatorial mainland as well. Before they stuck me in a dark train carriage and brought me here, I cleaned the desalination machines in the climate controlled Arctic regions."

I have only known one place in the world. A part of me wishes to visit other countries and cities, yet I would see them as a slave, a small cog in the gigantic, uninterrupted, workforce machine. I could be anywhere in the world: any country, territory, floating metropolis, it wouldn't matter, I would always be F-918, undeserving of a real life.

The boy looks at the large screens on the dome to see an elderly man with a blindfold over his eyes. "He travelled here with me."

I look up and see a short and thin man, grey haired with a dense beard. An old scar runs down his right cheek. The chains around his body and neck are causing him pain and cutting at his wrinkled skin.

I want to go ... I want to be invisible and float away ...

"He isn't guilty of any crime, though. He's just old and slow. A naturally aged body, incapable of working to their quotas. It sickens me!" The boy ignores any physical pain as he spits his angry words out.

I know that such corrupted actions are performed on a regular basis. I remember and old woman who used to be in a cell near to mine: F-368. The system disposed of her in a similar fashion. *She could hardly walk because her legs hurt so much. If you can't walk, you can't work ... you can't work hard enough for them ...*

"It will change ... one day," says the boy. His words hold an unusual confidence to them, not just a blind hope and need. He looks over his shoulder for a couple of seconds.

I can't see it, even with the power of my imagination. I have tried to travel and drift to such a world during my life, and I've also permitted myself to dream such absurd thoughts. They never come to me. Even my own imagination - a part of me that is so personal - seems to be under the control of those in power, banishing any optimism from my mind. My daydreams unlock the experience of freedom, yes, but only to a certain degree. They reach a level, an invisible line, a thick wall and they will not cross it or try to break through.

The boy takes another deep breath as he feels the congealed blood on his split lip, still thick and warm. He watches Warden Horrell on the screens as she returns to the platform. "It's already changing. I've heard stories about it, seen glimpses."

"What do you mean?" I ask as my heart jumps towards my throat.

"Change! Freedom! It's out there, in so many places."

A dull thump sounds behind us both. Then a series of sharp and decisive explosions follow.

What is that! I hunch forward and raise my hands around my head, forced by my instincts to protect myself from the unknown. *That's the kitchen ... and the mess hall!*

My eyes widen as I sink to my knees and pull my arms tighter over my head. The building that we were working in only minutes before has disappeared - obliterated.

The boy stares for a brief moment before he crouches down next to me with what looks to be delayed shock. He doesn't look scared like I am, though.

Why is he acting like this? How can he be so ... calm? Another thought enters my head. I listen to it for a second and decide that it can't be true.

His eyes switch between the explosions - now a rolling fireball filled with chunks of metal - and the elderly man on the screen. "The war started months ago ... They're losing control ... their grip weakens every day ..."

"War?" I hear his words yet I can't comprehend them. It's impossible. *What does he mean? What do the words really mean? Please ... let me understand!*

The boy stares at me. I have a feeling that he can see the mental fight that I am now involved in. He understands because he has a broken and institutionalized mind, as I do. *Can he travel further? Can he walk in a future that is ... free? Why can't I?*

A loud klaxon bellows through Europa-Four as the screens zoom to Warden Horrell's face once more. A security guard stands near her, passing on details of the incident. Her black eyes squint, lips purse and the creases on her brow increase in number. She points to the side of the raised platform and speaks quietly - still through gritted teeth - to a man with a computer tablet in his hands. He nods and the screens black out, ending their domain wide transmissions with a sudden accuracy.

I hear the rhythmic thud of military boots as a platoon of soldiers hurtle towards us both on their way to secure the area.

The boy stares at me again. "… And we're going to win," he says.